STAY

TIA LOUISE

USA TODAY BESTSELLING AUTHOR

SMART, SASSY. *Sexy.*

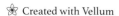

"The best kind of humans are the ones who stay."
-Robert M. Drake

PROLOGUE

Stephen

Ten years ago...

Stop crying, kid. Life isn't fair.
Humans invented fair as a pacifier, because they needed justice.
Animals don't know fair. In nature only the strong survive. You're
kind, loving, honest? Nice try.
If you're weak, you die.

Or poor.

"What are you thinking, *Esteban*?" Ximena lowers herself carefully into a dingy-brown, worn-out armchair, and I blink these thoughts away. "You were always the smartest boy in the room."

The gray strands outnumber the black in my old housekeeper's hair. It's thinner than it was when I was a boy, and she keeps it twisted in a low bun.

"Now I'm a man." I kiss the top of her head. "And I'd wager the whole city."

Her muscles tremble from exertion, but her eyes are bright. She still greets me with a smile, just like always when I visit. "Smartest man in the city. What is that like?"

"It sucks." I look around her crumbling one-bedroom apartment.

It's a second-floor walkup, outdated but clean. She works hard to keep it clean, even with the cancer eating her insides. Even with the years passing, drawing her closer to death.

The thought of her dying fans the darkness inside me. "Where's Ramon?"

"He moved downtown. He got a good job, working at the shipyards." Her accent is thick despite all the years she's lived in Manhattan, her English sprinkled with Spanish.

"That's a long way from here."

He won't visit. He might want to, but he won't have the time or the energy to check on his dying mother.

Her neighborhood is shady as fuck, and she's too weak to climb stairs. And I'm leaving for a long time. I'll have to count on her neighbors to do what I can't.

Slipping a fat business envelope from the breast pocket of my coat, I place it under a mug on her coffee table. "This should last a while. I'll send more, but I won't be able to check on you. I'll be gone eighteen months, probably longer."

"I'm so proud of you. So proud." Her cheeks rise, and she slowly shakes her head. "A Navy officer."

Every line in her face wrinkles with her grin. Her faded purple housedress is as thin and old as she is. I remember her fat and jolly, shining cheeks and hair, every word out of my mouth would make her laugh, even if it wasn't funny. I didn't understand her, how she gave love so generously to a boy who wasn't hers. To the son of a man who didn't even consider her worth his time, who thought he was doing her a favor hiring her to keep his oversized brownstone.

She takes my hand from where she sits, and I take a knee beside her. Every time I visit she's smaller, slipping away. Her grip tightens, and the scent of her drugstore perfume drifts faintly around us, dried flowers and talcum powder. It draws a memory of me as a little boy sitting on her lap, crying against her neck after the death of my mother. She would hug me against her soft body, rocking and humming a sad song I didn't recognize.

"Your father will cut you off if he finds out you're giving me money, *Esteban*."

I exhale a disgusted laugh. "Thomas is too proud to cut me off. It would make him look bad at the club. Unruly boys are to be tolerated, bragged about even."

Her eyes close, and her head leans back as she exhales a weak chuckle. "Men are the same everywhere. *Machismo*."

Pissing wars. I rise to standing in one fluid movement. "I'll never forgive him for doing this to you."

I blame him for her illness. I blame him for her deteriorating health. I blame him for her inability to find work after he ruined her reputation. No one would hire her after he branded her a thief in his home. All the Upper East Siders shut their doors in her face, and she was left to scrounge a living wherever she could.

I've brought her money from my allowance for five years, and I'd love him to come at me for it. Pompous bastard. So worried about his appearance. So offended by a missing watch.

"He did what he had to do." Ximena still defends my father's actions. "My son stole from him. Your father could not keep me in the house after he stole."

"Ramon stole to buy you medicine. He didn't steal to party or do drugs."

He might've gotten away with it, too. If only he hadn't stolen my father's favorite Rolex—not one of the other seven he never wears.

"He did not put my son in jail." She nods her head, as if my father, Thomas Hastings has the ability to throw anyone in jail.

He's just a grown-up trust-fund brat who knows how to invest the massive wealth he inherited from our bootlegger ancestors. At least he's good for something.

Pride beams in her eyes when she looks up at me. "Now you will go and be a hero. So handsome, serving your country."

I smooth my hand down the front of my jacket, contemplating hypocrisy. "It's what my mother always wanted. Her father was in the military."

"Yes, and she can see you from above. She is so proud of you. Just like I am proud."

I study the woman who filled my mother's role for a little while. I can't heal her. I can't change her situation, and I want to leave her with happiness, not bitterness.

"Thank you, *mamá*. I love you."

"I love you, *Esteban*." She takes a slow inhale and forces a chuckle. "Now why are you here with an old woman? Why are you not out celebrating with friends? You have too much spirit. You should be with a girl tonight, release some energy."

Energy. She's encouraging me to go out and get laid. "I'm not looking for a girl."

"A boy then!" My eyes snap to hers, and I see a joking sparkle.

After all the medicine, the chemotherapy, the drugs, she refuses to be beaten. She still manages to tease me. She's the only person who can get away with it.

"I'm not gay. I'm leaving in the morning."

"Which means you have all night." She carefully rises out of her chair and takes my arm, pulling me to the door. "No more hanging around here. Go out and live your life."

I wrap my arms around her in a long hug. The feel of her bones beneath thin cotton is physically painful to me. "I'll find someone to check on you while I'm gone."

"I have my friends. I have my neighbors. Stop worrying about me." She shoos me away. "When it's my time, I'll be ready." Touching my cheek, she says her final words to me. "Be brave, *Esteban*. Laugh often. Take care of yourself."

"Take care of you." I kiss the top of her head and hesitate one last time before I go.

It's the last time I'll ever see her...

≈

Emmy

"Harley Quinn is way sexier than Black Widow any day of the week." Burt Dickerson's voice is too loud.

He's on one of his DC versus Marvel fan-boy rants, and I'm staring into the bottom of my empty red solo cup. I need refill number four.

"Fuck that. Black Widow. Hands down." My older brother Ethan yells at him, but he's only yanking Burt's chain. Ethan doesn't give a shit about comic universes. "Give me a redhead any day. Fire crotch."

My nose wrinkles, and I want to punch my brother in the junk. "She was a blonde in the last movie. You just like Scarlett Johansson." *Why am I still standing here listening to them?*

"What's wrong with that?" He pokes me in the ribs, and I'm ready to call it a night.

It's almost midnight, and I've been watching the door so hard, my eyeballs hurt. Ethan threw this big college-graduation-slash-summer kick-off party for all his old school friends, and I made sure Stephen Hastings got an invitation.

Stephen Hastings... the love of my life.

Ethan said he wouldn't come. He laughed at me and said Stephen hates most of these guys. It looks like he was right.

God, I'm such a fucking moron. How long can I save myself for a guy who doesn't even know I exist? I'm a college woman now. Time to ditch the crush and start living my life.

I just...

I hoped.

With a sad exhale, my mind flies through all my cherished spank-bank memories of Stephen growing up... Tall, lean, dark, wavy hair that looks like he never touches it, but it's always just perfect. He was on the rowing team with Ethan, and when he'd take off his shirt... holy shit, my core clenches at the memory of his broad shoulders, his perfectly sculpted arms... So muscular and tanned. The lines in his stomach would flex, and my mouth would water like Pavlov's dog.

I'm ready to trade this beer for a pint of Ben & Jerry's, curl up in my bed, and cry.

He's not coming.

Walking down the steps, away from the landing at the door, I've reached the edge of the crowd when my brother's voice freezes my insides.

"Stephen! Hell, I don't believe it." Ethan laughs, and a few of the guys join in greeting him. "Didn't think you'd come."

"I didn't either." Stephen's low baritone tickles my lady bits, and I turn slowly to look up at him.

He's wearing a brown tweed jacket over a white button-down shirt and dark jeans. He hardly ever wears jeans, but shit, his ass is so fine in them. He always seems just a bit impatient, and when he scans the crowd, his blue eyes seem to glow from under his dark brow.

He's so fucking hot.

My heart beats faster as I contemplate my next move. He *will* see me tonight, dammit. I'm giving myself one last chance.

He turns again to Ethan, and the muscle in his square jaw moves. "I'm pulling out in the morning."

"Last day as a free man. Sucks to be you." Ethan shoves a whiskey in his hand.

He inspects the glass. "I thought it demonstrated my good character."

"Good character." Burt's loud voice interrupts them, and Stephen visibly cringes. "Still think you're better than us, Hastings?"

"Only you, Dick." Stephen takes a long drink. "Only you."

Girls actually swoon over Burt all the time, but he's nothing compared to Stephen.

"Let's join the party." Ethan puts his hand on Stephen's shoulder, and they start down the stairs in my direction. "Find a chick and get your dick wet."

"Right. That sounds like me." Stephen shrugs off my brother, and Ethan staggers away.

He pauses at the bottom, scanning the crowd with a frown. I follow his gaze over the mob of former classmates. Most are buzzed. Most are familiar. We passed each other daily at Pike Academy four years ago—until he left for Yale. Tonight we're reunited.

Girls sway in colorful silk dresses with thin, spaghetti straps, practically lingerie. Their hair hangs in waves over their shoulders and their eyes sparkle as they listen to guys tell exaggerated stories of their prowess, either in the stock market or on the playing field. The guys evaluate their breasts, their hips, their lips. I'm sure they'll be fucking like good little rabbits before the night ends. Our classmates can be so predictable.

All I know is Stephen is wide open. It's now or never.

"That's a fierce scowl." I'm amazed at how confident my voice sounds, loud and commanding. *Thanks, beer.* "Don't like what you see?"

I hop up on the bottom step beside him. It puts my head at the top of his shoulder, and I lift my chin, looking over the crowd with a scowl, imitating him. "You're right." My nose wrinkles, and I meet his gaze. "They're a bunch of horny assholes."

I manage to come off casual, teasing, and his frown morphs into a narrow-eyed grin. "Emmy Barton. Ethan didn't say kids would be here."

His voice is like warm butter, and I'm thrilled he remembers me. "I'm not a kid anymore, Stephen Hastings. I started at Sarah Lawrence last year."

"Bully for you." He takes a drink of whiskey, but I'm stronger than his sarcasm.

"I wanted to stay close to home."

"Why the hell would you want that?"

Blinking up at him, I smile, going for honesty. "I miss my dad. I miss Ethan. I guess family feels more important when you lose someone."

"Oh, right. Sorry." He looks down at his tumbler, and his expression darkens.

My mom lost her long battle against lung cancer a few years ago. It was devastating watching her suffer, and her death was a mixture of heartbreak and relief she was out of pain. It still hurts if I think about it too much...

Stephen's mother died of cancer when we were kids, but I remember how it changed him. How he smiled less, played less.

"We have that in common, don't we?" My voice is gentle.

"It's not so fresh for me." His softens, and I'm encouraged. I'm not inside the wall, but I'm closer.

"Here you are." Burt appears at my side, putting his hand on my lower back. *What the hell?*

Stephen's eyes go to where he's touching me, and all I can think is *fuck no.*

"You're drunk." I shove Burt's hands off my short denim skirt.

He immediately puts both hands on my waist and turns me to him, leaning closer. "You're not blowing me off for this asshole are you?" His breath smells like vodka, and his flat brown eyes are intoxicated.

He makes a move like he's going to kiss me, but I duck and twirl away, moving to stand beside Stephen, holding his arm. "Stephen and I are having a nice chat. You need to call it a night."

Burt's attention turns to Stephen, and his brow lowers. Stephen is ready when Burt lunges at him. His strong arm shoots out, gripping Burt by the shoulder and holding him back.

"Walk it off, Dickerson." It's a low growl, and I know Stephen could wipe the floor with Burt's drunk ass.

"Don't tell me what to do, Hastings." Burt grips his wrist.

Stephen's fist rises, and I hold my breath. I've never seen Stephen fight, and my heart is flying. I'm sure it's about to go down when Ethan and a big guy appear. They corral Burt, dragging him to the right, and I take my chance, catching Stephen's arm and pulling him into the crowd.

He stops and straightens his jacket, jaw clenched. "That asshole. I'm taking off."

"Wait!" I gently pull his arm again. "I know where we can get a refill... away from all this."

He hesitates a beat, then our eyes meet and his shoulders relax. I quickly lead him past everybody, waving at old friends as we weave through the crowd.

Ethan put a keg out on the terrace near the wet bar, and Stephen goes to refresh his whiskey while I step over to the corner balcony overlooking Central Park. It's a beautiful night, and I can see the moon and a few stars. I make a quick wish.

Warmth at my side causes me to turn. He's standing beside me in the moonlight, dark hair, blue eyes, that dimple in the side of his cheek. "So, what's your major?"

The way he says it makes me laugh. I push a strand of long, wavy blond hair behind my ear. "Art history."

The scene flips. He actually groans, rolling his eyes and turning his back to the railing. "Not planning to work after college?"

His disgust offends me. "I most certainly am. I want to get a job at Sotheby's or at one of the museums downtown. Maybe something in SoHo. Or maybe I'll move to London!"

A moment's pause, and he slants an eye at me. "Is that so?"

"It is." My feathers are still ruffled, and I straighten my button-up cropped top. "What will you do now that you're out? Take a job with your dad? Have a wife in New Haven and a mistress in the city?"

Two can play the stereotypes game.

He drifts a little closer, and my pulse ticks faster. "Is that what we do?" His voice is low, and his eyes drop to my lips.

My voice is softer, higher compared to his. "Isn't it?"

A slight grin from him, and that humming is back in my veins. "You're smarter than I gave you credit for."

"Is that a compliment?"

"It's actually an apology. I underestimated you."

Now it's my turn to hesitate. Still, it's not like I didn't know Stephen was arrogant. It's one of the things I love about him.

"Apology accepted." Reaching out, I trace my finger down the front of his blazer. "Now. Wasn't that easy? You don't have to fight with everybody."

Taking a chance, I put my hand on his chest. It's firm and warm, and he covers my hand with his. It's a gentle touch, but it radiates heat to my chest, fanning out into my belly, warming the space between my thighs. I want this so much... I've dreamed of it. I know if he'll let me in, everything will change. He'll change.

My voice is just above a whisper. "When you look at me like that, I wonder what you're thinking."

Our eyes hold, and I know he feels it, this pull between us. My breath stills, and I'm humming with desire.

But he throws on the brakes. "I'm thinking I've had enough whiskey." His tone is level, and he releases my hand, moving away.

I have to stop him.

I can't lose this moment.

"What do you want?" I'm sassy, flirting. "Do you even know?"

He stops, giving me the full force of his scowl. "I don't want a wife in Connecticut, and I definitely don't need a mistress in the city."

Closing the distance, I put my hand on his waist this time, sliding it back and forth, working my way lower. "Maybe you need me."

He stops my downward progress with a strong grip. "You're playing with fire, Emmy Barton."

"I'd rather be hot than cold."

His grip on me tightens, and he pulls me against his chest. I can barely breathe, but I blink up to his lips, slipping my tongue out to touch mine. His erection is against my stomach, and I'm so wet.

"Are you drunk?" His voice is a rough whisper.

"No. Are you?" Stretching higher, I touch my lips to the scratchy stubble of his jaw.

Leaning down, he kisses me fast. His lips shove mine apart, and his tongue invades, finding mine. My knees start to give out, but his arm is around my waist, scooping me up against his chest.

It's a rough kiss, not kind or gentle, and my fingernails

scratch up to his shoulders. A little noise escapes my throat, and he rumbles in response. Heat floods my panties.

Our mouths break apart with a gasp, and his blue eyes are blazing. "Do you want this?"

Nodding, I step back, holding out my hand. "Come with me."

He hesitates as I go to the glass doors leading to Ethan's dark bedroom. When I pause and look back, he's watching me like a predator. His hair is messy from my fingers, and his lips are parted with his breath. He looks like pure sex.

"This way." I'm holding still, hoping, until...

He follows me inside.

MY SHIRT IS RIPPED OPEN. Stephen doesn't bother removing my bra. He shoves the cups down under my small breasts, and devours me, pulling a taut nipple into his mouth and giving it a bite, sending electricity straight to my core.

"Stephen..." I whimper as his large hands cup and kiss me.

I'm on fire, threading my fingers into his hair. His mouth feels so good against my skin, and he lifts me like I weigh nothing, perching my ass on the edge of the sink.

We're locked in my brother's small half bathroom, and he's making my dreams come true.

"You still want this?" His voice is hot at my ear as he shoves my skirt up to my waist.

"Yes." I gasp, gripping his neck. *God, yes...*

His belt clinks, and I wait as he rolls on the condom. Our eyes meet once more, and his burn with desire. Everything's going to change after this. He's going to fall in love with me. I just know it.

Large palms go under my thighs, lifting them, and I feel the tip of his cock touching me, probing... It's about to happen... Then all at once...

Oh, holy shit! My eyes squeeze shut, and I bite my lower lip hard, letting out a little moan of pain.

"Fuck, Emmy," he groans in my ear. "You're so fucking tight."

I make a little noise of assent, gripping his shoulders. His massive cock rips through my virginity, and it hurts so much more than I expected. He has no idea, of course, and I have no intention of telling him. I know for certain Stephen Hastings would not deflower me so roughly.

Rotating my hips, I do my best to accommodate this distinct sense of fullness. My eyes are squeezed shut, and I focus on his scent, spicy sweat and fresh soap. It's warm and good. He groans again, thrusting faster at my movements.

"Yes..." His lips find mine, kissing me quickly, a touch of his tongue leaves me wanting more. "Like that."

His face is in my hair, and as he moves faster, somehow the pain begins to subside. It transforms into numbness, until gradually, gradually, the smallest flicker of warmth blooms in my lower belly.

"Come for me." Hot breath is at my ear, and my forehead tightens. *Can I?*

Warm hands cup my ass, lifting me off the sink and turning us to the wall. The pain is gone, and my body slides up and down against his hard pelvis. His cock glides in and out, the ridge of its head working my insides. My clit is against his shaft, and something begins to happen. Prickling warmth starts to grow. It gets stronger, and I forget everything but chasing it down.

My thighs tighten around him, and I'm pumping my body up and down, riding him, wanting that tingling heat to keep getting hotter. I'm desperate, gripping his skin and moaning as the orgasm creeps higher up my thighs.

"Fuck, Emmy." He groans, fucking me harder.

"Yes..." It's almost there. "Yes!" It's right there... the tightness in my lower stomach.

It bursts through me, and I moan so loud. It's like a million fireworks shooting through my veins. My vision goes white. I'm flying, and I feel it when his orgasm breaks, pulsing deep inside me as he comes with a loud noise.

I'm shaking. My thighs shudder and grip him, and he holds me. He holds still as we both fly through space together, soaring past galaxies, touching the stars. It's amazing.

Gradually, I blink open my eyes, and through the haze, I see us in the mirror, our bodies molded perfectly together. It's just like I dreamed it would be. My arms are around his neck, our bodies flush. It only lasts a moment.

The noise of the party outside creeps into our little cocoon. He reaches between us, lowering me to my feet as he grips the condom and quickly disposes of it. I feel like a newborn colt, my legs are so shaky.

His back is to me, and his shoulders broaden as he takes a deep breath. Then he moves to the sink to wash his hands. "It's been a while since I've done that." He sounds apologetic.

Shoving my skirt down, I straighten my bra, struggling to get a grip. "What? Bathroom fucked at a party?" I'm shook.

He cuts off the water and dries his hands on the towel as I button my shirt. I've managed to get myself together when he steps to me, putting one hand above my head on the wall and leaning close. "Had sex, period." Leaning down he kisses my cheek. "You were great."

He steps back, and just like that, he's ready to go.

"That's it?" I'm confused. The devastation hasn't hit me yet.

"I think I'll head on home." He reaches out and pats my upper arm. "Good luck at school."

I recoil from his touch. *Are you kidding me? Good luck at school?*

Loud banging startles me. A female voice shouts through the door, "Hurry up in there!"

The banging grows louder, and I go toward it, looking over my shoulder but not meeting his eyes. "Seems I overestimated you."

Pushing through the door, I run into the crowd. The party surrounds me like a wave, and I let it pull me under, drowning my tears in noise and sweeping us apart.

1

Emmy

Ten years later...

"Drop your pants for prompt service." Eli reads the sign aloud, and I want to die.

Sometimes I wonder if Lulabell Brady is the best influence for my seven-year-old son. Not that I have much of a choice.

"Oh." He nods, figuring it out. "Because it's a dry cleaner. I get it. Like how 'Miss Con-Cleaneality' is because Aunt Lou was a beauty queen."

"*Is* a beauty queen." I pull the glass door to see a line already forming at the front counter. "Never say *was* around Aunt Lou. Head on back and get started on your homework."

Lulabell Brady might be flamboyant, but she's my personal savior. She not only gave me a full-time job, including benefits, when I walked out on my cheating ex-husband, she also lets Eli stay in her office and do his studies during the day while I work.

Home schooling him was the right call when his seizures

started and his little classmates treated him like he was sick... or ignored him, which was worse. Impulsively I pulled him out before I'd arranged everything. Not such a great call. Thankfully, Lulabell has impulse-control issues as well.

"What is it about spring that makes people want to dry clean everything?" Lou huffs past me as I'm putting on my neon pink Miss Con-Cleaneality work vest.

It has my name stitched on it in silver cursive.

Lou's hair is teased up in a magenta-red bouffant, and her fake lashes are thick and black. Her lips are perfect, the Cupid's bow just so. She could be a drag queen herself if she were a man. Today, she's struggling under the weight of a blue-net bag on one shoulder and an armload of hanging clothes on the other.

"Is it nesting?" she groans. "Hey, Eli! How's life as a child genius?"

"Heavy." He hefts a backpack full of books higher on his shoulder.

"Tell me about it."

I jump to help her with the load. My son does a wave over his head and continues to her office, where she has set up a small school desk she found at a vintage store just for him.

I kind of love her for doing that.

"Do drag queens nest?" I take the net bag of comforters off her shoulder, and she hangs the ball gowns on a rack with a loud hoot.

"No more than beauty queens nest. They're far too busy *dieting*." She gives me a wink then holds up a red paper tag attached to one of the gowns. "Red tag means *Do Not Press*. It'll melt the beading."

"Got it." I make a mental note.

Lou moved to New York after winning Grande Miss Hemisphere in her home state of Kentucky to be an actress. She didn't make it to the stage, but she found a niche for specialty dry cleaning in the pageant and drag circuits. These beaded gowns, feathers, and undergarments require gentle, loving care, and Miss Con-Cleaneality is here to provide it.

It's amazing how having a gimmick is a magnet for business.

"Hey, the Art Bar's hosting a charity dinner, slash fashion show this weekend. I could use some help doing the models' hair and makeup. They'll pay you."

My eyes widen. "You think I'm ready?"

"Ready as you'll ever be!" She grins, and I hop over to give her a huge squeeze.

"You really are my fairy godmother!"

That makes her laugh. "I only took a chance on a deserving kid."

"You took pity on a single mom with nothing more than an art history degree, a pedigree, and zero job skills."

"I could tell you were a fast learner."

When I got pregnant and decided to marry Burt Dickerson, I put my dreams of working at Sotheby's on hold, and when Eli came and we discovered his seizure disorder, my dreams were shoved even further onto the back burner.

Then Burt decided he'd rather screw Peg Yardley than face our challenges together, and I left him, spending what little inheritance my dad left me on lawyers. It takes money to get a divorce. It takes even more money to get the custody deal I wanted.

Eli stays with me full-time, but Burt has visitation rights. It's not the exact arrangement I had in mind, but I remind myself he is Eli's dad. Still, it's hard letting him go with a man who would prefer to ignore his son's condition than be proactive about it.

So these days hair and makeup are as close as I get to art, and when I try to feel sad, I look at my little boy. The missed opportunities seem to fade away, and I'm sure something better is waiting for us out there. You never know what the future holds.

The bell on the counter out front makes an impatient *Ding!* and we give each other The Look.

"New Yorkers." Lou's voice grows louder as she complains. "Lord, don't make them wait half a second or there'll be hell to pay."

"I got it." I tug the back of my long hair out of my vest and start for the front.

"I'll be right out," she calls. "I got something for Eli."

I cast a glance back at my son, and I see him already digging into his animal science textbook. He's so smart. He's already on sixth-grade projects in science.

"You're spoiling him rotten."

"He deserves a little spoiling."

"Fairy godmother." Shaking my head, I turn and pass through the opening leading to the front counter.

I've just straightened the tail of my vest when I see the impatient bell-ringer and freeze in my tracks. My stomach pitches, and my throat goes dry.

Stephen Hastings is standing at the front counter of Miss Con-Cleaneality.

In a flash, I take in his wavy brown hair, neatly cut and swept away from his face, from his square jaw. That damn sexy square jaw, where the muscle is moving back and forth impatiently.

He's wearing a perfectly tailored gray suit that follows the line of his broad shoulders, down to his narrow waist. He's not wearing a tie, and I get the smallest peek at the hollow of his neck right at the V in the collar of his white shirt.

Knots cramp in my stomach, and I want to run away—at least to the back room to hide. It's the first time I've seen him since that night ten years ago, yet it's all back in a flash.

I remember touching his neck with the tip of my tongue... I

remember the scuff of his beard against my cheek as he kissed my neck and bit my earlobe. I can still feel his large hands gripping my upper thighs, pulling me hard against his pelvis. The thrust of his massive cock... Muscle memory causes my insides to clench. Yeah, *those* insides. Sue me.

Just as fast, I remember the shame of his rejection.

It burns my cheeks thinking of how innocent I was, thinking it would mean as much to him as it did to me. I almost laugh. In the end, Stephen Hastings was just like any other Upper East Side jerk who'd gotten his rocks off with some random chick at a party. He couldn't get out of that room fast enough.

No. I set my jaw. No matter how insanely hot we were together, I will *never* let him humiliate me like that again.

Now he's standing at the front counter, signature scowl firmly in place, looking arrogant as ever and sexy as fuck.

Why is he here? I happen to know he inherited more money than God after his dad died. He should have minions dropping off his dry cleaning. Instead he's here, disrupting my life by his mere presence.

His intense gaze is fixed on something outside the window, and I consider slowly backing out of sight...

Too late.

His head turns, those blue eyes hit mine, and my heart shoots off like a rocket. *Damn him.*

I'm surprised when he draws back, blinking quickly. Is it possible he's as startled to see me as I am to see him? If so, he recovers fast.

"Emmy Barton?" His tone is forceful. "What are you doing here?"

"I work here." I go to the counter and grab the small order pad and a pen, amazed at how calm I sound. "Dropping this off?"

"Uh, yes." He lifts the garment bag from his arm onto the

counter, unzipping it to reveal a deep red, beaded and feathered dress. "It needs to be cleaned, and she said there's a zipper problem."

I glance at his left hand, turning the thin strips of red fabric. No ring. A glance at his face, and I would almost think he might be embarrassed. *Does Stephen Hastings get embarrassed?*

"She is?" Like it's any of my business.

"My aunt Rebecca has taken up ballroom dancing." He says it like she's a stripper.

"And you're dropping off her dry cleaning?"

"She's a bit eccentric. She doesn't trust her doorman." His eyes roam over me, from the top of my head down my cheeks to my shoulders, and it's frustratingly hot. "It's been a long time. Why are you working... at this place?"

Pressing my lips together, I fight him, his sexy gaze, his kindness to his aunt. I remember him wishing me luck right before he walked out on me, never to be heard from again.

The battle is raging in my mind when Lulabell breezes in from the back, humming a show tune. She skids to a stop and her voice squeaks high, like a needle slipping off a record.

"Great balls of fire, Emmy! Why didn't you tell me James Bond was in our shop?"

"Stephen Hastings is *not* James Bond." It comes out snappier than I intend.

"Well, he can go undercover on me any day." She scoots up beside me, blinking her heavily lashed eyes at him.

With a sigh, I wave my hand between them. "Lulabell Brady, Stephen Hastings. Stephen Hastings, my boss Lulabell. Stephen is an *old* friend... from school."

I hit the *old* a little harder than necessary.

"How do you do?" He extends a hand, but when Lou sees the sparkling strips of scarlet feathers and beads in the garment bag, she changes direction.

"Oh, this is *fabulous*! Is it a Jean Claude?"

"Sorry?" He looks from her to the costume she's slowly lifting out of the heavy canvas.

"This is a work of art, Emily. Oh, I see there's a zipper problem here." Lou lowers her reading glasses over her eyes and tilts the metal zipper side to side on the counter. "I can replace it. Do you prefer metal or plastic?"

"It's my aunt's. I can text her and ask."

"Just call and leave a message when you know. I won't be able to start on it until tonight. It will be my honor." She returns the dress to the bag like it's priceless. "Emmy can finish writing this up, and tell your aunt I will personally handle all her costumes with the care they deserve."

"Thanks." Stephen reaches for his breast pocket.

"We also do fine menswear." Lou gives him a wink. "And you are so fine in your menswear."

She turns to the next customer, and he seems completely taken aback, which I enjoy until he turns those smoldering blue eyes on me.

As much as I hate him, he's really hard to look at straight on.

"You are the last person I expected to see here." He looks me up and down again, and I wonder if he remembers that night as clearly as I do. "You look great."

"Is that all? We're very busy." My tone is clipped.

That scowl I know so well returns. I'm far more comfortable with it than his smile, but a small voice interrupts us.

"Mom! Check it out!" Eli is at my side holding up a small bottle with a teeny tiny little pirate ship inside. "Aunt Lou said it's a true replica of Black Bart's ship."

"She did?" I drop to one knee to study the bottle clutched in my son's hands. "We'll have to get a magnifying glass to see it."

"Okay!" His eyes are wide with excitement, and the anger in my chest is forgotten.

"John Roberts was actually forced into piracy." My eyebrows rise, and we both look up at Stephen, who's watching us curiously. "He was a naval officer whose ship was attacked by the pirate Howell Davis. Roberts took over piracy after Davis retired and changed his name to Bartholomew Roberts."

Standing slowly, my arms cross. "How do you know all of this?"

"I was a little boy once."

"Too bad you grew up."

"Hey, mister." Eli holds the bottle out to him. "Does this look like his ship?"

Stephen takes the bottle and holds it close, squinting one eye and turning it back and forth. "Black Bart had several ships. It could be the *Fortune* or the *Good Fortune*, or the *Royal Fortune*."

"He wasn't very creative with his names." My arms are still crossed.

"Eh. He was a pirate." Stephen shrugs, giving me a wink. It provokes a little zing in my chest, and my jaw clenches against it.

"Mom and I collect pirates and mermaids. She likes the mermaids." Eli hooks a thumb in my direction.

"You seem like a really smart guy. What's your favorite subject in school?"

"Marine biology!"

"Naturally."

I've had enough. "Is that all for today, Mr. Hastings?"

He straightens. "I didn't know we were being formal, Miss. Barton. Or I guess, Mrs....?"

"You had it right the first time." His eyebrow arches as if he wants to know more. He can keep on wanting. "If you're done, people are waiting."

The panty-melting grin all the girls used to die for lifts one corner of his mouth. "Perhaps you'll be in a better mood when I return."

"We deliver." My tone is pure ice.

He thinks I'm challenging him, and Stephen Hastings never backs down from a challenge. "I don't mind picking it up."

Great.

With that he's gone, and I'm left trying to remember how to breathe normally.

Warmth at my side, and Lou is right at my shoulder. "Who was that fine specimen of male? And why are you keeping friends like that under wraps?"

"He is not my friend." I feel like I've run a marathon. Taking a breath, I swallow the tightness from my throat. "He's the worst mistake of my life."

She shakes her head and chuckles. "Girl, you're going to have to tell me this story."

ELI'S in Lou's office listening to clips of North American bird calls, and the sign on the door says we'll be back in thirty minutes. Lulabell and I sit with two coffees and two glazed donuts between us.

"He was your first?" Her eyebrows rise as she takes a sip of coffee. "That sounds like some kind of a dream come true to me."

I consider how life changing that night was—and not in the best way. "I had the hugest crush on him for so long. And I mean *huge.*" I trace my finger down the side of my cup. "He graduated with Ethan, but they weren't close friends. Still, I was at every rowing match, every track meet... oh, God."

I close my eyes and shiver. Lulabell laughs.

"As hot as he is now, I can only imagine a seventeen year-old version." She cocks an eyebrow. "Unless he had an awkward phase?"

Shaking my head, I sip my coffee. "He was never awkward. Not ever." Closing my eyes, I exhale all the crazy, pent-up emotion I carried as a silly teenage girl in love with Stephen Hastings. "He was never anything but gorgeous and brilliant and aloof and dismissive... and so damn sexy."

"Sounds like the kind of guy I'd fall for."

"So I got a little drunk and figured I'd make him see I was the girl of his dreams."

"With your magic, virgin pussy?"

Coffee almost shoots out my nose. I squeal and cough, and Lulabell starts slapping me on the back. "Don't die, Magic Pussy!"

"Oh my God!" I cough more, this time loudly. "I did! I really thought he'd have sex with little virgin me and fall madly in love."

"I take it he didn't." Her smile presses into a sad little frown.

Dotting the tears out of my eyes, I manage to recover from my choking fit. "He basically patted my shoulder and told me to have a nice life." I return her empathetic frown with a pouty lip. "I don't have a magic pussy."

She leans closer, hugging my neck. "None of us do, honey." We both laugh, then she straightens, releasing me. "Was it at least good sex?"

"Oh, you know." I lean back taking a bite of donut. "At first it hurt like hell. He has a pretty big..." I wave my donut at her.

"Jesus, give me strength..." She clutches her chest, making me laugh.

"But I was prepared for that. I held on through the first part and just focused on kissing his neck and touching him, smelling him..."

"He smells so good."

"Yeah... Then it got so much better. Then it was over." My

eyes actually heat at the memory, and I start to laugh. "Oh my God! I'm such an idiot!"

"You're not." Lou's voice is quiet, kind. "He's the type you never quite get over. And now look at what Fate has done! She brought him right back and dropped him at your door. If that isn't a second chance, I don't know what is."

"No." Shaking my head, I finish my donut and hop off the chair. "No second chance. Never again."

"Oh, come on, Em. You have to follow up on this. It's only right."

My eyes go through the doorway to Eli studying at his desk. "Stephen Hastings is one mistake I will not make again."

"I don't know." She hops up, following me. "A mistake like that I'd be willing to make again. And again... and again."

Our eyes meet, and we both snort a laugh.

2

_____

Stephen

Aunt Rebecca's brownstone sits on a tree-lined street between Columbus and Amsterdam. She's very proud of it—possibly more than she is of her late husband.

"I hope you were able to take my dress today, Stephen." She sits at the head of a long, mahogany table in a dining room with thirteen-foot ceilings and Venetian glazed walls. It has the original moldings around the doors and around the chandelier base, and deep green fabric drapes oversized, south-facing windows. The golden-yellow walls give the room a warm glow, along with the red Persian rug covering the wide-plank wood floors.

"Rudolfo is very particular about who handles our costumes," she continues. "Miss Con-Cleaneality is supposed to be the best."

At a glance, you'd never dream this thin, elegant woman wearing pearls, a purple pantsuit, and a cream turtleneck would ever strip down to velvet and feathers to do a tango. At least I wouldn't.

"Of course. I'm happy to run your errands. I have nothing else to do."

"Don't be sarcastic, darling. It's unbecoming."

I tilt my tumbler side to side, watching the amber scotch move around the glass. All afternoon I've been sidetracked by long blonde hair, bright blue eyes. She still wears it in waves over her shoulders... like she just spent the day at the beach. It's very unprofessional.

Her small nose turns up at the end. I'd forgotten. She didn't smile at me—no surprise, but when her son came out, her entire face lit up. That small dimple just below the corner of her mouth appeared.

I remember that night so long ago when I kissed her. When I fucked her in that tiny bathroom. Unease tightens my neck. Sinking my cock into her tight little pussy is a memory I've never been able to shake. Seeing her today only stirred it up again.

She held onto me and kissed me with such... *purity*. It's a stupid thought. I'm no romantic. She's just still so damn beautiful. What the fuck is Emmy Barton doing working at a dry cleaner?

"You know, I really enjoy these dinners. Such stimulating conversation." Rebecca is looking straight at me, and I sit up in my chair.

"I'm sorry, what were you saying?"

"Nothing of any importance, obviously. I just hope I'm not putting you to sleep droning on about my life."

"I'm sorry, Bex. Something unexpected came up today, and I've been a bit distracted—"

"Is that so? Nothing unexpected ever happens around here." She sips her wine. "Thank God."

I take a bite of my perfectly cooked steak. "Delicious." After a moment, I figure why not. "Emmy Barton works at Miss Con-

Cleaneality." My aunt frowns, so I elaborate. "Edward Barton's daughter."

Her face breaks into a smile. "Edward Barton was such a good man. He did so much pro bono legal work. I think he represented the man fixing my roof."

She looks overhead before lowering her blue eyes to mine. It's a family trait shared between her, my father, and passed down to me.

"Worried about your contractor's past legal woes?" I watch as she cuts a slice of her steak.

"Oh, I give everyone who works for me a thorough background check. It's always fascinating what comes up." She smiles, taking a bite.

A heavy crystal goblet of Barolo is beside her plate. I have one as well, but I haven't graduated from my scotch.

"Edward Barton was a rare man." I clear my throat. "He had character. He wasn't obsessed with money or appearances."

Perhaps he should have been. I vaguely remember my father saying something about his ratio of pro bono to paid legal work, and not knowing how he made ends meet. Perhaps that's why Emmy works at a dry cleaner now.

She'd said she wanted a job at Sotheby's or in London.

"Whatever happened to Emily?" My aunt spears a roasted Brussels sprout with her fork. "I remember she married one of the boys from your school... Edmund? Bertrand? Bart?"

"Burt Dickerson?" My voice rises slightly, and my aunt gives me a triumphant smile.

"Yes, that's the one. Do you know him?"

Shifting in my seat, I don't say what I'm thinking, which is *how could she marry that asshole?* Instead, "He was in my class."

"Too bad about that. You just never know." She slowly cuts another piece of meat and slips it into her mouth.

I'll take her bait. "Too bad about what?"

My aunt's face pinches with a frown. "Seems Bart slept with half the Upper East Side."

"Burt."

"Of course. Anyway, last I heard she was left penniless and living in the East Village. It's just too bad."

"Which is where I found her at your fancy dry cleaner."

"Isn't that something?" She's grinning, and I swear this old woman. Ever since my father died, she's been playing these little games with me. I wouldn't put it past her to have sent me there on purpose to bump into Emmy.

"I do enjoy our dinners." She leans back in her chair, holding her goblet of wine. "I'll be so sad when they come to an end."

"Why would they come to an end?"

"Well, I don't expect you to have dinner with me when you have a family of your own. But perhaps you'll invite me over sometime."

My aunt lifts a crystal bell beside her plate, and two servers enter to remove our plates. A fluffy little white dog scampers into the room behind them.

"Will you be having any coffee, ma'am?" One of the servers waits at her chair.

Rebecca looks toward me, but I shake my head. "That'll be all Jonathan, thank you."

She rises slowly, holding her little dog. I stand as well.

"Tell me goodnight now, dear." She walks slowly to the foyer at the front door, and I follow at her side. "Don't forget to pick up my dress when it's ready."

I don't laugh. I suppose in her eyes, I'm still a kid. "I meant to ask you, do you prefer metal or plastic zippers?"

She pauses in the oversized wood-paneled entryway, turning to face me. "That question feels inappropriate."

"The zipper on your dress needs to be replaced. The woman in charge said to ask."

"I have no idea. Metal, I guess. Why doesn't Rudolfo tell me these things?"

"I'll let her know." She starts to speak, but I finish for her. "I'll pick up your dress."

"And you're coming to my competition?"

"I'm pretty sure I have to be out of town."

"Stephen." Impatience enters her tone. "We're the only family we have left. We have to look out for each other."

"Of course, I'll be there. I'm only teasing."

"That's good. Have a good night, darling." She pats my arm and turns, leaving me in the doorway to see myself out.

STANDING IN MY THIRD-FLOOR STUDY, I look out the floor to ceiling windows over the treetops of Central Park. I didn't move far from the neighborhood. I'm in Midtown. Not like Emmy, who if my aunt is correct, went much further south, both financially and geographically.

Why can't I get her off my mind? She's rude. She married that fucking dick. She's working some low-rent job, probably living in a walk-up... So her plans didn't work. It's not my problem.

I just can't figure it out. Aren't all women supposed to be searching for their fathers? Burt is nothing like Edward Barton. The Dick is as far from honorable as you can get. He's not even like her older brother Ethan.

Ethan should have punched him into last week before he let him near his sister. Isn't that what older brothers do?

Discussing Edward Barton dredged up another bit of the past I'd rather leave buried. Ximena died less than a month after

I left for north Africa. I didn't even make it to her funeral. Ramon took her ashes back to sprinkle over her family's land. Then he stayed.

She's like one of those lost ships, buried at sea, and I can never go to the gravesite or give her flowers. I can never tell her how much she meant to me...

I can only hope she knew.

Rubbing my hand over my stomach, I turn my back on the city. I use the mouse to wake my computer, and I see a message waiting from my partner and Naval buddy Remington Key. The healthcare app we've been developing is almost ready for testing. It won't make a difference until real reform happens in the system, but we'll be ready with the infrastructure when it does.

It's my old struggle to make life fair. Money has the power to level the playing field. Or not. Edward Barton knew this. Pirates knew this. My father used his money to stay rich.

Emmy is strong, but can she survive? I don't know why I should give a fuck.

Slipping off my suit coat, I drop it on a stack of suits waiting in a chair, contemplating my next move.

3

Emmy

I'm staring at myself in the mirror, two stripes of translucent powder are on the tops of my cheeks just below my temples. Two more are along my jawline.

"Does this even work?" I lean in for a closer look.

The bed bounces, and I squeal, scooping up the pot of loose powder before it spills everywhere.

"What are you doing?" Eli's brow scrunches just like a little old man's. "Why do you have that white stuff on your face?"

"I'm baking." Twisting the cap on tightly, I drop it on the comforter beside me. "Now stop bouncing on the bed."

"Like a potato?"

"Like a face."

"Does it hurt?"

"It's supposed to set the concealer and foundation and eliminate fine lines."

Tapping the play triangle on the YouTube video, the recording of LaSalle's last fashion show continues. All the models are in long, straight sheaths, their hair is pulled sharply away from their faces in tiny buns on the tops of their heads, and their eyes are all you see.

Eli hugs Kona his stuffed killer whale and continues staring at my face. "Your eyes look really big."

I've applied a full face, complete with deep bronze shadow, cat liner, and false lashes. "See the girls in this video? They're the models from his last show."

"Who's he?"

"A rising designer. I'm helping Aunt Lou do hair and makeup for a fundraiser. I have to be sure I'm up with all the latest techniques." Leaning forward, I speak without moving my eyes. "Don't want to look like a dummy."

Finally, I coat my lips with a warm pink liquid lipstick, then kiss them together a few times, making a face and winking at the mirror before turning to him.

"What do you think?"

His little nose curls. "I can't see your freckles. You look like a Bratz doll."

"How do you know about Bratz dolls?"

"I went to school, Mom."

Picking up the large brush, I dust it across the line of the powder, blending it into my face. "You go to school now. It's just different."

I don't mention how I think he's learning a lot more as a homeschool student. I still want him to have the socialization of the academy, but I can't argue with how fast he's moving through his lessons.

Standing, I give the tip of his nose a light pinch. "I'll take that as a positive. Most glamour girls look like Bratz dolls these days."

"You're not going to start doing your face like that all the time, are you?"

The package of makeup remover wipes is in my hands, and I

start the process of removing the seven layers of makeup I'm wearing.

"Working at Miss Con-Cleaneality is not a full beat type of job."

"Aunt Lou is always made up."

"Aunt Lou is a beauty queen." I toss the first round of wipes and collect the tubes of primer and foundation, the eye liners and eyebrow pencils, the brushes and sponges, dropping them all into my square makeup case. "How are you feeling? Did you take your medicine?"

He falls back on the bed with a groan. "It makes my head fuzzy. I can't remember stuff."

"Eli." Fear squeezes my chest. Every time he has a seizure, I feel like my world is crumbling around my ears. It's terrifying.

I can barely even think of him lying on the floor, his body rigid and trembling, all his muscles tense and his eyes rolled back in his head. Sometimes he wets his pants... It's what happened the last time he was at his school, and all the kids saw.

Dashing to the kitchen, I snatch the prescription bottle off the windowsill and tap out a capsule. In a flash, I'm in the one bedroom of our apartment holding a glass of water and his meds.

"Mom..." He groans.

"Take it."

With another groan, he crawls across the bed on his knees and plucks the pill from my palm, drinking it down with the water while cutting his eyes at me.

"It's not a choice, Eli. You have to take your medicine." My eyes heat. "I can't bear it when they happen. It's like you're..."

I can't say it. I can't say it feels like he's going to die.

He softens and his shoulders drop. I sit with my back to the pillows, and he puts his head in my lap, hugging Kona to his chest. I tug his thick blond hair, letting it slide through my fingers as I stroke his head.

Elijah got his hair from me. He got his eyes from me. His personality reminds me so much of my dad. The one thing Burt gave him was this fucking seizure disorder.

This genetic condition my ex-husband refuses to acknowledge came from him. Instead, Burt complains I coddle him too much. As if Eli even wants to play football or lacrosse. He's interested in pirates and birds and sea mammals. He likes to read and collect ships.

"Are you ready for your bird test?" My voice still sounds shaken, vulnerable. "You don't have to take it tomorrow if you're not. We have a whole week left to study."

"I'm ready."

"Should we do the flash cards?"

"I don't need them."

He's frustrated, but I won't let him skip the meds, no matter how tired he says they make him. I took the job with Lulabell specifically so I could afford them.

Picking up my phone, I navigate to YouTube again. Searching quickly, I find the call of a raven and hit play.

"Mooom." He complains, but I see the smile lifting his cheek.

"You know..."

"It's a raven."

Quickly I type in another with one thumb and hit play.

"Whippoorwill."

"That was an easy one. Try this." I hit play, and the strange cry reminds me of a cat.

"Peacock." He shifts in my lap and rolls around to face me. "Remember that guy who knew about the pirates?"

My stomach tightens. I've been doing my best to forget

Stephen Hastings's surprise appearance ever since it happened —with no luck.

"What about him?"

"I liked him." His blue eyes look around, thinking. "He didn't treat me like a dumb kid."

The tone in his voice provokes an ache in my chest. As much as I tell him not to worry, I know it still hurts when his dad puts down his interests.

"Stephen Hastings is one of the smartest guys I've ever met." As much as I hate to say it, I'll admit it for my son. "He graduated with your uncle Ethan."

"I hope I get to see him again." He blinks slowly, and I can tell the pills are kicking in. "I can't wait to start learning about ocean mammals."

"Here." I flick on the television and pull up the Netflix app.

It only takes a moment before I've found *The Blue Planet*, and Sir David Attenborough begins telling us about the cycle of life on the ocean floor in dulcet tones. Eli will be asleep before the first segment ends. He's only seven, and I don't mind sharing my queen-sized bed with him sometimes.

When his breathing turns rhythmic, I gently move his head to the pillow and finish cleaning up and washing my face. I wash the few dishes from our fancy dinner of chili con carne—heavy on the beans and cheese.

Usually Eli sleeps on the couch in the living room. The tub is in the kitchen with a curtain around it, and the toilet is hidden in a closet behind the stove.

It's a long way from the posh, Upper East Side townhome where I grew up, or even Burt's luxurious penthouse apartment. I don't care. Anything's better than living with a cheater who's constantly belittling my son for not being "man enough," whatever that means.

Our apartment is tiny, but it's clean. It's warm in the winter, and we have what we need. With a sigh, I switch off the kitchen light and climb into the other side of the bed. My computer's in my lap, and I click over to the neurosurgery website.

Free trials are completely filled for the experimental procedure that could cure Eli's condition. It's new, risky, not yet FDA approved. They're really close, but for all those reasons, my insurance won't cover it. It could give Eli a chance at a normal life... The only problem is the hundred-thousand-dollar price tag.

With a sigh, I close the tab and shut down my laptop. I'm just getting on my feet, but if there's any reason to keep reaching for that corporate ladder, it's Eli. I have the credentials.

"I'll get there for you, bud." I give his head one final pat, and he lets out a little boy snore.

$\sim$

"Cleaning clothes is in our jeans." Eli reads the sign out front and nods. "It almost seems too easy."

"It's hard to come up with punny signs day after day." I pull the glass door open, and it's déjà vu all over again.

A line is forming. Eli and I quickly pass through to the back, where I pull on my pink vest and head to the front.

Again, I skid to a stop in my tracks when Stephen Hastings greets me on the other side of the wooden counter.

"The dress isn't ready." My voice is shorter than I intend.

"Good morning to you, too." He doesn't scowl, which puts me on guard. "Your co-worker said you do suits?"

"Lulabell is my boss, and yes, we do menswear."

Lou bustles out from the back, throwing her arms out when she sees him. "Another satisfied customer!"

"Technically, we haven't done anything for him yet," I say under my breath.

"I got your message last night. Her metal zipper is replaced. I tried to find one that won't get stuck, but if it does, just rub it with a little soap. Or a clear crayon works wonders."

He listens carefully and even nods and adds the occasional "Is that so?" at the appropriate time. It's kind of... nice that he cares so much about his aunt's things.

"You're dropping off those suits? Oh, Armani." Lou's eyes light as she reaches for the stack of dark suits on his arm. The doorbell rings, and she pivots, passing the stack to me. "Emmy, write these up, honey. That's a Lady Liberty contestant."

My eyes flicker to the elegant blonde entering with the small entourage around her. She's in a pink Jackie O suit and dark shades, and her equally blonde assistant is holding a garment bag.

"Sure." I take the stack from her, counting out the coats and pants.

"It's two suits and a jacket."

I can't help noticing his clean, faintly leathery cologne wafting up as I sort the sleek fabric. I fight against all the memories bubbling up at the scent.

"Just dry cleaned?"

"And pressed." His voice is smooth, and I keep my eyes focused on the notepad where I'm jotting down the details, copying his address from the receipt for his aunt's dress.

"They'll be ready on Sunday. We can have them delivered before noon—"

"I'll pick them up."

I do look at him then, and this time I'm frowning. "Why? Your apartment is in Midtown. There's no reason for you to come all the way down here. What's the point?"

It's a mistake to confront him. Those eyes sear into me, causing my insides to tighten in a way that can only be described as dangerous. My heart remembers the pain Stephen caused me, but my body only remembers how good being with him felt leading up to it.

"I wanted to see you again." He seems as conflicted saying it as I am hearing it.

"Well…" I hold out my bare arms. "Here I am."

"Yes, I see that." Dropping his gaze, he passes a large hand over his scruffy chin. He still wears that sexy scruff. My skin tingles with desire to feel it again. "Why?"

He glances up from under his dark brow, and I swear, it's pure sex appeal. For a moment, I'm a deer in headlights.

Then I remember who he is and snap the hell out of it.

The bell on the door has been ringing nonstop while I've taken down his order. Now I drop his suits in a blue net bag and pull the strings "So you've seen me again. Here's your receipt."

He reaches for it, and our fingers touch. It's a surge of electricity, and I pull my hand away fast.

"I'm sorry, that came out wrong." His hand is still extended toward me on the counter. Lulabell is beside me working, but somehow it feels like we're in our own separate bubble. "I meant to ask you to have lunch with me."

"No."

His chin pulls back, and for a half-second I wonder if any woman has ever dared say no to the great Stephen Hastings. I almost grin, but I turn my back instead, dropping the bag of suits into a larger canvas bin.

"Emmy…" Lou is at my shoulder holding a slip of paper in her hand. "Honey, I'm all out of fabric glue and sequins. Would you run to Jackie's and get us some more? Oh, and I need a new bobbin."

She shoves the sheet of paper at my hand, and my jaw drops. "Right now?" I scan the short line of customers waiting.

"Right now, honey! I need them before lunch."

I study her face for a moment, looking for any sign she's

setting me up. If I know Lulabell, she's sending me on a walk hoping Stephen will follow.

I'm not interested in such a setup. "Eli's working on his bird test. He might need something."

"Oh, you know he's going to ace it! Don't worry about him. Now scoot, scoot! I need you to get on down there and get what we need."

Her voice is pure sugar, but I'm not buying it. "Okay." I grab my wallet, the scrap of paper she's holding, and the company credit card before ducking under the counter. When I emerge, I'm standing right in front of Stephen.

"Can I give you a ride?" He's so close, I'm wrapped in his spicy fresh scent.

I cut my eyes to Lou, and I see her biting back a smile. I was right.

"Thanks, I can walk."

With that I'm out the door, Stephen right behind me.

4

Stephen

"To think I considered sewing a lost art." I'm walking swiftly beside Emmy, who's moving at a pace typically reserved for competitive athletes.

"Not in the pageant and drag community." She doesn't cast me a glance. "They make their own clothes, do their own alterations..."

"Drag?" We're passing a sign for The Cock, and it clicks. "I hadn't even thought of that. Lulabell must make a fortune."

"She does all right."

Emmy's pert chin is lifted, and her long hair bobs in a low ponytail over one shoulder. The neon pink work vest covers most of her outfit, which is made up of faded denim shorts and a white tank, and her toned arms swing bare at her sides.

She's still so damn pretty. Is that why I couldn't stay away?

"How long have you worked for her?" She stops so fast, I have to take a few steps back to where she's glaring at me with her hands on her hips. "What's wrong?"

She's so tiny in basic black Converse tennis shoes. Looking

up at me, she seems so young. Not much older than the last time I saw her, which I know is false. That was ten years ago.

"Why are you doing this?" Her cheeks are flushed a pretty shade of pink—I assume from exertion? Maybe something more? "What do you want, Stephen?"

"I wanted to walk you to the fabric store." I nod toward an old woman pushing a grocery cart of what I assume are her belongings. "It's a shady part of town."

"It's my neighborhood." She starts walking again, although a bit slower.

I confess, this pace is easier to keep in leather dress shoes, although I'll have another suit for her to clean after this cardio workout. "Since when?"

I know what Bex told me about Emmy's past. I also know her grapevine tends to get the facts twisted.

"Since when what?" She impatiently repeats my question, again without a glance.

"Since when has this been your neighborhood?" I say the words deliberately slowly. Two can play this game. "Last time I saw you, it was very far from here."

That pulls her up short again, and again, I take a step back to where she's standing. "None of your business."

She's so cute with her arms crossed, staring daggers at me with those pretty blue eyes. Her whole demeanor makes me want to fight back, to push her buttons.

"Actually, your brother is a friend of mine—"

"Acquaintance at best—"

"Our families have known each other since we were kids. One might argue it is, partially my responsibility to ensure your safety. When it's in my power to do so."

"Of all the old-fashioned, patriarchal, male chauvinist..." Her eyes narrow, and something passes across her expression, something like an old injury. "You can drop the chivalrous act,

Stephen Hastings. You showed your true colors a long time ago."

I'm not sure what that means, but she starts walking again. She's moving much slower now, and I see we're approaching a store that looks like it's been here since forever. A sign above the door proclaims it's Jackie's.

She pulls the door open and goes inside. I catch it and follow her.

It's a cramped, dusty space, with shelves upon shelves of buttons, snaps, ribbon, tape beading... it looks like a seamstress's paradise. A teen girl sitting behind the register doesn't look up from her phone, but a voice from the back calls out a hello.

"Hey, Jackie! It's just me, Emmy. Lulabell needs a few things."

"Oh, sure. Help yourself, now." The disembodied voice calls back.

From the sound if it, she's either in a cave or under a bolt of fabric. Naturally, I assume the latter.

Emmy makes her way down the aisle, picking up a clear tube of what I assume is glue and a package of buttons. She squats in front of a rack and digs in a box of shiny silver discs.

"Do you sew?"

"Not really." She takes out a few small spools and puts the cardboard box back. "I do hair and makeup."

Unexpected. "For drag queens?"

"Of course not. Any good drag queen does her own hair and makeup. I'm helping Lou with a fashion show this weekend."

She stands, and we're almost chest to chest. The heat between us is palpable, and she blinks quickly, like she miscalculated our proximity. Her fresh scent of flowers and soap surrounds me. I remember that scent... I want to reach out and touch her, but she pushes past me roughly.

I turn, watching her cute little ass in those cutoffs. *Criminal.* "That's not what you studied in school."

She goes around to the other side of the aisle. "Art history isn't the most useful degree."

"What degree lands you in a dry cleaner?"

"Don't be a snob. Working with Lulabell is more interesting than you think."

"I think Lulabell is very interesting."

"I don't really care what you think." She stares at the racks of brightly colored sequins. "She didn't tell me what color to get."

I spot a package of deep red ones and pick it up. "If it's for my aunt's dress, these should do."

She takes them from me, avoiding the touch of my fingers. *Yes, I felt it earlier, too, beautiful.* Watching her doing her best to avoid my eyes makes me grin. Emmy Barton is feisty and very angry with me for some reason.

I follow her cute little ass to the front of the store. "Why do you hate me?"

"I'd have to think about you to hate you."

The teen tears her eyes away from her phone long enough to check us out and take our money, then she's right back to texting. Outside, returning to Miss CC, Emmy takes a slower pace.

"Will you tell me now?" I give her arm a playful nudge, and she cuts an annoyed glare at me.

"What?"

"What brought you to this colorful neck of the woods?"

"I've lived here since I discovered my husband was sleeping with Peg Yardley."

Glancing up, I try to place that name. "Peg Yardley. Is she the one..." Suddenly I remember a face, and it makes me frown. "Her forehead's very large."

"Yes." Emmy's cute nose wrinkles.

"Do her eyes still sort of... bug out?" I lift my hands to the level of my eyes.

"As a matter of fact they do."

I always knew The Dick was an idiot. Peg Yardley doesn't hold a candle to the beauty walking beside me right now.

I exhale a retort. "She should have her thyroid checked."

Emmy laughs and quickly covers it with a cough, shaking her head and lifting that cute chin again. I grin, feeling pretty proud of myself for that little breakthrough.

"What do you know about anyone's thyroid?" When she looks at me this time, she's still acting angry, but I see the smallest crack in her wall.

"I've always been interested in medicine."

"So why aren't you a doctor?"

"I don't have to be."

"Ah..." She lifts her chin. "Of course you don't."

"Why don't you move back to Lenox Hill?" Her family's townhome isn't too far from my aunt's if I remember correctly.

"Ethan sold the place when he moved to Seattle."

"That wasn't very thoughtful of him."

She shrugs. "I was married, living in a penthouse. We didn't need it, and the upkeep and insurance got expensive. We don't all have fathers who leave us vast sums of wealth."

I let that pass. The last thing I want on my mind right now is Thomas Hastings. "One should never sell real estate in Manhattan. Unless you're desperate." We're back at Miss CC's and I hold the glass door open for her.

She pauses in the entrance, squinting up at me. "Still the smartest guy in the room?"

"In the entire city. Now go with me to lunch."

"No." She walks through the door without a backwards glance.

I'm right behind her, ready to argue, when she stops. We both look up to see Burt pacing in front of the counter.

5

Emmy

Burt's hand is on his hip, and when he sees Stephen, he stops pacing. "What are you doing here?"

Stephen glares back at him. "Dropping off some suits."

"You're early." I breeze through the stand-off between them. "Eli is taking a test."

"Who's proctoring it?" Burt follows me to the counter.

"It's a timed online exam. He doesn't need a proctor."

"How do they know he's not cheating?" Burt has a big problem with my decision to homeschool Eli. Primarily because he can't play sports—not that he could anyway.

My jaw clenches. "Your son doesn't cheat."

His eyes narrow at my tone. *Asshole.*

Stephen steps forward, interrupting our standoff. "You know, you're right. It's too late for lunch. How about I take you to dinner instead? I'll pick you up at seven."

The shock registering on Burt's face fills me with unexpected pride. *Dammit, Stephen*. I turn slowly to look at him, and I don't miss the glint in his eye.

"Seven sounds great." I force a smile, although I feel like I'm making a deal with the devil.

Why is Stephen doing this? I kind of don't care if it makes Burt think I'm dating his old nemesis. Which I'm not. *Definitely not.*

Stephen holds out his phone to me, a cocky grin curling his lips. He needs my number.

A second ticks by as I hesitate. The weight of Burt's presence watching us, is the only thing that drives me forward. I take Stephen's phone, quickly sending a text to myself:

STEPHEN

Stephen Hastings is not your hero.

He takes the phone back and reads what I wrote. Just as fast he cuts me a look, and it's like a charge of electricity straight to my core. *What am I doing?*

He quickly taps a reply, but I'll have to wait and read it later. "See you tonight. Wear a dress."

I'm about to tell him I'll wear what I want, but he turns to Burt. "Take it easy, Dickerson. I see you haven't changed much."

"I could say the same to you." Burt straightens, getting right in Stephen's face.

A knot is in my throat, and I'm not sure I can breathe. Stephen only exhales a laugh, and takes a step back from my ex-husband. "Good thing I didn't need to."

Burt's face goes red. "Neither did I."

God, Burt's such an idiot. My forehead drops to my finger-tips, and I shake my head. Stephen only chuckles and walks out the door, leaving me to deal with my ex.

"You're going out with that guy?" His voice has always

reminded me of an annoying little brother older guys would stuff in a trash can.

Or maybe that's what I wish would happen.

I can't believe I actually got stupid drunk and slept with him that one night. Or that I got pregnant. Or worse, that I married him. My head spins at the layers upon layers of dumb decisions I made trying to correct that mistake.

The one bright light to come out of that dumpster fire of a year is sitting in Lulabell's office identifying 120 North American birds.

"Do you really care who I'm dating?" It would be the first time Burt cared about anything not involving his penis.

"I care who my son's around." I don't believe it. "That guy is the biggest asshole I know."

I can't resist. "Have you ever looked in a mirror?"

He's about to snap back at me when we're interrupted by the one male voice I'm always happy to hear.

"Mom! I got them all right! I made a hundred!" He's jumping all around holding up a sheet of paper.

"You did not!" I fake disbelief as I try to catch the paper in his waving hand. "Let me see."

He hands me the sheet verifying completion of the ornithology unit of the state's junior high science curriculum, and I turn into his biggest cheerleader. "You did it!"

I hold the sheet towards Burt. "He's making straight As in a sixth-grade science class."

"Yeah, great." Burt waves the page away. "You're still not a teacher."

Eli's chest sinks, but I step forward to catch his arm. "This is really amazing. I'm so proud of you."

He looks up, and I give him my brightest smile. It gets me a small grin, and he lets me hug him. I kiss the top of his head, briefly closing my eyes. It's moments like this I want to remember.

Not how shitty Burt can be or how I never should have married him.

"All right, get your stuff. We've got to go." Burt walks to the door, while Eli runs to the lockers to grab his backpack.

I duck under the counter and put the bag of sewing supplies in Lou's cubby. Eli returns, giving me a brief hug before running to where his dad waits at the door.

"Got everything?" Burt asks, and he nods. "Pack your football gear?"

My breath catches, and I spin around in time to see my son's pleading face. "You know he can't play football."

"He can play football. You don't let him."

Heat rises in my cheeks, and I'm on the other side of the counter in a flash. "Burt, stop. You know it's not safe. If he hit his head…"

"He could hit his head riding a bike."

"Which is why he wears a helmet."

"He'll wear a helmet when he plays football."

I feel like I can't breathe. "No. That is not in our agreement…"

"The only thing wrong with Eli is his overprotective mother."

I'm so upset, I'm shaking. "I don't want to fight you over this—"

"Then stop fighting me."

He pulls the door open, but I catch his arm in my firm grip. "I will if you force me."

Our eyes meet, and I don't expect to see anything in his flat brown gaze. Incredibly, he backs down. "I'll see if there's something else we can play."

My shoulders slump, and I feel like a dishrag. "Thank you."

Eli is out the door when he steps back, getting right in my face. "This is why I'm with Peg."

I'm sure he means it as a burn, but all I can think is *Peg can have you.* "Just take care of my baby."

"He's not a baby."

My jaw tightens, and I say a little prayer as I watch them go. Eli walks dutifully beside his father, who's checking his phone. Speaking of phones...

Digging in my vest, I pull out mine to see a text waiting on the face.

> STEPHEN
> Dick Dickerson is not your hero.

I quickly tap out a response:

> He never was.

The gray bubble appears with dots in the center. I wait to see his reply.

> STEPHEN
> At least his genes don't seem very strong.

A sigh escapes my lips.

> Only the sick ones.

My phone goes quiet. No gray bubble. I put it on the counter and start sorting clothes as I think about tonight. Dinner with Stephen Hastings. What have I gotten myself into?

The phone buzzes, and I lift it to read the face.

> STEPHEN
> You don't need a hero.

Raising my eyebrows, I appreciate the vote of confidence. I tap out the obvious question.

> Are you calling me a hero?

It only takes a moment for him to reply.

STEPHEN

You're no damsel in distress.

My thumbs move quickly.

> So I don't need you.

STEPHEN

Let's find out.

6

Stephen

"I take it you don't cook much." I'm standing in the small kitchenette of Emmy's fourth-floor walk-up.

She's behind wood and glass doors. White curtains cover them, but I can see her silhouette moving in the background. It's sexy, and I look away... to a heavier white curtain surrounding something in the corner of the kitchen. When I pull it aside, I nod. It's a bathtub.

"Sorry?" She opens the double doors, and my throat goes dry.

She's wearing a silky yellow dress that stops mid-thigh, showing off her shapely legs, accentuated with platform espadrilles. The part that kills me, as my eyes slide up her body, over the embroidered flowers on the bodice, is the neckline. It's off the shoulder, and damn. Emmy Barton has lovely shoulders.

"Is this okay?" She looks down and a lock of blond hair slips to the front. "Lou found it at a vintage store, and I've never worn it."

"You're beautiful." Her cheeks tinge a pretty shade of pink.

She has already informed me I'm not her hero—not sure where that came from—but I don't mind rocking her little boat with a compliment. "I see you have the requisite kitchen-bath."

Her eyes actually light, and she crosses the tiny space to the even tinier kitchen. "Isn't it nuts? You hear about these apartments in Greenwich Village with tubs in the kitchens, but the truth is they're pretty rare now. Most of the walk-ups have separate baths these days."

I take a step to the door beside her Barbie dream stove. Behind it, a narrow tunnel leads to a toilet on a riser. "Something like this?"

She joins me at the door, and her fresh scent surrounds me, flowers and soap. My dick twitches, and I take a step back, clearing my throat. I can't make an adjustment with her this close.

"It's a pretty tight fit. Don't bump your head." She points to the archway above the steps leading to the elevated toilet.

"Why would they construct it this way?" I look at the strange configuration.

"I think it has something to do with the pipes below." She turns and goes to a minuscule closet just outside the doors separating her bedroom from the living area.

I see a queen-sized bed inside. "One bit of luxury?" I motion toward it.

"When we first moved here, Eli slept with me. Now he prefers being on the futon. Most nights."

"What happens when he needs his own room?"

Her lips tighten, and that old irritation is back. "I appreciate you trying to help me save face or whatever in front of Burt today, but you and I are not friends."

"I thought we were... a while back."

"Really? And when did you get back to Manhattan?"

"Six years ago."

She tilts her head to the side. "I thought I hadn't seen you around."

"You were married."

"Did you know?"

I shake my head no, glancing at my loafers.

"Did you care?"

"I was a bit preoccupied." Trying to find Ximena, learning she'd died, dealing with my emotions, my anger at the injustice of it all.

"Yeah, I have a life, too." She's angry, but I don't want our night to go this way, both of us fighting. I want to know her better.

"Friends or not..." I slip my hands in the front pockets of my slacks, doing my best to redirect. "You have to eat, and I did make reservations." Her brow lowers, but I push through. "Think of it as a cost-benefit scenario. You spend a few hours with me, and in return, you get a great meal."

She thinks several seconds, then puts her purse on her shoulder and walks to the door. "I suppose I don't like eating alone. Where are you taking me?"

THE HEARTH IS a short walk from her apartment. The streets are crowded like always, and every time I reach out to touch her, to protect her from the mob, she pulls away. When we reach the restaurant, she at least lets me hold the door for her.

The dining room is dark wood and yellow lighting. It's dim and cozy, and the long, rustic tables are polished to a high shine. We're led to a small one by a window, and I order us a bottle of red wine and warm Italian butter beans.

"Butter beans." She leans forward and emits a low laugh as the appetizer is served.

"You know how these New York chefs are. Always taking simple things and reinventing."

We take a bite, and I'm about to take it all back. "Damn!" She covers her mouth with one hand. "That's some good ass butter beans."

I shake my head, covering my laugh with my napkin. She lifts the globe of pinot noir and takes a sip, her eyes fixed on me.

"What?"

Leaning forward, she puts the glass on the table. "I honestly can't remember the last time I ate a butter bean."

"You never answered me at your apartment. Do you cook?"

"As much as I'm able. The kitchen's kind of small."

"I noticed."

"Still, I have a brain. I'm able to figure things out."

The corner of my mouth rises with a smile. I remember how smart she is. "So tell me about your son."

Her entire demeanor shifts with that one question. Warmth fills her eyes, and she fingers the stem of her wine glass.

"What can I say? He's amazing. He's incredibly smart. He's sensitive." Her eyes flicker to mine. "He's my best friend."

She's so pretty in this light, talking about Eli like he hung the moon. I don't remember my mother as clearly as I'd like. I only remember Ximena comforting me after her death. Watching Emmy's entire mood change at the very thought of her son makes me wish I could remember her better.

"What made you decide to homeschool him?" I lift my glass of wine and take a sip. It's an excellent pinot.

Her eyes become clouded. "He had a bad seizure at school. He fell during PE class. He was down for almost a minute, and when he stopped, he'd... Well, sometimes it causes him to lose control of bodily functions." Her chin drops, and it feels like a punch in the gut.

He's a cute kid, curious and thoughtful. "I'm sure he was humiliated."

"Some kids were nice about it. Others... well, you know."

I look down as my jaw tightens. "Kids can be cruel. Hell, adults can be cruel."

"It wasn't a good situation. He couldn't continue taking PE, but the school wouldn't work with me. I could have made a big stink about it, but Burt wasn't helpful. After a few weeks, Eli didn't want to go back."

"Can't say I blame him."

Thinking of that cute little guy dealing with jerks teases that old wound in my heart. The disadvantages of not having money, not having power. I've always had both...

The waiter interrupts us, putting a plate of beef and ricotta meatballs in front of me. Emmy ordered the polenta with charred carrots.

"This might be the fanciest dinner I've had in years." Her eyes are warm.

We do a little toast, and I dig into my dish, letting out a low groan. "Delicious."

Her fork is across the table at once, spearing one of my meatballs and stealing it to her plate.

"Hey," I cry with a laugh. "You didn't even ask."

"Oh, sorry." The bite is in her mouth in a flash. "May I try one of your meatballs? I can? Oh, it's delicious!"

She says it all so fast, as if we're having a conversation. I quickly reach out and stab a charred carrot. "Hey!"

I give her fork a parry as she tries to go for another one. "Stay on your side of the table."

Pressing her lips together, she returns to her plate. "So touchy."

We chew for a few minutes, and I admire the glow of her skin under the yellow lights, surrounded by dark wood.

"Did you ever work at Sotheby's?"

She shakes her head. "I had Eli right out of college... I thought I'd go to work once he started preschool, but the seizures started. I didn't feel comfortable leaving him."

"I'd think preschools would be trained for epileptic children."

"It's a different thing, a brain disorder." She takes another sip of wine. "We weren't even sure if the seizure meds would work."

"So there's no cure?" She's quiet, and her eyes go to her lap. I'm not sure how to read this response. "I've spent the last three years researching every treatment, ever since his first seizure happened. I was terrified. I'd never seen anyone have a seizure before."

Shifting in my seat, I try to imagine. I can't. "Is there a cure?"

Nodding slowly, she studies the base of her wine glass. "Only two hospitals in the U.S. do it. It's an experimental surgery, focused on a very specific area of the brain. It's very expensive, and there's no guarantee—"

"You want to do it?"

"I'd love to do it, but insurance won't cover it. It's not FDA approved yet."

"Can you get in one of the trials?"

"They fill up so fast."

"I see." I'm frustrated by her predicament.

We've finished our meal, and I signal for the waiter to bring us the check. It takes a few minutes to settle up, and I stand, holding the back of her chair as she rises.

The night air has grown chilly while we were in the restaurant, and the crowd has grown thicker out on the sidewalks. It's Friday in the Village. As we walk back toward her apartment, she doesn't pull away when I put my arm around her to shield her from the mob.

When we reach her apartment, she stops at the main

entrance. "Sorry." She glances up, and our eyes meet. "I'm not the most entertaining dinner date."

Placing my hand on the doorframe, I lean in closer. "You're wrong. I like your son. I wanted to know more about him."

That gets me a smile. "He really is great. I try not to let the challenges get us down."

Pushing off the door, I motion for her to enter. "I'll walk you up to your door."

"There's really no need—"

"Don't start with that again. Your neighborhood is sketchy as fuck."

Shaking her head, she laughs. "It's really not. The West Village is way sketchier."

"That doesn't make it better."

The door closes behind us with a slam, and our feet make short scuffing noises as we climb the square-shaped flights of stairs.

"Didn't an apartment building explode around here a few years back?"

She stops ahead of me on the stairs and turns, looking down. "Someone had hacked into the gas line of the restaurant below. It wasn't a reflection of building safety in the neighborhood."

I take a step up, changing our perspective so now I'm looking down at her. "If that isn't a reflection on building safety, I don't know what is. Do you have renter's insurance?"

Her eyebrows rise, and she starts climbing again. A low growl rumbles from my throat, and she actually laughs. "You sound like Ethan."

"Renter's insurance is shockingly affordable and pretty easy to secure."

We're at the door and she stops outside, looking up at me. "Thanks, Dad."

Leaning closer, I pin her under my arm again. "I liked your dad. He would've agreed with me."

"I like my apartment. Stop bossing me around." She turns under my arm, unlocking the door and stepping inside.

I step inside behind her and close the door, leaning my back against it, watching as she goes to the tiny closet and puts her purse inside. She toes off her boots, making her even shorter in bare feet.

Then she faces me, one hand on her hip and the other motioning around the room. "See? It's nice. Don't you think?"

I glance to the kitchen, to her bedroom. She's waiting for me to say something. "You keep it very clean."

Shaking her head she walks to the near-empty refrigerator and opens it. "I'd offer you a drink, but I need to go to the store."

"I don't want a drink." I'm watching her, wondering what to do with these feelings twisting in my stomach.

I want her.

She stands across the room looking at me, and a quiet extends between us. We've spoken nonstop since our paths crossed. She says I'm not her friend. She says I'm not her hero, but there's no denying the pull between us.

Her blue eyes capture mine, sparkling and warm. Her shoulders have teased me all night, soft and shapely. I want to touch them, kiss them... bite them. Her breasts are hidden in the drape of that dress, but I remember them, small, bouncing with every thrust of my hips.

When I meet her gaze again, her expression has darkened. "Stop looking at me that way."

"Tell me to leave." Pushing off the door, I take a step closer, closing the distance between us.

"I don't like you." Her voice goes softer.

I take another step closer. "It feels like you do." Reaching out, I touch her shoulder with the backs of my fingernails. It rises automatically, and chills skate down her arm. "I think you feel the same thing I feel."

Her chest rises and falls rapidly. Her breathing comes faster. "I don't feel anything for you."

Our eyes meet again, and I lean closer. "Then tell me to go."

Her lips part, and her pink tongue darts out to touch her bottom one. I inhale slowly, fresh flowers and soap. Placing my hand on her shoulder, I slide a lock of her silky blonde hair back and forth between my fingers.

"I don't want to go." Releasing her hair, I straighten, moving away. "But I won't stay unless you want me to."

Her eyes don't leave mine. "I don't want you to."

Nodding, I start to leave when her hand grasps my wrist. I stop moving when she steps closer, rising onto her tiptoes. Her breasts graze my chest.

Her face tilts higher, and our eyes meet as she whispers. "This isn't happening."

It's the last words she speaks before our mouths collide.

7

Emmy

Stephen's kiss intoxicates me. No one kisses me the way he does, and I want it. I've wanted it since he walked through that door. He pushes my mouth open and nips my upper lip before seeking out my tongue with his. Then he pulls my bottom lip between his. He devours me. Heat burns between my thighs, and wetness slips in my pussy.

"I can't do this." I gasp, holding his neck, and trying to get my bearings.

"Decide." He growls before sucking my tongue into his mouth.

I feel his cock against my thigh, hard and long and so thick. I remember him so well. Oh, fuck, I want to climb him like a tree.

His large hands are on my ass, gathering my dress into his fists until he finds my skin. His fingers trace the line of my thong. If he touches my clit, I'll come at once...

I'm holding his shoulders, when he cups my ass and carries me to the tiny table in my itty-bitty kitchen. He sits me down, standing between my thighs, leaning closer to ravage my mouth again.

My lips chase his, my tongue curls with his, my fingernails rake through the scruff on his cheeks, into his hair. I moan when he palms my breasts through my dress. I can't stop making little sounds. It's been so long since I've had good sex. Since I've had him.

His lips are at my temple, and his voice is a hot whisper on my cheek. "I want to have you for dessert."

My clit is screaming yes... *Yes!* When my brain cuts through like a bullhorn. *No.* I can't have sex with Stephen Hastings. As bad as I want it, as long as it's been, it would be a mistake.

Placing my fingers on his mouth, I shake my head. "You know we can't do this."

"I'm not sure I know that." His hands are still on me, but his eyes study mine. He won't force me.

He won't try and wear me down like Burt did.

He wouldn't have to try. Clearly, I'm his...

Stepping back. He runs a hand down his blazer, down the front of his pants. That cock... Oh, I want that cock so bad.

Groaning, I put my fingers over my cheeks and stand. Then I catch his wrist as I pass him on the way to my door. Have I forgotten what happened the last time I let my hormones take over? He fucked me and dumped me like a used condom.

"You have to go now." Opening the door, I hold it between us, refusing to meet his gaze.

He clears his throat, pausing in the entrance. "I'm sorry—"

"No..." I cut him off. "Just go. I'm not falling for you again."

He's on the landing, and I close the wooden barrier firmly between us. My eyes squeeze shut, and I lower my forehead to the door, breathing hard. Tears are in my eyes. Stupid tears. Stupid girl.

My hand is still on the doorknob when I finally hear the noise of his footsteps receding down the stairs. He hesitated. Why would he hesitate?

Pushing away from the door, I roughly wipe the damp from my cheeks. "It's hard to walk with an erection, I guess."

I won't let myself go back there. I won't dream about him at night and analyze everything he says or does searching for clues that he cares. I'm not that little girl anymore. I'm a woman, a mom. I have more important things in my life now.

Picking up my phone, I shoot a text to Eli.

How's it going?

I wait several seconds, but I don't get a reply. Glancing at the clock, I see it's after eleven. I guess he's gone to sleep. I fight against the pang of guilt over not catching him before bedtime.

Flopping on my bed alone, I stare at my phone face, wishing he would reply. As Stephen pointed out, he's growing up. It happened so fast. I've got to get him that surgery before he's too old for it to help him. But how?

"LET'S BE CLOTHES FRIENDS." I read the sign aloud into my phone as I dash into Miss Con-Cleaneality.

Eli forces a chuckle on the other end of the line. "Good one."

I wave to Lou as I run to my locker, pushing in my bag and pulling out my vest. "You don't have to laugh if you don't think it's funny."

"I like it, Mom. It's punny."

"Punny," I exhale, shrugging on my vest. "Who taught you that word?"

"You did!"

"I did?" I can't help a grin. He really is brilliant for seven. "Sorry I didn't catch you before bedtime last night."

"It's okay. I was pretty tired."

"Did he make you play football?" My chest is tight, and I swear to God, I will take away his visitation rights... But how? I can't afford another lawyer.

"No. We went to a baseball game instead."

Thank you, Jesus. My laugh is weak. "No wonder you fell asleep."

"I like baseball!"

"Nerd." I lean my back against the lockers wishing I could comb his hair off his forehead. "Well, I have to get to work now. Have fun. If you want to come back early, that's okay."

"I'm good. We're going to the park tomorrow."

"Really? Well... that's great! I'm glad to hear it." He calls to someone in the background. I tell him I love him, and we disconnect.

I try hard not to put Eli in the middle of his dad and me. I don't want to put that kind of pressure on him. Burt always pushes him to play contact sports, even though his doctors have advised against it. He doesn't want his son to grow up "queer." *Asshole.*

God, I'd give anything for a redo of our custody arrangement. What made me think allowing him to have visitation rights was a good idea? I believed a son needed his dad in his life... Now I'm not so sure.

Walking out front, Lou has a red handkerchief tied around her head Rosie the Riveter style. She's in a vintage yellow waitress dress with her pink vest on top. I'm in my usual cutoffs and tank top. When we get to moving fast, it gets hot in here.

"How's my little man?" She winks a false eyelash at me. "His idiot dad behaving?"

"No football, thank God." I pull out the pick-up receipts for today and sort them.

"That's good." Lulabell watches me putting the receipts in the little box organized by last name, and she muses, "We probably should get more digital around here."

"It would make things easier." Glancing up, I smile. "We could do discounts for return customers and special promos…"

"That sounds like math." She slides a pencil behind her ear. "I was thinking it would eliminate all this alphabetizing."

"That, too." I give her a wink.

Lulabell is hopelessly stuck in the year 2000. She still carries a flip phone. "Are you ready for tonight?"

"Yes! I can't wait. What time do I need to be at the Art Bar?" The bell on the door dings and a perfectly coiffed blonde walks in with an iPad in one hand and an earbud in her ear.

She hands me the slip without even pausing her conversation. It's weird. Almost like she's speaking to me, but not. I want to say something, but Lou takes the slip from my hand.

"I've got her." I return to sorting while my boss goes around the rack of beaded, plastic-covered evening gowns. "The show starts at seven, so if you're there by six, we should have plenty of time."

She rings up the bougie assistant, and I take the next customer. By noon, most of the pickups are done. Saturdays are different because we don't have the lunch hour rush. We have a lull in the middle of the day.

"So how was your date with James Bond?" Lulabell leans on the counter. "Give me all the scoop."

"He doesn't look like James Bond." I roll my eyes, doing my best not to flush at the memory of kissing Stephen. "No scoop."

"If you have no scoop after a night with that man, you're doing it wrong."

I say a silent prayer for a customer to walk in. The last thing I want right now is to discuss Stephen with Lou.

Despite my stern pep talk about not having feelings for him, I spent half the night trying to forget how he kissed me. Correction, *devoured* me. I would close my eyes and see his gaze potent as a touch, undressing me with his eyes. I could feel his hands ghosting across my legs. Finally, I gave up and dug out my vibrator. In less than ten seconds, I collapsed into a leg-shaking orgasm.

Lou studies my pink cheeks. "Something happened."

"He took me to Hearth..."

"Nice place."

"Then he walked me home..." My voice trails off, and she scoots closer.

"And?" Her eyebrows waggle.

"That's it."

"That's it!" Her shoulders drop, and her expression is pure dismay. It morphs into contemplation. "It was only a first date, I guess."

"First and last. I'm not doing that again."

"Emmy, honey. Wake up." She laughs, touching my arm. "I'd do that again and again and again..."

"He's worried my apartment will explode."

Her teased head tilts to the side. "Isn't that sweet! He's worried about your safety!"

"He told me to get renter's insurance."

"That's less romantic... But girl! You don't have renter's insurance?" Her eyes are round with horror. "My sister Sarabeth's apartment burned down because a neighbor left her curling iron plugged in."

I'm about to protest the theory that Stephen Hastings is always right when wouldn't you know? The bell rings, and he waltzes into Miss Con-Cleaneality.

"Speak of the devil!" Lou straightens off the counter, and I cringe from my scalp to my toenails.

He aims that panty-melting grin right at me. "Were you speaking of me?"

"Isn't that funny..." I grab the box and flip to the Hs. "I always suspected you were the devil."

He leans on the counter so I catch a sniff of his warm, leathery cologne. It's annoyingly sexy. "You realize, in that context, the devil isn't actually Lucifer, the prince of darkness."

I tilt my head to the side and smile up at him. "Yet here you are."

Lou waves a hand in front of her face. "Lord, I'd better put the caps on the chemicals. You two are going to burn the place down with all that heat."

My cheeks blaze, and I turn away, going to the rack of evening gowns. "You're here for your aunt's dress?"

Lou touches my arm. "I've got it, honey. I have a special place for the Jean Claude."

"Of course you do." I look down, not wanting to return to the counter.

Fat chance of that.

Lou gives me a little shove. "Get out there now, and ring him up." She leans into my shoulder. "And stop fighting. Let what's going to happen, happen."

My jaw tightens, but I return to the front to do my job.

I go straight to the register and start ringing up his ticket.

He walks down to where I'm standing. "I was thinking about our conversation last night."

"We don't have to revisit it." I reach for his card without making eye contact.

"You should move in with me."

"What?" I look up to find his blue eyes studying me intently. His card slips through my fingers to the floor. "Shit."

Leaning down, I dig under the counter for the thin piece of plastic. When I reemerge, his brow is lowered, and he nods, like it's another case of him always being right.

"Temporarily, of course. I have plenty of room, and I work from home. Elijah can stay and do his studies while you come here during the day."

"No." I close my eyes, shaking my head. "Just... no."

"Why not?"

"It's too far from here."

"It's less than ten minutes on the train."

"It's a ridiculous suggestion. I'm not moving in with you."

He pauses a moment, considering me. "Is it because of the other thing? Your inability to keep your hands off me?"

My eyes narrow. "I can keep my hands off you."

"Then it's settled. I'll have my housekeeper clean out the spare rooms."

"It is not settled!" My voice goes higher.

Lulabell chooses that moment to return with the red dress over her arm. "What's not settled? Is there a problem with the register?"

"Stephen just asked me to move in with him." I slant my eyes at her for backup.

Instead, a massive grin splits her cheeks. "Damn, girl! When you've got it, you've got it!" She puts the dress on the counter laughing.

Stephen's expression is mildly amused. "Tell you what. I'll make you dinner tonight and show you the place."

He takes the dress from Lou, and she turns to me, arms crossed, a mischievous grin on her face that says *just do it.*

"I have to work tonight."

His brow furrows. "Where?"

Lulabell jumps in. "It's a fundraiser fashion show at The Art Bar. She'll be done by seven, seven thirty at the latest."

"Thanks, Lou." I don't even try to mask the sarcasm in my voice.

Stephen taps his hand on the counter. "I'll pick you up at your place at eight."

He doesn't wait for my answer before he's out the door.

I turn to Lulabell, and she only laughs, waving her hand. "Stop fighting, baby girl. Enjoy the ride!"

8

Stephen

The day moves too slowly. I hop online and video chat with my work partner Remington Key in South Carolina. He's finalizing coding, and his hair's a mess. He's in a white t-shirt and pajama pants, and a tiny, dark baby's head is on his shoulder.

I can't resist teasing my formerly ship-shape Naval buddy. "Perhaps you're taking this working from home a bit too far. At least put on pants, man."

"What time is it?" He rubs an eye and looks around, I presume searching for a clock.

"It's after noon. See the top corner of your screen."

"Sorry, this little peanut didn't want to sleep last night." He puts a large hand on the tiny baby's back, and something inside me twinges. *What the fuck?* I snatch up a stress ball and give it a squeeze.

"You know, children bring lice into the house." I lean back, pushing against the unwelcome rush of sentiment in my chest.

"I can't wait to give you hell when it's your turn to have one of these."

"You'll be waiting a long time, my friend. Now, what's on the agenda?"

We pull out our master list, and he names potential clients for a new defense program he's working on. Remi has made a name for himself with military applications. I've always been more interested in healthcare. In my opinion, it's a more urgent problem. He's always been more focused overseas, but we make our relationship work.

Actually, Remi and I are good friends.

His wife walks in and takes the baby. She waves at me on the screen, and I nod glancing at the clock. "We should call it a day. You look well, my friend. I'm glad."

"And you're still living the single life?"

"I wouldn't say it in those words."

He's easy and happy. "What words would you use?"

"I'm developing my business. I'm not hanging out in bars hitting on women."

Remi leans forward, looking directly into my eyes. "Your business is developed. Are you planning to be alone the rest of your life?"

The question hits me in a way I don't like. "Perhaps, if that's what I choose to do. Modern society is too fixated on the construct of marriage and two point five children."

"Try it some time."

I've had enough. "If we're done here—"

He laughs, and I click the mouse to close the window. It's six-thirty. Tapping on my phone, I place a to-go order and schedule delivery for two hours from now.

Remi's words have made me restless. How I choose to live my life is nobody's business. Frustration tightens my chest, and instead of calling my car service, I head out the door to walk downtown.

The streets of New York are easier to manage solo. My hands are in my pockets, and I move through the clumps of tourists and residents like a pebble in a stream.

I couldn't relax in the cab home from Emmy's place last night. Sexual frustration was part of it, but also thinking of her in that apartment clenched my jaw. It's cramped and dangerous. The location is bad, and it's not enough space for Eli. Hell, what if he had a seizure? He could hit his head on any number of objects if he fell in that rattrap.

Emmy's resistance nags at the back of my mind. Why won't she stop fighting and do what I say? She knows I'm right. I think of Ximena and Ramon in that fucking dump in the Bronx. If I could have helped them, I would've.

When I got home last night, I surveyed all the wasted space in my townhome. I only use two rooms on the top floor, apart from the common areas, I have space for two more people easily.

Putting our physical attraction to the side, the Bartons and the Hastings have been friends for years. And dammit, what's the point of having vast sums of wealth if I can't use it to help people in need?

Emmy should understand this. Her father used his legal expertise to help others. It's not such a foreign concept. As I walk, I anticipate her objections and my response. She's so fucking stubborn with all this *I hate you* bullshit. What is she? A child? And clearly she does not hate me. She moans like a sex kitten when I kiss her. I have to adjust my fly at that memory.

The neighborhood grows more colorful as I approach the bar. Glancing at my watch, I see it's only seven.

"Name?" A young woman with a severe black bob and multiple piercings in her face looks at me expectantly. She's dressed in a black leather mini and a silky beige tank that shows off her sleeves of ink.

"Stephen Hastings." She holds out a clipboard, but I put a hand up to stop her. "I'm not on the list. Can I buy a ticket at the door?"

"Sorry. Invitation only. The tables are sold and all set up for the dinner."

A group strolls up beside me, and I move so she can check them in. As they enter, I peer into the space. It's an exposed-brick courtyard beyond this wall, and I see several tables in the back unset and unoccupied.

The girl returns to me, frowning. "I'm sorry, you'll have to come back after the event. It ends at eleven."

"How much for a table?" I take my wallet out of my back pocket.

"Sir, we've already set up for the—"

"I understand, but I noticed empty tables in the back. How much?"

Her lips press together, and she tilts her head to the side. "Eight hundred."

"Can you run my card?"

"Cash only." She points her pencil over my shoulder. "There's an ATM on the corner there."

"Be right back."

Five minutes later, I'm inside, strolling around the brick-lined courtyard, hoping the girl at the door puts the cash I gave her into the fund. Groups of people stand in circles chatting softly, champagne flutes in hand. Oversized palm trees and Ficus are arranged throughout and white Christmas lights are draped from the columns, over arches. It's an elegant, low-key affair.

Picking up a program, I learn that it's a fundraiser for art programs in public schools. Good cause. A waiter passes through to what looks like a backstage area, and I drift over to take a peek. Bingo. I've found her.

"Yeah, so I asked him, if you're not banging your secretary, then why are you working late every night?" A very long young woman with a thick New Jersey accent sits in a chair waving her hands as she speaks. She's wearing a brown tube dress, and her hair is parted right down the middle in a stick-straight bob.

"What did he say?" Emmy's blonde waves are piled on top of her head in a bun. A few tendrils hang around her pretty face. She's in a tight black dress with a white men's shirt over it tied at her waist.

She looks way hotter than the toothpick she's working on.

"He said he doesn't even have a secretary."

A fine line forms in the center of Emmy's forehead, and I watch as she rubs a thick black brush over the girl's whole face.

"Do you believe him?" She drops the brush and picks up a purple sponge shaped like an egg and starts dabbing it around the model's nose and eyes.

"What choice do I have?" The girl lifts her bony arms. "But I tell you what. My uncle Artie knows a guy who's a detective, and he's going to do some digging."

Emmy steps back, gives her a compassionate look, and picks up a pink bottle. "Close your eyes." She sprays a light mist in the air above the girl's face, and then touches her leg. "You're all done. Good luck with Lenny."

The girl stands and hugs her. "Oh, Em, you're the best! You come back with Lou again, okay?"

"If they let me!"

No one else sits in her chair, and Emmy leans her head to the side, rubbing her neck. Lulabell waves at me from the other end of the room, and I wave back. *Busted.*

Emmy turns to face me, and as usual, her smile melts away.

I release the curtain and walk to where she's packing up her kit. "Good evening."

"You're early." She doesn't look up from her progress.

"I got tired of waiting, so I walked. Made pretty good time."

Her eyes travel from my leather shoes up to my neck. "Do you always dress like a *GQ* model when you go out walking?"

Casting my tan suit a glance, I shrug. "I like this suit. It's comfortable, and this is an eight hundred dollar per table fundraiser."

"How did you get in? You're not on the guest list."

"It seems like a good cause. I bought a table. Although, if they really want to make money, they should let you be a model."

Our eyes meet, and energy flashes between us. I feel it low in my belly. I've got to sleep with her again. It's the only way to get this out of our systems.

She turns away, but her cheeks are flushed. My throat tightens. Yes, tonight.

"Are we sitting at your table?" She blinks those pretty eyes up at me.

"Good God, no. The food at these events is awful. Rubber chicken and mushy vegetables. I'm taking you back to my place."

"I'm not moving in with you." That sassy mouth. She's always so defiant.

"That's correct. Tonight, we're having dinner, and I'm showing you the place."

"It's not happening."

I take her arm and lead her toward the entrance. "Then view this as an educational experience. People buy tickets to look inside historic brownstones."

She shakes her head, slinging her bag over her shoulder. "I've been inside them."

"KATHERINE HEPBURN HAD a place in Turtle Bay Gardens." She strolls through the open floor plan of my living and kitchen area with a glass of pinot noir in her hand.

"The neighborhood's close to Broadway. You could take Eli to a show whenever you want."

She makes a little face. "Burt would love that."

"Sorry?"

Her nose wrinkles, and she seems annoyed. "He makes these comments about how I'm over-protective. How I'm keeping Eli from doing manly things. Like it's going to make his son turn out gay."

"Have I mentioned your ex husband is an idiot? He was an idiot in school, and clearly he didn't mature out of it."

"My point is who cares if he's gay? All I want is for Eli to be happy..." Her voice trails off, and she takes another sip of wine.

"And to get that surgery?"

"I've stopped thinking about that."

A pinch in my chest reminds me I haven't. "Come with me. I'll show you the extra rooms."

She leaves her glass on the island and follows me to a flight of dark-wood stairs. On the second floor, a sitting room faces the street, and directly across from us is a small bedroom.

"My aunt decorated this one. Actually, she decorated the whole house. She likes projects."

A strange feeling tightens my chest. Am I worried about what Emmy might think? I shouldn't be. Bex has excellent taste.

She enters the blue room, and her breath catches. "Oh, my goodness..." It's a whisper of wonder as she turns, looking at everything.

The walls are covered in beige wallpaper with a small pattern of navy anchors, ship's wheels, and spy glasses. The bed is made with a navy and beige spread covered in nautical patterns. In the bookcase are hardbound editions of *Moby Dick*, *Treasure Island*, and other sea-themed stories.

My favorite part is around the medallion at the base of the ceiling fan. It's a large, navy stencil featuring points of the compass and the words *Not all who wander are lost.*

"Eli would love this." She goes to the bookcase and carefully picks up a conch shell from Key West, a starfish from Bermuda. On top of the bookcase is a massive, black pirate ship in an enormous bottle. "He'd freak out if he saw that."

"It's Blackbeard's ship. *Queen Anne's Revenge.*" I'm feeling really good about my proposal at this point. How could she possibly say no? Having housemates is a fact of life for most New York residents. Not the rich ones, but still.

She picks up a framed photo of me in my dress whites. I step up behind her and reach for it. "I can remove the photographs of me."

"You're very handsome in uniform." She looks up, and our eyes meet.

She doesn't seem as angry anymore. I remember the last time she looked at me this way, that night so long ago. It fans the heat smoldering in my belly.

"We all looked the same." I put the photo aside.

"I never asked how you liked being in the Navy."

Clearing my throat, I rub my stomach, trying to break this pull I feel toward her. "I liked it more than I thought I would. I went in thinking the danger, the lack of control would bother me, but the routine, the discipline... it was very satisfying."

"Were you in any battles?"

"No, I was lucky." She follows me to the door and back out onto the landing. "My time was mostly spent sailing, being a presence."

"Still, you were always in danger."

"I suppose we're in danger every day of our lives."

"But not like that."

I lead her to the bedroom at the end of the hall. It's pale yellow and faces a small park behind the block of townhomes. "Rebecca wanted the window-seat to be the focal point of this room."

Emmy leans into it and looks outside where a large tree grows. "As much as I hate to admit it, I miss this. Growing up in this world is so different from the East Village."

"You belong here."

Her eyes flash at me. "I didn't say it was a bad different. This life can be very controlling and miserable."

Tell me about it. Still, "I don't remember you being miserable growing up."

She shakes her head, but I let it drop. I don't want to fight with her.

Instead, I motion toward the stairs at the end of the hall. "My bedroom and office are on the third floor. You never have to see me. Unless you want to."

Her arms cross and she meets me at the door. "Why are you doing this? I didn't ask for your help."

"You didn't have to."

"So, what's in it for you?"

My brow furrows. When did little Emily Barton get so cynical? I guess she has a point.

"We're old friends—"

"No, we're not old friends." She snaps.

Okay, perhaps not. I think through all my reasons from earlier today on my walk.

"Our families have known each other forever. I like your son. I have the space..." The tension in my stomach turns to anger. "Why are you being so stubborn? Your dad helped people in need."

"So none of this is about me?"

"Indirectly, I suppose—"

"I meant about *sleeping* with me." She gives me a look.

I actually laugh. "Definitely not. You've been a harpy ever since we ran into each other."

Her jaw drops, and she steps forward to shove my arm. "Bastard. I have not."

"You have."

"I'm sure any woman who hates you is a harpy."

"You keep saying that." I put my hand on the doorframe above her head and lean down, closer to her face. Our warm breath mingles, and I know she feels our chemistry. I've been fighting it for two days.

"Tell me why you hate me." My voice is low and smooth.

She jerks her chin away, clearly flustered. "I'm not having this conversation with you."

I chuckle. Flustering her sassy little ass might be my new favorite thing.

I'm ready to challenge her when the buzzer sounds downstairs. Our eyes meet, and we say at the same time, "Food."

Paper bags with the Burger & Lobster logo are spread all around us on the oversized bar in my kitchen. Emmy's on a barstool picking chunks of lobster out of a Kaiser roll while I uncork a bottle of Sangiovese. A beast burger is on a plate in front of me.

"Mm!" She nods around her bite. "This was always my favorite place. How did you know?"

I put a fresh glass of the dark red wine in front of her. "It's everybody's favorite place."

"Burgers and lobster. I was expecting something a little different from you."

"Don't start with the whole I can't believe you eat hamburgers crap." I swirl the wine in my glass, letting it open, before setting it down and picking up my food. "I've known you longer than that."

"Excuse me." She makes big eyes as she takes a sip of wine. "I only meant I expected something fancier for my seduction dinner."

"This is not a seduction dinner."

"It's not?"

"No."

"That's disappointing." She snorts and drinks more wine. "So all this 'move in with me' really is about your concern for my welfare?"

"It's more about your kid." I take another bite of burger. "If I wanted to have sex with you, I'd have sex with you."

"Is that so?" She puts her glass down, eyes narrow. "Whether I want to or not? Have you heard of Me Too?"

"Yeah, and you want it, too." I sip my wine, keeping my eyes fixed on hers.

"I don't know how we got onto this conversation." She blinks away and picks another chunk of lobster out of the Kaiser roll.

"Sounds like the cry of the defeated to me."

"You wish."

I laugh. I swear, she's always been this way, feisty, cute.

Her hair is still in that ridiculous bun on the top of her head, and she still has that white shirt over her black dress. She's not cute. She's beautiful.

"What happened with Burt?" I can't help my curiosity. "Other than he's an idiot."

"Haven't you heard? I'm a harpy."

"No." Shaking my head, I take another sip of wine. "The harpy thing is new. Why did you leave him? I'm certain you would have tried to make it work. For Elijah."

She cuts her eyes at me, then unexpectedly softens. "He couldn't handle Eli's condition. He was embarrassed to have a son who wasn't a big-time jock like he was. We fought constantly. Next thing I knew, he was sleeping with Peg."

"Peg, the bug-eyed home wrecker." I take another sip of wine, thinking. "So Elijah blames himself for what happened?"

"I don't think so... God, I hope he doesn't." Her chin drops. "I did my best to shield him from it."

"He's smart, though." I think about myself growing up. I knew everything that went on in my house, whether the adults told me or not.

"Why are you doing this?" Her voice rises, angry. She rocks back on the barstool, circling a finger in front of me. "You go from not giving a shit about me to now you're so interested in my welfare?"

That does it. Placing my wine glass down, I round the bar to stand in front of her. "When did I not give a shit about you?"

Her brow lowers, and she pushes against my chest. "You took what you wanted, and you walked away. Now you're trying to do it again."

"I don't know what you're talking about. I'm trying to help you. I'm not trying to take anything." I'm between her legs now tugging on the knot in that white shirt. "Except this. Take this off."

The knot slips open, and the shirt falls down her arms, leaving her in only that black knit dress that hugs her body. "Stephen..."

"That's better."

"Now this..." I reach up to her hair, feeling for pins and sliding them out, one by one.

"What are you doing?" Her voice goes louder, and her hands catch mine as her thick blonde waves fall all around her shoulders.

"Much better."

"Remind me... You said this *isn't* about sleeping together?" Her eyes flash as she pushes her hair back, and I catch her face.

Using my thumb, I tug her bottom lip down. "I said if I wanted to have sex with you, I would."

Heat moves through my pelvis, centering in my cock, which is hard and aching. I'm tired of playing games with her. I unbutton the top three buttons on my dress shirt and pull it over my head. Her eyes widen at my bare chest and her bottom lip slips between her teeth.

It's fucking hot.

"I can't." She whispers a weak protest.

"Do you want me to stop?" My eyes hold hers, level and determined. "I'm calling bullshit if you say yes."

Her throat moves with a swallow. I imagine the tip of my cock hitting the back of her throat, and it makes me harder.

"Tell me to stop and I will." I step closer and heat sparks between us.

She reaches out and puts her palm flat against my bare chest. My fingers thread in the side of her hair, lifting it off her shoulder.

"Tell me the truth." My voice is stern. "Do you want this?"

"Yes." Her eyes flutter up to mine, heavy with desire. "I want it."

9

Emmy

Stephen shoves our dinner aside with his arm and lifts me off the stool onto the bar. His hands are under my skirt, and he grasps the sides of my thong, ripping it off in a rough snatch.

"Oh, shit," I gasp, and his face returns to mine.

He's the same, so fucking beautiful—his torso lined, his muscles lean. I want to run my tongue all over his body. Dark blue eyes watch me, following the path of his fingers along my neck, into the side of my hair. They close in a fist, pulling it so my eyes water.

"Ow," I whisper, but his mouth is on mine, swallowing my voice in the same, ravenous, devouring kiss—pulling my lips with his, tracing my tongue, sucking, biting.

He moves to my jaw and nips my skin, moving higher into my hair before speaking in a hot whisper in my ear. "Lie back."

My nipples are hard beneath my dress, and energy swirls up my thighs to my core. I'm hot and wet, and this is insane.

"Stephen..." My voice cracks, and he catches my eyes again.

His are fire, and I melt beneath them, doing what he says. The hard granite is cold against my back, but I don't have time to care. He shoves my skirt up, over my hips, and covers my pussy with his mouth, licking and sucking me fast and hungry as electricity races through my legs.

"Oh... oh, God!" My back arches off the stone. His arms wrap around my thighs, pulling me closer to his mouth, and he circles my clit with his tongue.

His cheek scuffs my hypersensitive inner thighs, and I rock my hips against his face like I haven't had an orgasm in ages. Stephen's eating me out like I'm a chocolate soufflé, and my hands go to his hair, pulling, pushing. I moan loudly when his thumb presses inside me.

"You're so wet." He kisses the crease of my thigh, tracing his tongue over the skin there.

I'm on fire, dying for more. He hovers over my sex, his hot breath on my stomach when our eyes meet. His shine with satisfaction, like he's won a war, but I'm too helpless to care.

"Please don't stop," I gasp.

"I'm not." Leaning down, our eyes hold as he slips out his tongue, sliding it flat over my clit. It's dirty and erotic, and *oh, God...*

He does it again, firmer, faster, and my eyes squeeze shut. Two more times, and I cry out so loudly, I'm sure they hear me in the street. My thighs shake, my whole body shakes as I come apart, bucking, and pulling his hair. He slides his tongue over my clit again and again until I'm begging him to stop. I can't take it anymore.

"Stephen..." My core aches.

I fumble for his shoulders, scratching his skin, needing him to fill me. In a swift move, he stands, ripping open a drawer and shoving the contents aside. I don't understand until I hear the tearing of a condom wrapper. He rolls it on, and while I'm still throbbing, he rams into me balls deep.

"Oh, fuck." He bends forward over me. His palm slams against the granite, and he starts to thrust, faster, deeper.

"Yes... yes!" My insides stretch for him, and I remember this sensation of total fullness. Stephen Hastings has a massive cock.

Arching my back, I rock my hips, matching his thrusts, sending him deeper. He groans and wraps his arms around my waist, lifting me and putting me on his lap. He's sitting on the padded leather stool, and we're chest to chest. I'm straddling him, holding his broad shoulders, my hair spilling all around us. His face is at my breast, and I quickly slip my arms out of the sleeves of my dress, pushing the top down.

He helps me, pushing the lace cup of my bra aside and sucking a taut nipple into his mouth. He gives me a bite, and it's a charge of pleasure straight to my core.

"Oh, fuck." I hiss, falling forward and tracing my tongue along the cords of muscle in his neck.

Salt fills my mouth. We're sweaty and hot, and the scent of leather and flowers and sex surrounds us.

I thought I'd embellished our first time in my imagination, remembering it as better than it was.

I was wrong.

It really was that good.

Large hands grip my ass, moving me up and down. Our rhythm, our chemistry is on fire. My eyes close, and I'm burning in a sea of desire, orgasm licking my inner thighs like flames.

My pelvis shudders as I come again. My inner muscles clench around him, pulling him deeper. He speaks low and dirty words, telling me what he wants, telling me to take him more, all the way. When he comes, he groans loud and rises to his feet. Pressing my back against the bar, he holds himself deep, rocking his hips firmly in place.

Nothing is sexier than this arrogant man losing his precious control between my thighs. He pulses, filling the condom. My arms are around his neck and his cheek rests against my temple. Our breathing slowly returns to calm.

Lowering my legs, my hands slide down his muscled arms as I stand, trying to get my balance. He disposes of the condom before coming back to me. Then he does the unexpected. He pulls me to him, holding me against his bare chest.

It's not like the last time, our first time. We're skin against skin, and his palms are flat against my skin. It's intimate and quiet. His lips touch my temple, and I wonder how it's possible he feels so right...

No, he's not right. He's bossy and proud. He said if he wanted to have sex with me, he would. *Oh, my God...*

He did.

The reality of what I've done slams into me like a freight train.

I take a step back, out of his arms, straightening my bra and pulling the sleeves of my dress up quickly. "I have to go."

"Wait." He steps forward. "Stay..."

"I've got to get out of here." My head is all mixed up, and I grab the white shirt off the floor. I jam my arms into the sleeves, not even bothering with the knot.

What the hell was I thinking coming here tonight? Of course, I had sex with him, because clearly, I'm just the girl who can't say no to Stephen Hastings.

"Let me drive you back." He grabs a set of keys off a hook.

"No... I'm leaving, and I'm doing it without you!"

Cringing, I know I've made a critical error. I actually thought I was over this guy. I actually thought I was in control. I was a fool. And I was so, so wrong. This is Stephen Hastings we're talking about, my kryptonite.

"What about—"

"I am not moving in with you."

"Emmy, stop this. Right now." His voice has taken that tone. Mr. Bossy.

I'm not having it. Scooping up my purse, I fly out the door, jogging down the steps and racing to the subway stairs before he can follow me.

If I wanted to have sex with you, I'd have sex with you...

"Great job, Em. What else would you do if he wanted?" I'm pacing in a circle around my apartment, thinking how easy it was... How long it's been... My arms are crossed tight over my chest, and I'm fighting to get my raging emotions under control.

Or my hormones.

Or both.

Scanning the small space, my lips tighten. Yes, my apartment is a dump compared to his townhome. "But it's cozy and it's clean!" I shout, fluffing the couch pillows. "I am not moving in with Stephen Hastings."

I couldn't even make it through dinner without attacking him. I'm supposed to hate him. Remember? One shot of a ripped torso, and all bets are off. *Damn hormones.*

I grab my phone, typing out a text to Eli.

> How did it go today?

Seconds pass. I put my phone down and walk to the kitchen to get some water. I hear my phone buzz and run back, scooping it up as I hop on my bed.

STEPHEN

> You shouldn't have left that way.

Stephen's words make my heart sputter.

For a second, all I can do is stare at the face. Then I shake it off and get myself together. Setting my jaw, I tap out a reply.

> It was time for me to go.

STEPHEN
> Why?

"Why?" I say out loud. Okay, I know he can't hear me.

> Lines were crossed. It was exactly what I thought would happen.

I sit back and smile at my ability to cut to the point.

STEPHEN
> We're consenting adults. Why shouldn't we have sex if we want?

My brow furrows. Stephen might be a little better at cutting to the point than I am.

> Because I don't want to have sex with you!

I hesitate before hitting send.

STEPHEN
> Liar.

I can almost feel his eye roll through the ether.

STEPHEN
> You enjoyed it as much as I did. And stop saying you hate me.

A knot is in my throat, and I try to swallow it away.

> Maybe I don't hate you.

STEPHEN

> You don't say?

> Nope. I do hate you.

A few second pass, and I'm fuming again at his arrogance. The gray bubble appears then disappears. Appears, disappears. I don't know if it means he changed his mind on what to say or if he's sending me an epistle.

My phone buzzes, and I'm ready to go off, until I see it's a reply from Eli.

ELI

> Not bad. Tired. Will be glad to be home.

My chest pulls.

> Everything okay, baby?

ELI

> Mooooooom.

Again, I swallow a knot in my throat.

> Sorry! It's a habit. Everything okay, my big strong man?

ELI

> Moooooooooooooom!!!!!

That makes me laugh, even though my eyes are watering. Nothing will ever stop me from worrying about him. I quickly tap back.

> I think you just need a good night's sleep.

His dad probably had him running his ass off all weekend.
Jerk.

ELI

> Before I go sicko mode.

> What does that mean?

ELI

> Just tired. Love you.

> Love you more.

My heart is racing. My stomach is in knots. From screwing
Stephen, to the immediate realization I totally screwed my
resolve to keep him in the *Not-Friends Zone*, to my worries over
Eli, I'm never going to sleep tonight.

Stephen Hastings. What is his deal anyway? I picture his
face, those blue eyes, that square jaw... Is he bored or trying to
make a point?

He needs to get lost. He needs to get out of my life and leave
us alone. Arrogant asshole with his sexy, arrogant mouth and
that sexy arrogant tongue... that made me come really, really
hard. *Shit.*

Next time I see him, I'm telling him just that.

To get lost, I mean.

My teeth grind, and I punch my pillow a few times
before dropping my head in it again. I scoop up the
remote, scanning through Netflix, looking for something to
binge.

A few clicks and I've found *The Blue Planet*. Sir David Attenborough's soothing voice drifts through my bedroom, telling me

calmly about the hideous creatures that live at the very bottom of the sea…

LOUD KNOCKING JERKS ME AWAKE. I sit up, and it's bright outside. The screensaver is on the flatscreen. More knocking, and I scoot out of bed. It's morning. I'm still wearing my black knit dress, and I didn't wash my face last night. *Great.*

"Some makeup artist I am," I grumble, reaching for a silk kimono draped on a chair.

"Mom!" Eli's voice comes through the door.

"Coming!" I dash over and open it and almost fall backwards when my son grabs me around the waist in a hug.

Just as fast he releases me, running to my room and hopping on my bed to watch television.

"Still in bed?" Burt's arms are crossed and his legs spread like he's ready for battle. "It's after ten."

"It's Sunday." *God, what a dick.* Still, I force an upbeat tone in my voice. "How'd it go?"

"We always have a good time together." His arms drop and he walks into my apartment uninvited.

"You don't have to be defensive." I pivot, holding the door open. "Eli said you went to the park? That's fun."

"God, this place is a dump." He turns around, inspecting my tiny apartment. "How can you live like this?"

"My apartment is not a dump." Now I'm defensive. "It's very clean."

Eli's in the bedroom watching Netflix, and I carefully walk over and close the double doors. If Burt's going to start, I don't want him to hear us. Stephen's words are heavy on my mind, and the last thing I want is my little boy stressed out about his fighting parents. He's got enough to think about.

"I don't like Eli living here. You know it was only a block over where that building blew up?"

If I hear that one more time... "That explosion was caused by an illegal gas tap."

"Still, I don't want my son growing up like this. I've decided to talk to my lawyer about changing our arrangement. I want Eli full-time."

My stomach plunges. "What? You have no grounds for that!"

"I have plenty of grounds." His eyes flash. "You took him out of Pike Academy without my permission. You're home schooling him, and you're not even a qualified teacher. You have him living like a street urchin in this dump. You're a good mom, but my son deserves better than this."

"He does not live like a street urchin! And he's doing really well in school. He's already at the sixth grade level in science."

"He doesn't even have his own bedroom. A boy needs his own bedroom."

Stepping forward, I lower my voice. "Then maybe you should chip in a little more every month."

Burt's eyes flash. "Don't start with that. You're the one who walked out."

"Because you were sleeping with another woman!" My whisper goes high.

"I'll pay for anything my son needs. But I am *not* paying for your harebrained schemes and experimental treatments."

"How dare you..." I'm fighting to keep my voice low. "Everything I do for Eli is well-researched and documented."

"I want him back in Pike, back with his friends—"

"He had a seizure and wet his pants. His so-called friends made fun of him." My stomach cramps at the memory.

"Boys get teased in school. You overreacted, as usual."

"He would come home every day crying."

"He'd have learned how to take up for himself eventually."

My fists are clenched, and I've never wanted to hit a man so much in my life.

"I've been doing my own research." Burt goes to the door, putting his hand on his hip. "You know who else had epilepsy? Julius Caesar. Back then they had no medication, no surgeries, and he conquered the world."

"You're comparing me to Julius Caesar? Thanks, Dad!"

I jump at the sound of Eli's voice, unclenching my fists and doing my best to calm down, to smile. "Hey, buddy! How long have you been standing there?"

"A minute." He looks around. "I'm hungry. Did you go to the store yet?"

I swear, his timing is the worst. "Not yet... I thought we could go together, and you could pick out something special."

"Okay!" Eli walks back to the bedroom.

I turn to Burt, my teeth clenched. "You are *not* taking him from me."

"I'm not leaving him in this environment, around drag queens, growing up in the Village. Next thing I know, he'll be wearing a dress."

"It's time for you to go." I push past him to the door and hold it open.

"You're right. You'll be hearing from me."

He leaves, but before he's too far down, I step into the hallway. "You know who was famously gay? Julius Caesar."

Idiot. I go inside and slam the door, leaning my back against it, and crossing my arms. My heart is beating so fast, I think I'm going to be sick. I never expected Burt to do this, to try and take Eli away from me.

I can't afford a lawyer, and knowing Burt, he'll probably hire somebody to make me look like an incompetent, unstable head case. How can I fight him?

I stagger to the couch and drop in a heap. I want to slide all the way to the floor and cry, but Eli emerges from the bedroom. Pushing my hair back, I do my best to quell the tears, to put on a happy face. "Ready to go to the store, buddy?"

He sits beside me and puts his arms around my waist. "Everything okay, Mom?"

"Of course!" I suffuse my voice with optimism. "How about you? Did you have fun at Dad's?"

"It was okay. Peg is weird."

My brow furrows. "In what way?"

"She laughs at everything Dad says. Even when it's not funny."

Because she's an idiot, too. "Is she nice to you?"

"She's okay."

I comb his hair with my fingers, thinking. How am I going to keep him with me? How can I fight this?

Eli flinches. "Ow!"

"What?" I look down where I'd been scratching his scalp and see a bruised, scuffed mark on his head. "What's this?"

"Just... had an accident playing lacrosse."

I catch his shoulders and lift him off my lap. "Lacrosse? What were you doing..." I don't have to ask that. "Did you wear a helmet?"

"Yeah, but they're small."

Rage tightens my chest, but I hold it down. "Have you taken your medicine today?"

He shakes his head, and I stand, going to the cabinet and getting a pill. He likely hasn't taken one since Friday morning. Burt never gives him his medicine.

"Come on. We need some fresh air and a walk."

I've got to burn off these emotions tying me in knots. We're halfway down the smelly stairs when a homeless guy steps out of my neighbor's doorway. I let out a little scream.

"Got any money, lady?" He leans into us, and he smells really bad. Eli grips my arm.

"I'm sorry, I don't have any cash. You're not supposed to be in here."

His eyes flash, and I grip my son, running the rest of the way down. I hear noises behind me, and I know my neighbor must've opened his door. He'll take care of it, but I'm shook. A situation like that is exactly what Burt would use as proof Eli should stay with him.

We're walking to the small, corner grocery, and I think about Stephen's offer. It's the one thing I know could derail Burt's plans.

I think about the ship room. It really is perfect for Eli. He wouldn't be around dry-cleaning chemicals. He could study in a quiet room, in a luxury townhome near the Upper East Side. Burt wouldn't have a leg to stand on...

Oh, God. Can I do this?

As much as I hate it, I might need Stephen's help.

10

_____

Stephen

Roommates. We can be roommates. Period.

It's late, and I close the book I'm reading about the life of Thomas Paine. It's a snooze fest anyway.

Picking up my phone, I study Emmy's words, a victorious smile curling my lips. I knew she'd see I was right. A gray bubble floats on the screen, indicating more is coming, and I wait to see what changed her mind.

Probably a rat.

EMMY

Not roommates with benefits. No more blurred lines...

I roll my eyes, waiting a few seconds before I answer.

What happened? Why the change?

It takes her a moment to reply.

EMMY

You're right. Our families are friends, and perhaps my place isn't ideal.

I'm always right. And your place is not ideal.

Now I'm sure it was a rat or some other vermin. I wait for her snarky comeback, but instead, she seems serious.

EMMY

I'm doing this for Eli and only until I find a better place for us to live.

Because we're not friends?

EMMY

We're not ANYTHING. Agree?

Glad to see her fight is still there. Although, I confess, my thoughts about our arrangement have changed since I fucked her senseless. It might be nice to have a roommate with benefits.

I'll pick Eli up in the morning and let him see the place.

Another pause, signs of texting.

EMMY

Don't tell him why. I'm still deciding.

I'll show him the room.

EMMY

Nothing more.

Leaning back in my chair, I grin. I won.

Problem solved.

For now.

MISS CON-CLEANEALITY on a Monday morning is worse than Grand Central Station. "Push the pull door?" I read the sign as I wait for Emmy to finish with a customer.

"It's existential." She doesn't look up.

Her hair is piled on top of her head again, and she's wearing blue denim cutoffs and a black tank under her neon vest. As I wait, I let my eyes travel down her body, remembering how it felt against mine.

I remember pulling her hair down, letting it tumble around us in soft, flower-scented waves. I remember burying my face between those smooth thighs. I remember the sounds she made when she came for me, when I sank my cock into her tight little pussy...

Shit. Must stop that train of thought before I get a semi.

Several more minutes pass while Emmy writes the woman's special instructions on a small pad. With a pen. It takes forever.

"Have you ever considered automation?" My tone is impatient. "A computer system would save a lot of time and money."

Emmy rips off the claim ticket and passes it to the customer then drops a net bag of suits in a large bin. "Good luck convincing Lulabell to modernize."

"I could convince her."

She disappears into the back room, and I prop my elbow against the counter, waiting. Vintage pinup girls are painted on the cinder block walls. The entire place has a fun, 1950s vibe going.

"Here are your suits." She hands me a stack of hangers with plastic-covered clothes on them. "And here's Eli."

"Black Bart!" The boy grins and points at me, squinting one eye.

It's cute. I smile and return his point. "You're John Roberts. I'm Howell Davis. I captured you and turned you into the most successful pirate of your generation."

Eli nods. "Okay!"

The blue backpack on his shoulders is almost as big as he is, and I take it off him. "Let me help you with that."

Lulabell watches me from behind an ancient cash register. "Good morning, handsome."

"Hey, beautiful." I wink at her, and she shakes her bright red head. Just as fast her eyes go round. "I've got it!" She points at me. "A young David Gandy!"

"Eli, you left these." Emmy holds out a prescription bottle, and the boy groans. "Don't give me that. If I'm late, take your pill."

She looks up at me, and it's the first time we've faced each other all morning. It's the first time I've met her eyes since I was covering her with kisses. Shadows are beneath them, and she looks like she hasn't slept.

Now I'm concerned. "Are you okay?"

She cuts away from my gaze and Lou sidles up beside her. "Gandy, yes?"

"What?" Emmy frowns. "Oh." She doesn't sound playful. "Sure. He's way more Gandy than Bond."

"Girls are weird." Eli complains at my side, and I decide to let it go for now.

She's not giving me anything.

"You have no idea." I drape my suits over my shoulder. "Let's go. Car's waiting."

Emmy ducks under the counter, and quickly pulls her son into a long hug.

"He's not joining the Foreign Legion," I groan impatiently.

She cuts me a look before turning back to Eli, with whom she's all softness. "Don't let this guy make you a mean old cynic, okay?"

Eli's got my back. "I think he's alright."

I hold out my fist, and he bumps it.

She stands and gives me a look that's pure mamma bear. "Take care of him."

"You have my word."

With that, we're in my car headed uptown. Eli leans against the window, looking out at the changing scenery.

"Your neighborhood's called Turtle Bay? Are there a lot of turtles or something?"

He's cute with that blond hair and his mother's big blue eyes. "The East River curves around creating a cove. Apparently, it looked like a turtle to the Dutch settlers."

"Oh." He nods and returns to the window.

"My house is close to the United Nations building."

"Okay." He lifts his small eyebrows and nods. It makes me chuckle. I guess the UN building isn't super exciting to a kid.

"How old are you? Eight? Nine?"

"I'll be eight in a couple months." I can tell this is a point of pride. I don't point out it means he's still only seven.

"You're a young man. That's a lot of responsibility."

He squints up at me. "Do you remember being seven?"

"I do. It was about two years before all the other guys started being assholes."

Eli coughs a laugh and nods. "You'll get in trouble if Mom hears you."

Leaning closer, I impart some wisdom. "It's not a bad word if it's true."

He only laughs more. "Mom says when they're mean, I have to shake it off."

"Shake it off..." My expression is not pleased. "That's a

Taylor Swift song?" He nods, looking down. "I like your mom, but next time, if the big boys are mean to you, start humming 'Let the Bodies Hit the Floor.'"

He raises his eyebrows and smiles. I hold up a hand, and we high five. Still, his little face is tense.

I give him a nudge. "What else?"

"What about dads?"

My throat tightens, but I remind myself The Dick is his father. I can't say what I really think about the guy. I have to practice restraint. "What about dads?"

"Oh..." He looks out the window again. "I don't know."

I'm pretty sure I do. Leaning back in my seat, I think aloud. "My dad wanted me to be on the rowing team, the lacrosse team, the football team... I wanted to read books and study biology."

I've got his rapt attention now. "What happened?"

"I read books and studied biology... And I was on the rowing team." His little brow lowers, and he nods as if he understands some deep wisdom. I can't help thinking he probably does. "You have to respect your father. But you can talk to me about it if you want. If you trust me."

His head tilts to the side, and he studies me a second. "Okay."

"I'll do my best to deserve your trust." We're at my town-home, getting out of the car, and I lift his blue bag. "What's in the backpack?"

He pulls it around and unzips it, showing me a medium-sized textbook with different ecosystems on the cover, a note-book, and a stuffed orca that looks pretty worn. "I have some science work. I'm starting the unit on sea mammals."

"That's a fun one."

"Mom lets me watch *The Blue Planet* on Netflix. They do a bunch of stuff with ocean animals and stuff. Do you watch that show?"

"I don't." The driver hands me my stack of dry cleaning. "You'll have to show it to me."

"Okay!" He shouts, skipping up the steps to my front door. "The guy who talks has this accent because he's from England. Mom says it makes her sleepy. My medicine makes me sleepy."

"Can I see your medicine?"

"Sure." He unzips the front pocket of his backpack and hands me a prescription bottle. I slip it in the pocket of my coat. "You take this when?"

"Before dinner." He's stuffing the books and the orca in the pack.

"Who's the whale?" I point to the black and white animal.

"This is Kona. He's not really a whale. Killer whales are dolphins."

"I've heard that." I unlock the door and let him enter before me.

"You know how they call dolphins the dogs of the sea?" He marches into my townhouse chatting up a storm. "Orcas are the wolves of the sea because they hunt in packs. But they don't attack humans. They only eat seals and stuff. This one time, an orca ate a moose that was swimming in the water... Mom made a joke about Bullwinkle and Rocky. It made me laugh so much..."

He's so animated telling me his story, I hate to interrupt him. "Head up to the second floor. I'll take these to my room and meet you there."

Eli charges ahead of me, and I carry the suits to my closet up top. When I get back down, he's already in the nautical room, looking at the giant ship in a bottle on the bookcase. His little lips are parted, and rapture is in his eyes.

I take it down and we sit on the bed so he can see it up close. "What do you think?"

"Wow..." he whispers, touching the glass carefully. He reads the words printed on the red band across the side. "*Queen Anne's Revenge.*"

"It crashed off the coast of North Carolina."

Eli traces a small finger along the line of the mast. "It has black sails."

"The whole ship was black."

"Who was the captain?"

"Blackbeard."

His little mouth falls open, and he looks up at me with the roundest eyes. It causes a strange, tight feeling in my stomach. I stand and pick up another, smaller bottle.

"This is the *CSS Alabama*. It was a Confederate Sloop of war built in Liverpool, England."

"Wow..." It's the exact same inflection as the first time. He holds the smaller bottle, inspecting the brown ship with twelve white sails. "It was captured by pirates?"

"Not exactly, but the *New York Herald* once called Captain Raphael Semmes a pirate of the high seas. At his peak, he burned one Union ship every three days until they finally sunk him off the coast of Normandy."

He steps over to a picture of me in uniform. "Is this you? You're on a ship."

"Yeah." I put the bottle holding *Queen Anne's Revenge* on its perch.

"You were in the military?"

"The Navy."

Eli looks up at me. "Is that why you know so much about ships?"

"No, I already knew all that from when I was about your age." He nods, and my voice gets quieter. "My mom wanted me to be in the Navy."

"Oh." He nods slowly like that explains everything.

I guess at seven, what your mom wants pretty much explains

your life. I stand, walking to the door. "How do you like this room?"

He follows me. "It's really cool. You live in this big house all by yourself?"

"I do." We walk down the hall toward the stairs, I point up them. "My rooms are up there. My bedroom and my office."

"You must get pretty lonely." His backpack is in his hand, and I notice it's unzipped. The stuffed orca is out, and he's holding it. "Mom's place is really small, but I can sleep with her if I get lonely."

A benefit I've been considering myself lately—sleeping with his mother. "I thought it might be fun to have roommates here."

He nods, but he's different. He blinks slowly, and looks away toward the blue room.

"Are you okay, Eli?"

Reaching up, he rubs his eye with the heel of his hand. "Oh, yeah!"

He looks tired to me. Emmy didn't say anything about him napping. Still... he's only seven. "Why don't you lie down on the bed and rest. I'll wake you in an hour so you can do your school work."

Grateful blue eyes blink up at me. "Thanks, Mr. Hastings."

"Call me Stephen."

"Thanks, Mr. Stephen."

It's not what I meant, but I'm not going to argue with him right now. I pat his little back and watch as he walks slowly to the nautical room, trailing that long black and white dolphin behind him.

Not once in my life have I given much thought to children. It's not what I do. I make computer applications and solve problems for major corporations. Now this little boy is here making me wonder if I've got it all wrong.

Ridiculous.
I have work to do.

11

Emmy

Stephen's townhome is even more imposing on the second visit. Probably because I know what's inside. Or maybe because of what went on inside the last time I was here? With a shiver, I knock on the door.

"You don't have to knock." He opens the door, and I'm hit full-force with the intensity of his presence. So imposing, so dominating, so seriously sexy.

I push back on those feelings. "Why are you answering your own door?"

"As you know, I don't have overnight staff." His tone matches my impatience.

It's good. It's where I need to keep him—in the Not-Friends Zone.

"So how'd it go today?"

"I was about to ask you the same."

"Busy as every Monday. What have you two been doing all afternoon?"

The pounding of feet on wooden stairs interrupts, and Eli's

voice echoes in the stairwell. "MOM! You should see this room! It has ships on the walls and a compass on the ceiling and a giant ship in a huge bottle..."

Wrinkling my nose, I squint up at Stephen. "I bet nobody is ever that loud in here."

"I think you were that loud Saturday night." He gives me a sly grin, and heat flashes from my neck to my cheeks.

I don't have time for a comeback. Eli is tugging on my hand. "You've got to see it!"

"I saw it, baby! I was here Saturday."

"Mom." He stops tugging and gives me The Look.

"Sorry! I meant I saw it, Mr. Big Man."

He rolls his eyes. Stephen slides a hand in his pocket and walks to the kitchen area. "Would you like a drink?"

"No thanks, I'm on the clock."

He frowns at me, and I tilt my head toward Eli. "I like to be prepared at all times."

"Oh." He puts the bottle of wine aside. "He took his medicine."

"Thanks." I swing Eli's hand. "Run get your stuff, now. We have to catch the train home."

"Okay!" He takes off for the stairs.

Stephen strolls to where I'm waiting just inside the door. "Come in and stay a minute."

"I can't. I've got to get home, feed Eli, go to bed." Crossing my arms, I rock on my toes, looking away from his smirk. "Work tomorrow."

"You seem uncomfortable."

"Do I?" Uncrossing my arms, I look around. Not at him. "I'm probably just, you know, amped up from a busy day at work."

"If it's about our arrangement, I've been thinking... I could make a contract if it would make you feel better."

Now I do meet his eyes. "A contract? Are you worried Eli might break something?"

"No..." He chuckles. "To make it feel more official. You were worried about blurred lines."

"Oh," I look down. "It's okay. I mean, it seems kind of silly to make a contract for house guests."

"Roommates. And only until you find a better place to live. It's temporary."

When he says the word, my stomach sinks. *Really, Em?* "That's right. Temporary."

"Got it, Mom!" Eli walks down the stairs. I notice he's moving a little slower.

"Let me carry your backpack."

"I got it." He looks up at Stephen. "Thanks man, this is a cool place you got here."

Eli's grown-man impersonation slays me, but what hits me even more is when Stephen holds out his hand for a high five.

"Thanks again." I start for the door, but Stephen stops me.

"Let me send for the car to take you back." This time when I look up, his smile is warm. It makes my insides all squishy.

"We're good. It's a short train ride."

"I'll see you tomorrow?"

"I'll let you know."

SOMETIMES ELI LOSES the battle between being a kid and being a big boy—meaning sometimes he still holds my hand. Usually when he's really tired, like now.

"Feeling okay, buddy?"

He nods, resting his head against my arm as we wait in the subway station. He smiles, but I see the lines around his eyes. Now I wish I'd taken Stephen up on that offer of a car... I just couldn't stay around him being warm and high-fiving my son. It's fucking with my Not-Friends Zone approach.

Eli lifts his head. "Stephen has a bunch of sea stuff. Did you know he likes biology just like me?"

"I didn't."

"And his dad made him play sports even though he didn't want to. Just like me!"

Eli is so excited, it scares me a little. "He told you that?"

"Yeah. He has these two big ships in bottles... One is Blackbeard's ship, and the whole thing is black—even the sails!"

"Sounds like you had a fun day. Would you want to go back?"

"Oh, yeah. His house is huge! It's bigger than Dad's."

"I'm pretty sure it's been in his family a while." Our train breezes up, and I stand, still holding my son's hand.

"It's okay, Mom. Our place is cozy."

Grinning, I rub his head, and he winces, which makes me frown. "Does that bump still hurt?"

"It's okay." He shrugs, and I know he's protecting his dad.

Burt never called today to follow up on his threat to talk to a lawyer. Maybe he was only bluffing. Maybe he was just taking a cheap shot at me—as usual. Maybe I'm moving too fast on this whole Stephen arrangement. How can I know?

All I know is I'll do anything to keep Eli safe. I put my arm around my son's shoulder and give him a squeeze. "I like our cozy little place."

"Me too." He blinks up and smiles.

"GIRL, you are not going to believe who called me this morning!" Lulabell dances in from her office and catches Eli's arm, giving him a little dosey-doe. "Guess!"

She spins to face me, and I don't even know where to start...

"RuPaul?"

"Wouldn't that be a trip?" She laughs, slapping her hip. "No."

"Umm..." I look around the room. "Lady Gaga! She wants you to do all her dry cleaning, you little monster!"

"I wouldn't be standing here right now. I'd be dead on the floor!" She laughs more, waving her hand at me. "You'll never guess, so I'll tell you. Leon Steinfeffer!"

I jerk back. "Leon who?"

"Steinfeffer. It's a silly name, I know, but he is the Candice Bergen of the New York-Miss United States circuit. He loved your hair and makeup at the Art Bar, and he wants you to join the crew of the Lady Liberty pageant!"

My head is spinning. "I thought pageant girls did all their own hair and makeup..."

"For the most part they do, but it's a service they offer, and the pay is *phenomenal*." The bell rings, and a girl enters, dragging several beaded gowns over her arms and shoulders. Lou writes her up while I take the dresses, wrangling them onto the hanging bar and red-tagging them.

"So what do you say? Hair and makeup for Lady Liberty? Oh, just say yes."

I huff a laugh as I haul a sack of laundry across the counter. "What are the hours? I'll have to do something with Eli."

The bell rings, and it's Stephen to pick up my son. Today, he's in a light gray suit with a brown tie that matches the lighter highlights in his wavy hair. I get a hot flash just looking at him, and that settles it. This roommate thing will never work. Not. Ever.

He's behind a woman carrying two large net bags, and when he offers to help her, Lou leans into my ear. "Such a gentleman. I bet he'd help with Eli."

Turning my chin so he can't see my face, I glare at her. "I would never ask Stephen to babysit. Are you kidding me?"

"Why not? They seem to be friends. All they talk about are ships and pirates and the Navy. Unless he has an ulterior motive." She waggles her eyebrows.

"It's not like that." I hand the woman her claim ticket.

"Whatever you say, girl. What should I tell Bob?"

I exhale deeply. "Tell him yes. I'll figure out something."

Stephen's at the counter. "Contract for you." He slips a business envelope out of his pocket. "And I'll take Eli."

"Let me call him." I turn the envelope over in my hand as I step around the entrance. "Eli? Want to hang out at Stephen's again today?" His head pops up, and he nods. "Get your stuff together."

Returning to the front, I wave the note. "You didn't have to do this. It seems like a lot of extra work."

"I just amended an old contract I had." He's watching me in that way that feels like heat on my skin.

Things are different between us since Saturday. Or are they?

I don't like to let myself go there. Eli joins us, backpack on one shoulder.

"Ready?" I lean down to give him a kiss.

I'm just getting close when his eyes go wide. His fist jerks up to his chest, and my stomach plummets as he hits the floor.

12

Stephen

Everything feels too fast and too slow. I'm fumbling, trying to remember what I know about seizures, trying to control the chaos.

Eli's eyes are rolled back in his head, and his body is alternately rigid and shuddering. A steady stream of tears coats Emmy's cheeks, and she rocks back and forth on the floor of the dry cleaner holding Eli's hand. "I'm here, Eli. It's going to be okay."

"I'll call 9-1-1!" Lulabell runs to the back room.

"What time is it? Somebody check the clock." Emmy's voice breaks. She's calm but her shoulders shudder.

Dropping to my knees, I rip off my coat and ball it up. "Put this under his head. Roll him onto his side."

"It's ten o'clock!" A woman cries from the back.

Emmy hiccups a breath. "It's going on too long." She holds her son's little hand, rocking back and forth. "Stay with me, baby."

Thankfully, the customers either leave or move to the outer

walls. I place my hand on Emmy's shoulder. "It hasn't been a minute."

"I can't take this." Her head drops, and her tears are like glass ripping my chest.

Fuck. I want to help them. "He's going to be okay." My voice is quiet, soothing, I hope.

She only shakes her head. "God, please help him... I hate this so much."

The noise of sirens grows louder, and a murmur moves through the crowd. Some are sighs of relief. Some are grumbles of *it's about time.*

Eli is starting to relax. He's coming out of it.

"Time?" I call.

"Ten oh-two? Three?" It's an analog clock, so it's not much help.

"Eli?" Emmy strokes his head with trembling fingers.

EMS bursts through the door, surrounding us. "Where's the patient?"

I stand, giving them space to get to him. "Is a parent present?"

"I'm his mom." Emmy's voice is so weak.

"I'm her friend." I step forward.

"Sorry, sir. Family only." They push me aside. Indignation burns in my chest, but I stand back watching as they coordinate and lift Eli onto the stretcher. "Would you like to ride in the ambulance?"

"Where are you taking him?" I ask, only to be rebuffed again.

Lulabell is in the room with us. She touches Emmy's arm. "Don't ride in the ambulance. It's too upsetting. He'll be okay."

Frustration is a tight fist in my guts. I understand the concerns for privacy, but being pushed aside like this when I'm trying to help my little friend is infuriating.

I touch Emmy's hand. "I'll drive you. Find out where they're taking him."

"Sir?" She straightens, staying close to the gurney. "What hospital?"

"Mount Sinai is the closest."

I look up at the guy. "Komansky Children's is the best for this type of thing."

"We don't have time to get all the way uptown."

Emmy turns pleading eyes on me, and I back down. "Whatever. We're right behind you."

MY FISTS CLENCH AND UNCLENCH. I stand in the waiting room, watching through the glass as Emmy talks to the doctor alone. She's been crying off and on since the seizure, and I can't say I blame her. Eli's a sweet kid, and seeing him in the grip of invisible torment is gut wrenching. I want to pull her in my arms and hold her. Hell, I want to pull them both into my arms and tell them I'm going to fix this.

I sure as hell understand Emmy's reasons for homeschooling and her fixation on that surgery now. If Eli were my kid, he'd have a private tutor and already be on a waiting list, if not in treatment.

A bustling noise behind me causes me to look up.

Burt Dickerson barrels into the waiting room. "Where's my boy?" His voice is too loud. His face is red. "Where's Elijah?"

Through the glass, I see defeat filter through Emmy's features. She drops helplessly into a chair. I want to go in and give her the strength she needs. Instead, The Dick barges in and begins attacking the doctor. Through the walls, I hear his booming voice.

"My son gets the best care available. I want to know what caused it..."

The other voices are quieter, but I see Emmy point to her head. I see Burt explode again. "Don't tell me it's because he played lacrosse. Exercise is good for him."

Leaning forward, I prop my forearms on my thighs. Sometimes the legal and medical fields feel really fucked up.

"Families are hard." An old woman slowly approaches me, using her IV stand as a prop. "Your girlfriend is very upset. I take it that's the child's father?"

I don't bother trying to correct her. "Her son has epilepsy."

"Such a terrible affliction." The woman shakes her head. "So cruel. I'm sure you've been there to help with him."

"I was today." Our eyes meet, and hers are sympathetic.

"I'm sorry." She touches me with a bony hand. "It'll be easier when you're married. They'll let you be a part of the conversation then."

"We're not—"

"Okay, now. Take care." The old lady gives me a smile and pats my arm before slowly scuffling past with her IV stand.

My eyes move back to the glass. In that little box, I see my girl slumped in a chair. She looks so miserable. The Dick is gusting like a freight train, and the doctor appears ready to throw in the towel.

I turn back to find the old woman, but she's gone. Instead, Lulabell comes hurrying in. "Sorry, I came as fast as I could. I had to take care of the last few customers and close the shop. What's happening?"

"I don't know." I look back at the window. "Only family's allowed."

"God, I fucking hate that rule." Lou hisses under her breath. "Emmy could use somebody now. Burt is such a damn bully."

He always has been. Only, I'm formulating a plan to rescue Eli and Emmy from his domineering presence. "Give me your number."

"With pleasure." Lou winks, taking my phone and texting herself from my number.

"Text me if anything happens. I'll be back."

13

Emmy

"Just tell me he's going to be okay." My stomach churns, and Burt's yelling only makes it worse.

As much as I want to be strong, I can't take the seizures. Every time I see my baby lying on the floor shaking, suffering silently, I panic. This time it seemed worse. It felt longer than before, too long.

I look around the waiting room for Stephen. *Where did he go?* Lulabell waves and gives me a questioning thumbs up. I give her a weak smile and a shrug in return.

"He's going to be okay." Dr. Roberts puts his hand on my shoulder. "You did everything right today."

"I didn't have his seizure meds." My voice is weak. "I'm supposed to give him his meds when—"

"EMS took care of it." The doctor smiles warmly. "I'd like to do an EEG just to be sure nothing has changed. You said it's been a while since he had one?"

Nodding, I look down at my hands, feeling so helpless. "The meds have been working... but he..." I decide against throwing

Burt under the bus. At least for now. He'd just make a scene. "He bumped his head this weekend."

"Is that so?" The doctor pulls out his clipboard. "That could be significant. What exactly happened?"

Lifting my eyes to Burt, I don't even try to mask my glare.

"What?" He steps back, holding out his arms. "Oh, this is my fault now?"

This is all your fault.

I don't say that.

"The doctor needs to know how he hit his head."

Burt drops his arms with a loud exhale. "We were playing lacrosse, okay? It's a contact sport."

Dr. Roberts frowns at my ex. Big shock. "I'm not sure lacrosse is the best choice for a child with his condition. Not to mention his age."

I can't even look at Burt. I'm on my feet pacing while the doctor continues. "I'd like to keep him overnight for observation. Just to be sure he doesn't have another one."

I hope Burt intends to pay the bill. Another thing I don't say out loud.

"I need some fresh air. When can I see my son?"

"We have him sedated for now. If you'd like to step outside, there's a small park just off the waiting area there. I'll tell the nurse to call you when he starts to wake up."

"Thank you so much. I can't tell you how much I appreciate your help."

"I don't know if I appreciate it." Burt starts, but I'm out the door. I can't deal with his bullshit another minute.

Bursting through the crash doors, I put my hand on my chest and gasp for fresh air. My breaths are shallow and new tears coat my cheeks. Lifting my chin, I close my eyes to the heavens.

"Oh, God." I pray softly. "If there's any way in the world you can help my baby right now..."

The metal door clangs open, and I look up. Striding into the courtyard like a knight straight out of *GQ magazine* on a steed borrowed from *Town & Country* is Stephen. Only he's not wearing armor or riding a horse. He's in a brown tweed suit, walking swiftly toward me. His expression is determined, and in his hand is a ragged, stuffed killer whale.

"You brought Kona." I almost start to cry again.

"How is he?" When he gets to me he pauses a second, blue eyes scanning my face.

"I don't know." The tears start again. "They have him sedated."

He reaches out and pulls me to his chest. I hold a hand over my lips as I wet his shirt with my tears. Stephen only holds me. Occasionally, I feel the press of his lips against my head, the warmth of his breath on my hair. I'm not sure how much time passes before I get myself together and step back, wiping my eyes.

"I'm sorry. I didn't mean to cry on you. I messed up your shirt."

"Don't apologize to me. I care very much about Elijah, and what happened today was horrible."

"I hate it so much, Stephen." Turning to the side, I fight against more tears.

"I've moved your things into my place. You're coming home with me."

As much as the finality in his voice comforts me, I shake my head. "I'm not leaving the hospital until Eli does."

"Emmy." His voice softens. "Eli's sedated. You're exhausted. You need to rest."

"I appreciate what you've done—"

"We're getting married."

I'm pretty sure the world just tilted. Everything goes silent—pigeons stop chirping, frogs don't croak, cars halt on the freeway.

"I'm sorry, it's been a really stressful morning. What did you just say?"

"Emmy Barton, will you marry me." Stephen's expression is stern, not romantic, and I watch as he pulls a ring out of his breast pocket. "It's the best I could find on short notice."

I don't move as he tries to put a thin platinum band with an oversized square-cut diamond on the third finger of my left hand, but it's too big. He ends up sliding it on my middle finger.

"I'll have it resized."

"Resized?" I'm coming out of my shock. "Have you lost your mind?"

Blue eyes flash at me. "Emmy, do you know why people pay me thousands of dollars a day? Because I identify their problems, I see what needs to be done, and I fix them."

This day has been just shitty enough that I'm done being nice.

"Stephen Hastings," I snap right back. "My son and I aren't a computer application."

"All the same, there are tax breaks associated with us being married. There are deductions for unreimbursed medical expenses. I have many contacts in the healthcare field. It's possible I can work out an arrangement that will cover Eli's surgery and the requisite doctor's visits. If you're my wife, Eli will become my dependent." He stops pacing and faces me square on. "That means, they cannot shut me out of that god damned room ever again. When you need me... When Eli needs a strong ally, I'll be there for him." He hesitates, softening a tiny bit. "Our marriage will not be a permanent state of affairs, but it will allow me to help Eli in the most seamless and cost-effective way possible. Problem. Solved."

It's an airtight case.

I can't argue with him on any of it.

All I can say is the obvious. "I can't marry you."

"We're not arguing about this." He walks past me toward the waiting room door. "We can and will meet at City Hall on Friday and have it done. I'll secure the marriage license and start the paperwork tonight."

My head is spinning. I feel like I've been thrown a lifeline. Only, it's a lifeline wrapped in brambles and thorns. Thorns I feel certain will pierce my heart and leave me to bleed out.

"Just slow down a minute." I hold out my hand, my eyes catching on the enormous diamond he put on my finger. "I didn't say yes to this."

Stephen's eyes flash. I've never seen him truly angry, but this is pretty close. "What's your reason for saying no? Is it because you believe in only marrying your one true love? Is that what you believed when you married Burt? That he was The One?"

His words shock me, but he has a point. "I married Burt because I was pregnant with Eli."

"You'll marry me for Eli as well. Trust me, you'll find I'm a far more agreeable husband than The Dick could ever dream of being."

I'm quiet a few moments while he waits for my assent. I can't find a reason to say no and only one massive reason for saying yes. "I'll marry you, but I won't share a bed with you."

For whatever reason, my answer pricks the tension between us like a pin to a balloon. His shoulders drop, and the firm set of his jaw eases. Even his angry brow relaxes some. "We'll cross that bridge when we come to it."

"We won't come to it because we're not going to it. The road to it has orange barrels and a sawhorse. And railroad crossing bars."

He exhales a chuckle. "I feel like we've had this conversation before. Just before I had you on my bar, eating you for dessert."

"Don't..." My voice breaks off.

One eyebrow cocks, and his blue eyes smolder. "I promise, I will never make you do anything you don't want to do."

"It feels like you're making me now."

Only, it's not quite true. He's throwing me a lifeline. He's charging in here to be my savior... granted in the most unorthodox way I could have ever imagined. Still...

"The first thing you told me about Eli involved this surgery and how much you wanted it for him. You told me Burt was against it, and it's not covered by your insurance."

My stomach is tight, and I can't tell anymore if the energy coursing through my veins is shock or adrenaline or excitement. Eli has a chance at a cure!

"You're nothing if not unexpected, Mr. Hastings. Personally, I haven't decided if you're a hero or a bully."

"I'm not a hero. You said so yourself." He puts his hands on my upper arms just before he pulls me against his chest. It's a warm and comforting hug. He smells so good, and I slide my hands around his narrow waist. His deep voice vibrates against my cheek. "I care about Eli. I want to make this right. You will not argue with me. You'll do as I say."

My jaw clenches. Him saying those words makes me want to argue.

He doesn't give me the chance. "Stop being stubborn and say yes."

Looking down, I give his proposal one final thought before I concede. "Okay, Yes. I'll marry you. For your money."

14

Stephen

When I left Lulabell in the waiting room, my memories of Ximena and what happened to her weighed heavy on my mind. All I could think about was how sick she was, and how I couldn't do a thing to help her. She wasn't my mother, hell, she wasn't even in the country legally. All I could do was give her cash and pray it was used for her treatment, trust Ramon could get her what she needed.

The memory cramped my stomach and solidified my decision. I would not let it happen again. Having those doctors shove me out into the waiting room, watching The Dick bluster into that office and do everything wrong cemented what I had to do.

Yes, it's unorthodox, but I've never given a shit what people think. My reasons are sound and I'm not leaving Emmy and Eli to suffer at the hands of fate or Eli's father.

I walk to their apartment in the East Village, and it's infuriatingly easy to jimmy the lock on her front door. I look around the small place until I find a suitcase. She'll be able to come back

here and get what she wants. In the meantime, I grab the neces-
sities—toiletries, clothes, lace panties... Little boy underwear,
pajamas, books.

Then I spot Eli's killer whale on the bed and scoop him up.
"Come on, Kona, you're coming with me."

Looking around one last time, I see pictures of her with
Elijah, some of her and Ethan, a few that look like they were
taken in college. None are of her with Burt or any other men for
that matter. I pick up a photo of her and Eli she has on her
nightstand and put it in the suitcase before zipping it up.

I send the case to my place with my driver before walking
back to Mount Sinai, Kona in hand. Ximena's hearing is in my
mind. It was actually mediation...

It was possibly less official than that.

Edward Barton was so calm, fair, and diplomatic. Ximena
was so sick and weak. My dad was such an asshole, going on
about his precious Rolex like he didn't have seven more.

Ximena was so grateful he didn't send her son to jail. So
thankful my dad didn't report her to immigration.

The memory makes me sick to my stomach. How is it
possible to be blessed with so much, yet have so little compas-
sion for those less fortunate? Someone who's taken care of your
home and your son? Much like Ximena, my relationship with
my father never recovered.

STANDING in the hall outside Eli's hospital room, I watch
through the small window as Emmy puts Kona under his arm in
the bed. I watch as she sits in a chair at his bedside, leaning her
head on her hand, smoothing his fair hair away from his placid
face. Her love for him is so strong, it reinforces my decision to
help them.

Eli is asleep, but he's no longer sedated. The doctors finished their tests, and his brain activity has returned to normal, and at this point, they don't expect any physical side effects.

It's after ten, and I knock gently on the door. Emmy looks up and our eyes meet. My stomach tightens at her expression. It's gratitude, but it's something more.

"Why are you hanging around, Hastings?" Burt's voice is an unwelcome irritant.

Still, my voice is calm when I turn to face him. "I thought you left."

"I'm about to. Just had to sign off on the paperwork. As his father." He hits the word a little too hard for my taste.

"I would expect Eli's father to take a more active interest in his well-being."

"What the hell do you know about it?"

"Only what I observe, what I hear."

"Is this about him playing lacrosse?" He steps closer, hooking his thumb at his chest. "Eli is my son. He's strong, and I'm getting him out of this place. I'm taking him home with me, and I'm not having any more of this homeschool, alternative therapy, hippy-dippy shit."

The door opens, and Emmy joins us. "What's going on out here?" she whispers, looking up and down the hall. "I can hear your voice inside."

"I'm taking off, but I'll be back to see how he's doing."

Emmy's lips tighten into a straight line. "How he's doing? He's recovering from a head injury that happened on your watch. When are you going to take this seriously?"

"I take my son having a normal life seriously. Not being treated like some... bubble boy."

"I can't do this anymore." She lowers her chin, rubbing her face with her left hand.

Burt's eyes widen, and he grabs her finger. "What's this?"

I put my arm around Emmy's waist and pull her closer. "We're getting married."

Burt's eyes go round, and his jaw drops. "What the hell? Why am I just hearing about this?"

"She just said yes."

He takes a few steps away then back to us. "I never liked you, Hastings, and I'll be damned if you come in and try to touch what's mine."

A defiant grin curls my lips. "Worried, Dick? Afraid your ex-wife might find a man who treats her with respect?"

His face turns red, and he steps closer to Emmy. "What kind of stunt are you pulling now?"

Before she has a chance to answer, I move between them. "Back off, Dickerson. You're not going to intimidate Emmy, and you're not doing anything to endanger Eli again. I'm making sure of it."

He glares at me. "If you think you're telling me what to do with my son, you're crazy."

"I've been called worse." My jaw is set.

For a moment, we're at a stand-off. Then he takes a step back and starts to go. Before he's too far away, he claps back. "This isn't over, Hastings."

Emmy's shoulders droop, and chin falls. "I'll never understand him."

"Why in the world did you marry that asshole?" I put one hand on her shoulder, lifting her chin with my other. "He's the world's biggest douche."

Our eyes meet, and she exhales a weak laugh. "I told you, I got pregnant."

"Have you ever heard the expression 'Two wrongs don't make a right'?" My voice is gentle.

"Don't be an ass." She turns toward the window facing Eli's

room. I take a chance and put my arm around her waist. She doesn't pull away.

"Did you ever love him?" I'm not sure why I want to know the answer to this question so badly. Maybe I need to know what she's capable of.

She hesitates before answering. "I don't know. Maybe... If love feels the way I think it does, I've only ever loved one man."

"If it doesn't?"

"If it doesn't, I've only ever loved my father. And Eli."

"Your father was a good man. I admired him. Eli reminds me of him. He's thoughtful and smart."

She turns to face me. "Thank you. For what you're doing for him. I can't tell you how much it means to me."

"Don't thank me for this." I touch her cheek. "I'm heading to my place to finish up. Call me if you need anything."

She nods, and I lean forward to kiss her forehead. Her skin is warm, and I hold her a beat longer.

Everything is about to change.

15

Emmy

I'm standing in the middle of City Hall in a crowd of people waiting for their number to be called.

Lou insisted I wear something wedding-ish, so I ditched the denim skirt, pink sweater, and sandals in favor of a beige shift dress and nude heels. She styled my hair in a French braid around my head with white daisies pinned along it in a headband style. I added a little makeup, and the result is I look very elegant.

As my matron of honor and our one required witness, Lou is wearing a peach suit, her hair styled in a Liz Taylor bob. Eli is smiling beside her in a navy blazer and khaki pants, Kona tucked under his arm.

Every day he gets a little stronger. Other than fatigue, he didn't have any side effects following his seizure. The doctors released him with a slightly stronger prescription.

In the meantime, Stephen's been working his contact list, finding out all he can about the surgery and how soon Eli can be evaluated for it. We discovered one of the best neurosurgery hospitals is in the Upper East Side, a few short blocks from Stephen's home. He's already tracked down a doctor he knows to meet Eli.

Eli is thrilled to be moving in with Stephen. He thinks we've been dating this whole time, and he never knew. My stomach cramps, and all my self-doubts come rushing back.

This is a huge mistake. I never should have said yes to this.

What happens when it's over?

I want to run, but God, it's too late now. What can I possibly do?

I have to focus on the positive—my son is going to get his surgery. He's going to have a shot at a normal life. Burt has backed down... Or at least he's neutralized for now.

"There he is!" Lou's voice sounds relieved.

She has no clue what's driving our sudden nuptials, and she's been beside herself as well, wanting to do all the traditional things. She probably thinks I'm pregnant. Stephen and I agreed to keep the real details of why we're getting married between us. As a result, it's been hard to put her off, but I have to. This is all pretend. Or at least, it's only temporary.

Turning, I see my fiancé striding confidently up the marble lined corridor in our direction. My stomach tingles. He's so damn sexy in a dark gray Armani suit, white shirt, and light blue tie. The color makes his blue eyes glow, and several heads turn to watch him pass. In his hand is a small bouquet of white roses.

"You're beautiful." Stephen's words are like warm liquid in my veins. He steps forward to kiss my cheek before he hands me the flowers. I hold them to my nose. They smell beautiful. *Do not get attached, Emmy.* "Ready?"

"Ready as I'll ever be." My voice is soft.

I look up, and he's watching me. Our eyes meet and something shifts in his expression, but he doesn't address it. Instead, he pulls my hand into the crook of his arm and leads me to the window where we'll hand over our paperwork and meet the Justice of the Peace.

"Just a minor formality." His tone is all business, and I snap out of my little girl romantic notions.

"Right."

We're led into a small courtroom, where the two of us stand before an older man in a long, black judge's robe. Lulabell and Eli are right behind us.

"Join hands." He seems bored.

I shift my bouquet and put my hand in Stephen's again. This is nothing like my first wedding. Dad was still alive when I married Burt. He wasn't happy, but still, we went all out. Every aunt, uncle, cousin, all the Bartons from up and down the Eastern Seaboard came to see me make that massive mistake. Five years later, it was over.

Today's little bit of history repeating itself is far more subdued.

"Repeat after me, I, state your name..." Stephen does as instructed. "Take you, state her name, as my lawfully wedded wife. From this day to all the years to come, for good, for bad, in sickness and health, for richer, for poorer, until death do us part."

He says it so fast, Stephen hesitates then repeats it all perfectly. Cocking an eyebrow, I see this is a challenge. It almost makes me laugh. I'm a little grateful to him for easing the tension of this strange day.

"Repeat after me..." The magistrate leads me through the whole thing, and I only stumble once around the *til death do us part* line. I'm not sure if it's subconscious.

"I now pronounce you man and wife, you may kiss the bride."

My breath catches. I forgot about this part.

Lulabell makes a little noise of excitement, and I hear a

groan from Eli. My eyes meet Stephen's and his expression is as serious as always.

I'm nervous. The only way he's ever kissed me is ravenous, devouring, right before we have wild sex. Obviously, we can't kiss that way here.

Swallowing the knot in my throat, I lift my chin. He reaches up and slides his thumb along my cheek, holding my eyes with his just before he leans down and captures my lips. My eyes flutter closed. It's a gentle, but firm kiss. He pushes my lips apart, but only briefly swipes his tongue to mine before pulling back.

Heat floods my panties, my breath disappears, and he finishes with one last, quick capture, his lips tugging mine, leaving my insides humming. My eyes open and he gives me that trademark, cocky grin.

Damn him.

I want to hit him for being such a stupidly good kisser. I want to hit myself on the head with my bouquet for being so weak when it comes to his bossy butt. I'm sure it's clear on my face how much I enjoyed that kiss, and I hate it.

"I now pronounce you Mr. and Mrs. Stephen Hastings." The old man holds up his arms, and Lulabell bursts into cheering applause.

I look down, embarrassed, and she rushes forward to hug me, wiping tears from her eyes. "It was just perfectly sweet and beautiful!"

Eli shoves his hands in his pockets, and Stephen passes some money to the magistrate before we file out, back into the bustling foyer of City Hall. Strange how that little room managed to create a sacred space only steps from all this chaos.

Miss Con-Cleaneality is closed for the occasion. Stephen takes us to lunch at Tavern on the Green, and Lulabell is in heaven. She claims she's never been to the centuries-old establishment. We have a fairly adequate lunch in a beautiful setting in the southwest corner of Central Park.

I have chicken salad with sweet potato fries. Eli orders a fancy pizza. Stephen has steak, and Lou orders roasted lemon chicken under a brick. We finish it off with New York cheesecake topped with blackberries and lemon curd. It's very elegant, if not the fanciest cuisine in the world.

When we leave, Lou takes my son's hand and shoos Stephen and I away.

"I've got him, I've got Kona, I have his medicine, and the number for his doctor—not that we're going to need it. Now go. Enjoy your honeymoon weekend."

Eli groans at her words. He hates being treated like a baby, but he hates being treated like an invalid even more. I squat down and pull my little man into my arms. My eyes heat when I think of all the things I would do to give him a perfect life, free of this condition.

"Take care of Aunt Lou for me, okay? Show her a good time." I kiss his cheek. "I love you."

"I love you, Mom." He squints up at Stephen then holds out his hand for a high five.

"See you Monday, bud." Stephen slaps his palm, and they exchange grins.

I kind of like their special relationship. I like my son having a positive-ish male influence in his life. I wish Ethan were closer. I can't even think about what my older brother would say about all of this if he knew.

"Don't do anything I wouldn't do!" Lulabell calls, dragging Eli in the opposite direction.

"I don't think there's anything she wouldn't do." I muse, looking up at my new husband.

The wind ruffles his wavy brown hair. His pretty blue eyes

crinkle with his smile, and every time I look at him, he's studying me like I'm a mystery he wants to solve.

"What?" I finally ask.

He takes my hand and pulls it into the crook of his arm. Looking down, he gives me a wink. "What what?"

"Why do you keep looking at me that way? Like it's the first time you've ever seen me."

We're walking with my hand in his arm, dressed to the nines. It's a gorgeous Friday afternoon. The park is full of people jogging, riding bikes, throwing Frisbees, walking their dogs. You'd never know there was so much hustle and bustle steps away from us.

"I've never been married before. It's... unexpected."

"Oh." I look away at the couples lying on the ground holding hands, kissing. "We're not really married."

"We are legally married. I don't expect to do it again."

Glancing up, at his handsome profile, I try to understand. "Why not?"

He shrugs. "After a while such things seem superfluous. I'm set in my ways. I don't like change, and I don't have the patience to get used to a new human in my life."

"Now you have two."

"I'm used to you two."

We've walked across the park to the Upper East Side, now we're headed slightly south to his neighborhood near the East River. We've been walking slowly, but it's not terribly late. Stephen stops at a tiny liquor store on the way to his place.

I wait as he buys a bottle of champagne. A few streets over, he stops in a pastry store and buys a small, round cake with white frosting.

"What are you doing?" I laugh, holding the cake as we approach his townhome.

"We just got married. We should have cake and champagne."

I follow him inside, and we go to the bar. He takes everything from me, arranging the cake on a crystal stand then taking down two crystal flutes. I wait as he pops the cork, scrunching my shoulders at the festive noise.

"Here." He holds his glass out to me. "To the unexpected."

"The unexpected." I clink and we both sip.

"Nice wine." I take another, longer sip while he pulls out a knife to cut the small, round cake.

He carefully places two pieces on plates. A ribbon of pink strawberry lines the center, and he holds out a plate to me.

I take it, but he stops me eating. "Don't we feed each other the first bite?"

"You really want to do this?"

"I told you I'm never doing it again."

Slanting my eyes, I shake my head at him. "Okay."

We both pick up our pieces of cake and slowly move them toward each other's mouths. Our eyes lock, and I see a glint of mischief in his. "Don't you da—"

I don't even finish my sentence before he's smeared frosting all over my upper lip.

"Motherfucker..." I smear the piece I'm holding on his cheek and chin as he turns his head laughing.

It's a full-throated, loud laugh. It's something I've never, ever heard, and it makes me laugh more. I hop up onto the bar, sitting so we're eye to eye.

"Come here." He steps between my legs, and I take the clean washcloth off the counter, dampening it in the small bar sink.

Slowly, I wipe the white frosting off his chin, then his cheek. His eyes are burning when I meet his gaze. He takes the cloth from me and holds it under the water, rinsing it before wringing it out and cleaning my face.

"You looked very beautiful today." His voice is quiet, intimate. "I like these daisies in your hair."

I reach up to pull one out, holding it between us. "They're kind of simple flowers."

"They remind me of you."

"In what way?"

Our eyes meet again, and the heat is building.

"They're beautiful. Sweet but strong."

"I'm not sweet." My voice is a whisper.

"You are." He traces his thumb along my cheek. "You're also strong. I'm lucky to have you as my first and only wife."

Emotion flares in my chest at his words. "Stephen... I told you I'm not sleeping in your bed."

"Who said anything about sleeping?"

Leaning forward he kisses me, and it's that good kind of kiss, the devouring kind. I exhale a whimper, and his hands are beside me on the bar, sliding up my thighs, clutching my ass, pulling my core closer to his body. I hold onto his face, chasing his kisses, not even trying to resist.

He growls, moving his mouth to my neck and pulling at the soft skin there. "You're delicious. I want to taste you again. I want you coming all over my face while you scream my name."

"Stephen..." It's a hot gasp, because God, I want that, too.

Pulling back, our eyes meet. His are dark with desire. "Come with me."

I slip off the bar, and he leads us quickly to the stairs, climbing three flights to the top floor, to his bedroom. I've never been up here, and I'm fascinated.

It's all dark wood, rich and old. The wood floors are covered with thick, silky Persian rugs in blood red patterns. His bedroom is oak-paneled wainscoting with beige plaster walls leading up to beige coffered ceilings. It's elegant and gorgeous.

I don't have time fixate on it. He turns me, sliding his fingers into the back of my hair, searching for the bobby pins that hold the braid along my scalp. I reach back to help him, freeing the braid then slowly unweaving it as he traces his lips down the back of my neck.

"Stephen," I whisper as currents of heat race up my legs, through my belly.

"Yes," he hisses as my hair falls in waves around my shoulders. "So beautiful."

I'm looking down when I feel his fingers sliding the zipper on the back of my dress. It falls in a silky puddle at my feet, leaving me in my beige lace bra and half-slip. I look up and over my shoulder at him. His gaze is hungry, possessive as he leans down and kisses me. His hands cover my flat stomach before rising, slipping under my bra to cup and knead my breasts.

I exhale a sigh, leaning my head back. His erection is firm at my back.

He takes his hands away. "Get on the bed."

Stepping forward, I climb onto the firm mattress.

It must be memory foam, because nothing moves as I make my way to the center. I sit with my back to the embossed headboard, watching as my gorgeous husband slowly removes his coat, loosens his tie and lifts it over his head. Then he unbuttons his white shirt, slowly revealing the lines of muscle lurking underneath.

When he bends down to remove his pants, the lines in his stomach flex and deepen. My bottom lip is caught in my teeth, and I shift to ease the tension building in my pussy. I want him inside me. I want him thrusting and making me scream his name as I come. I might have done all this for my son, but God, I'm going to enjoy having Stephen Hastings as my husband for a little while.

16

Stephen

Emmy bites her lip as she watches me undress. Her eyes follow my movements, and the heat flickering in her eyes has my cock a steel rod in my slacks. "When you look at me that way, I want to fuck you senseless."

Her full bottom lip pops out, and she drops her chin, her pretty cheeks turning pink. She's so fucking beautiful and so fucking stubborn. Shoving my pants off, I climb onto the massive king-sized bed in my room, catching her leg and pulling her under me. She lets out a little squeal, and I cover her mouth with mine.

She tastes sweet like strawberry cake, and her body is soft and warm against mine. I slide my lips along the line of her jaw, and she makes a little noise. "That sound..." I bite the skin on her neck and she does it again. "Spread your legs."

"Stephen..." Her hands are on my sides, fingertips tracing around to my back.

"Do it." Reaching down, I pull that filmy slip higher as she opens her thighs for me.

I hook my thumb in the side of her thong and rip it away as I bury my cock balls-deep in her slippery heat.

She inhales sharply, arching her back higher. I let out a low groan.

One of the benefits of getting married—blood tests. We're both officially clean, and I plan to fuck her bareback all over this house this weekend.

"You feel so good," I hiss, sinking deeper into her.

Her knees rise at my sides, and she moans as I rock my hips faster, harder. "Yes..." She gasps in my ear, and I catch her around the waist, rolling us over so she's on top of me now.

"Sit up." I nudge her waist. "I want to see you ride me."

She buries her face in my neck. "No."

"God dammit!" My back arches and I growl, shoving my cock deeper into her. "Don't tell me no, woman!"

She moves her face, kissing my cheek and speaking in my ear. "You like when I tell you no. You like fighting with me."

A surge moves through my cock, and I groan. She's right.

Reaching down, I unclasp her bra so I can feel her hard nipples against my chest. "Let me at least kiss your tits."

"Stephen," she moans, rocking her hips against my pelvis, driving me crazy with her hot little pussy.

"Sit up." I order, and she finally obeys, arching her back and rising above me.

Fuck me... Her long hair falls over her shoulders, between her small, round breasts that bounce every time I thrust into her. She rotates her hips like a dancer, and I push my head back, trying not to blow.

"Fuck, Emmy. You're so damn sexy." She slaps her hands against the mattress on either side of my head, and I rise up to kiss her mouth, pulling her lips and sucking her smart tongue.

She sits up again, rocking faster, and her expression changes. She's feeling it now, and it's hot as fuck watching her focus, bucking those hips and pulling my cock. I reach around to cup her ass, lightly following her movements with my fingertips.

"Oh, God!" She gasps, moving quicker. "Oh, yes!"

"That's right, come for me."

Her head falls back with a moan, and I reach my hands up to catch hers, holding them as she breaks into shudders, her pussy clenching, massaging and drawing out my orgasm. I've been following her lead, enjoying the view until now.

I catch her around the waist and roll us so she's under me, and I pound out my own orgasm hard and deep in her throbbing core. She rises to meet me, finishing out the last threads of her climax as I go. My back arches, and I hold steady, pulsing deep inside her beautiful body.

With a deep sigh, I rest my forehead against her shoulder. "That's one part of married life I very much like."

"So you married me for sex?"

I nip the skin on her neck. "You married me for money."

She starts to laugh, and I slip out. We both groan. I rise up, propped on my forearms over her, looking into her blue eyes. She seems happy... I think?

"What is that expression? What are you thinking?" I don't know why, but I truly care all of a sudden.

Her slim brows pull together. "What are we doing?"

"Taking care of Eli. Getting him the help he needs."

Her lips press into a half smile, and her eyes cut away. I chase after them. "What?"

"I mean, what are we doing right now?"

"Having hot sex whenever we feel like it." I grin, raising an eyebrow. "It's a perk of being married."

"So your marriage proposal was not purely altruistic?"

"Altruism is good, but hot sex is even better."

She snorts and wiggles in my arms. I ease up so she can roll over, onto her stomach. Her head is propped on her hand. "It seems silly to have a honeymoon for a fake marriage."

"I don't mind indulging in this part of the charade. Do you?"

She chews her lip and looks down at her hand on the bedspread. "No. But I'm afraid people will be hurt when it's all over."

"They won't if we handle it right." I trace my finger down the length of her back, assuming she's concerned about Eli. "Don't worry. When the time comes, we'll discuss the right thing to do. It's going to be okay."

She inhales deeply and gives me a little smile. "So we're basically hostages in your house for the next two days, pretending to be blissed out newlyweds?"

I shrug, dropping onto my back. "Sure."

"I'm ordering pizza." She jumps out of the bed, going to my closet.

I roll over watching her, grinning at her skipping around in only a half-slip and panties. She's a welcome compliment to my dark brown and gray, ultra-masculine room. She takes my chocolate-brown silk robe out of the closet and puts it on before heading to the door.

"Meet you in the kitchen!" With that she's gone, leaving me to pull on my boxer briefs and a tee and chase after her.

Emmy sits on the enormous white granite bar in my oversized kitchen. A piece of New York style pizza is in her hand, and the bottle of champagne is between us. My robe is tied around her waist, and she swings her bare feet. I've never thought this townhome looked better.

"So which old ancestor left you this pile of bricks?" She picks up her glass of champagne and sips.

I grin stepping in front of her, putting both hands on her thighs covered in the smooth silk of my robe. "My aunt Rebecca inherited it from her great aunt Matilda."

She puts a hand on my shoulder. "Wouldn't that make Matilda your great great aunt?"

I open my mouth, and she holds the pizza so I can take a bite. The savory mix of marinara and spicy Italian sausage hits my tongue, and I let out a groan. "Joe's is the fucking best."

"Have I mentioned how much I love living in modern times? If it were ten years earlier, we'd have had to walk."

I slide my hands from her thighs to her ass. "What were we talking about?"

A grin curls her lips. "Aunt Matilda. Why isn't she your great great aunt?"

"She is. She died before I was born, so she didn't leave me anything."

"Mm." Emmy nods, taking another bite. "You're so blessed to have a large family. All I have is Ethan."

"Back in the day they would've said we were good Catholics."

"Why are people such assholes?" She rolls her eyes and shakes her head, taking another big bite of thin crust.

I reach for the champagne bottle and refill both our glasses. Maybe I don't mind her sassy mouth when it's on my side.

"Cheers." I hold out my glass and she clinks without looking. "What did you do for fun when you were at Sarah Lawrence?"

"While we're on the subject," she teases, slipping off the bar and walking into my white living room. "I've never been in this room."

"I never noticed how white it is until now." A wall of windows faces the garden in the back.

The two couches and thick coffee table are white, the walls are stark white, leading up to the white tray ceiling above. Even the warm-brown wood floors are covered in a pale sisal rug.

"I think the idea is to send your eyes out the window to the beauty of nature." She flops on the overstuffed couch, holding her pizza.

"Or to give me a hell of a cleaning bill when you drip pizza sauce everywhere."

She looks around the pristine space. "Have you ever sat in here?"

"I don't think I have."

I plop on the couch at her feet, and for a moment, we're quiet, gazing at the wind moving through the leaves of the big tree outside the window.

Emmy finally nods. "Eli will use it. This couch will be beige by the time we leave."

Her words make my stomach twist strangely... which is ridiculous. They haven't even moved in properly, and I don't like the thought of them leaving?

"So back to Sarah Lawrence. What do young co-eds do so close to the city? Do you even hang out on campus?"

"We have a lot of school spirit." She acts indignant, and I hold up my hands.

"No offense to the Gryphons... That is the school mascot, right? The Gryphon? Is that a reference to Hogwarts?"

She throws a small, white pillow at me. "Are you making fun of my school? I'll have you know we have an extended list of notable alumni, including Barbara Walters, J.J. Abrams, Emma Roberts—"

I catch the pillow easily, dropping it to the floor. "Emmy Barton... Now what did you do for fun?"

Her eyes narrow, and she scoots onto her feet. "Strip chess."

"Now we're getting somewhere." I look around the room, and sure enough, a marble chess set sits behind a white basket of glass spheres on the coffee table. "Aunt Rebecca saves the day."

"No!" She grabs my arm as I start to get up, pulling me down again. "We can't play strip chess in our underwear! We'll be naked before the game even starts."

"It'll be naked chess." I arch an eyebrow, lifting her fingers to my lips. "I like it."

She takes her hand back. The pizza is gone, and she studies my face. "New game... Truth or dare."

My lip curls. "Lame. Everybody plays truth or dare."

"It's a classic getting to know you game. We should get to know each other better."

"I prefer strip chess." I put a hand on her smooth calf and slide it up to her knee. "It'll help us get to know each other better."

"I'd have you naked in two moves."

"I'd have you naked in one." My eyes level on hers, and heat smolders between us.

She slides off the couch onto the rough sisal. "I'd like to know you better clothed first."

Looking down at her pretty legs on the scratchy rug, I grab a large cushion from the corner and toss it to her. "Sit on this."

"Such a gentleman!" She stands, rearranging my robe, and tightening the belt. "You'll have me spoiled."

"Clearly I'm a pushover. You have me playing Truth or Dare... Who goes first?"

"Flip a coin." We both look around. Coming up empty, she grabs a black pawn and a white pawn, and holds them behind her back. "Pick one and the color."

I tap her left shoulder. "Black."

She brings her palm around, and it's the black pawn. I laugh, pointing at her. "I go first."

"So competitive, Mr. Hastings."

"You know it, Mrs. Hastings." The sound of that gives us both a moment's pause. Emmy exhales a laugh, and I continue with the question. "Truth or Dare?"

She leans back, studying my face. I've got so many wicked

ideas for sexy dares. I'm sure she can tell, because she shakes her head at me quickly and says, "Truth."

I start to speak, and she interrupts. "No... Dare. I mean dare."

Even better. I try to decide which I want to make her do first. Naked handstand? Masturbate in front of me? Send me a nude selfie?

She jumps in again. "Truth! I'm sorry. I want to do Truth."

I place my hand gently on her arm. "I know you were pretty sheltered growing up, but you can only pick one."

She squeezes her eyes shut and makes a little noise. "I don't trust you! Okay, okay. Truth. I'll stick with truth."

I pretend to be offended. "What have I done to make me so untrustworthy?"

"Seriously?" She gives me a look that makes me chuckle.

"Okay, truth. Are you ready?"

She blinks fast, and pulls her knees up. "I don't know."

"Get ready. This was your idea. I just wanted to have sex all weekend."

Her eyes roll. "Just ask already."

"Why do you hate me?"

17

Emmy

The words hang in the air, and my mind flies back ten years to my humiliation in Ethan's guest bath. Stephen was such a jerk. He walked out like I was any other disposable party girl...

Good luck in school. I was so shattered.

"Next question!" I reach for my champagne and take a long sip. I need it to kill this ache in my chest—this ridiculous ache that has resurrected from the dead for some stupid reason. I do not care about Stephen Hastings.

"That's not how it works. You can't pass on a question."

"I just did."

"Okay, if you want to pass..." His eyes glide down my neck to my breasts, and I swear, I can feel it on my skin. "You have to remove one item of clothing."

For a moment, I consider this. "Seems fair." I scoot to the side and reach under the robe, under my slip, removing my thong underwear.

Stephen's eyebrow arches, and he laughs in that low, rich

way he does. It makes my insides tighten. My insides need to grow up.

"My turn." I shift around again, getting comfortable. "Why are you such an arrogant jerk all the time?"

"Please don't spare my feelings." He feigns offense, but his cocky smirk is firmly in place.

"Just like that." I point at him, squinting one eye. "Inside your head, you're being one right now."

"You know nothing about the inside of my head, Emmy Barton Hastings."

"Then educate me." I put an elbow on the cushion, keeping my eyes fixed on his. "What makes you think you know more than everyone else?"

"Easy." He taps my nose lightly with his finger. "I do."

"That is not an acceptable answer."

"But it's the answer. Half the world is ignorant. The other half hasn't read as much as I have or they don't pay attention. Or they don't care, which is worse."

I drop back against the coffee table. "What makes you think you're better than everyone else?"

"That's two questions, cheater. But I'll answer it. I don't."

"I don't believe you." He's sitting up there on the couch, beautiful and kingly, square-jawed sexy, and he's not telling me a thing I want to know.

I'm down here on a cushion with no underwear.

"Truth or Dare?" He reaches down and slides one long finger through my hair.

I'm not sure I'm ready for his dares.

With a sigh, I opt for truth.

More fingers thread in my hair tightening, forcing me to look in his eyes. They're hot, possessive. "Who was your first?"

My stomach tightens. "No."

I'll never tell him that. I'll never give him the satisfaction of knowing it was him.

He's still holding me captive, with his words, with his eyes, with his hand in my hair. "Lose the robe. I'm going to fuck you."

"I don't want to have sex with you right now." Reaching up, I push his hand out of my hair. I stand and cross the room, taking my glass. "I want you to answer my questions."

"You know, you really suck at Truth or Dare." He swings his legs off the couch and follows me. "I answered all of your questions. By contrast, you answered none of mine."

"It's because you're not playing right." I pour more wine, trying to kill the desire for him flooding through my veins. I hate him. "Why don't you ask me something ridiculous like have I ever had sex on my period?"

"Because I already know the answer. It's no."

"How could you possibly—"

"I went to school with The Dick." He grabs the bottle from my hand. "I had to listen to his big mouth going on about period blood more times than I would ever wish on my worst enemy."

My jaw clenches, and I'm furious that he's right. "I guess you two have that in common?"

He pauses in drinking his wine, studying my lips. "Nothing would stop me from having sex with you if I wanted."

My nipples are tight, pressing against the thin silk covering them. My entire body burns for him. "Except me." I say softly.

He takes a step closer, his smile possessive. Reaching up, he traces a hair off my cheek. "Except you want to." His thumb moves down my upper lip, tugging on my lower one. "Who kissed you first? It'd better not have been some idiot."

"I thought you considered everyone an idiot."

"Not at all. You're one of the smartest people I know." His hand moves to my shoulder. "It'd better have been someone who deserved it."

Why is he saying all these things to me? My shoulder rises. "It was Travis Wiggins. We got picked for seven minutes in heaven. I don't know how smart he is, but he was a decent kisser."

Stephen's brow furrows. "Why don't I remember him?

"He was a year behind me." I think about the lanky kid who moved away before high school. "He was tall for his age."

"I see." Both of his hands are on the bar, caging me between his muscular arms. "What do you want to know about me? What can I tell you?"

The energy between us is so kinetic. I could slide my lips along his jawline and start a fire. "Who was your first?"

He doesn't hesitate. "Renee McAdams."

"Renee?" I'm not sure how I feel about his answer. "She was three years older than you."

"I was tall for my grade." He's teasing me.

I press my lips together fighting a grin. "Ass." I push against his arms, but he leans closer, tracing his lips up my cheek.

"Let's fuck now."

My chest squeezes, and the space between my thighs floods with heat. I'm slippery and tingly, my skin burning for his touch.

"I wasn't finished..." My hands go to his waist, tracing the skin just beneath his shirt. "Did you enjoy it? Do you miss her?"

"I barely remember it." He cups my cheeks, capturing my lips in a kiss, but I turn my face.

"Did you?"

Dropping his hands, he exhales heavily. "Emmy. I was fifteen. I got my dick in a girl, I don't know if I liked it. It lasted sixty seconds."

"Poor Renee." Our eyes meet, and I can't hold back. A laugh bursts through my lips.

He grabs me around the waist, causing me to squeal. "Poor Renee."

It's a growl that only makes me laugh more. "You're such a cocky bastard. She probably thought you were going to be good at it."

"If so, she *was* an idiot." He drops me to my feet, caging me in his arms again. His face is close to mine. I kind of love it.

"Your favorite word for people."

"If Renee thought I was any good at sex as a fifteen-year-old virgin, she was an idiot." He looks at my lips in that scorching way. "Actually, now that I think about it, she wasn't very smart." He wraps a long strand of my hair around his finger. "Now quit stalling. Let's fuck."

He pushes his hips against mine, and I feel his erection through the thin boxer briefs. I reach down and slide my palm up and down his massive member. It feels good, and I feel wicked.

"Hmm..." My eyes travel to his shockingly white living room. "Where would you like to do this fucking?"

"That's better." He unties the robe I'm wearing, sliding his hands around my bare waist, circling them higher to my breasts, cupping them and pulling the tips. He leans close, hot breath in my ear. "I want to bend you over that white couch and fuck you until you scream."

With every pinch of his fingers on my beaded nipples, a little charge registers in my core. My hands are on his shoulders, and I lean closer, kissing his cheek. "Take off your shirt."

In a flash, it's over his head, and my breath hisses. He's so damn sexy, tanned skin, perfectly toned. Threading my fingers in the waist of his boxers, I push. His hands cover mine, and he shoves them off, allowing his massive cock to spring free. It bounces heavy and erect in front of me.

My eyes are fixed on the mushroom tip, and I lightly trace my fingertips along his shaft. When I look up, his expression is dark with lust. Dropping my shoulders, I allow the silky robe to flutter down and off my body. I'm standing in only that half slip, no panties, no bra, taut nipples.

I drop to my knees, keeping my eyes on his. He exhales a groan, wincing as I take him in both hands, leading his tip to my mouth. I part my lips and suck the tip, tasting the salty precum, watching as he closes his eyes and groans. My hands move up and down his shaft, and I take him further into my mouth.

"Open," he growls, shoving one hand in the back of my hair. "Wider."

I drop my jaw, not sure how much more of him will fit. He holds my hair and straightens, pushing his cock further into my mouth until I feel it hit the back of my throat.

"Fuck, yeah." He pulls back slightly then thrusts in further.

My eyes close, and I lift my chin, doing my best not to gag. The smell of sweat and leather and musk surrounds me. My hands grip the front of his thighs, feeling his muscles flex with his movements.

Both his hands are in my hair, and he's thrusting like he's lost control. I'm so fucking turned on, heat slips between my thighs. I want to massage my clit, but I can't let go of him for fear I'll fall backwards.

"Fuck, yeah," he hisses again, thrusting further. I'm sure he's going down my throat when he stops suddenly. "I'm about to come."

He steps back, scooping me off my feet, and half drags, half pushes me to the couch. A little gasp escapes my throat when he pushes me onto my stomach over the back of the couch. I reach out, but my hands sink into the cushions.

"Stephen…" It's somewhere between a cry and a moan.

"Open up." He rips up the back of my slip and kicks my feet apart, pushing them further with his knees.

I obey, and back and forth, he slides the tip of his cock along my slit until he finds entrance and slams, balls deep into my pussy. A hoarse cry rips from my aching throat. He's rough and demanding, and I'm so full.

The way he's fucking me from behind, he goes deeper, thrusts harder. He grabs my hipbones and pulls me up and against him as I push my hands in the cushions, needing to massage my clit, needing to ease this tension building and twisting in my pelvis. I'm so close to coming...

"Fuck, you feel so good." He groans. As if reading my mind, he moves his hand around the front of my thigh. He finds my clit, circling and pinching it, and I cry out, breaking at once into orgasm. My legs shudder, and I collapse as my climax rockets up my thighs, centering on the place where we're joined.

"Oh, God." I surrender to his domination. It feels so, so good.

He stops thrusting and holds my hips, bending forward over my back, pulsing deep between my thighs as he groans loudly. I feel him moving, filling me. My insides clench around him, and he gives me one more little thrust. It makes me moan, and he reaches for my shoulders, pulling me up, wrapping one arm around my waist and one around my shoulders.

I'm locked against his body, his face at the back of my neck. "Good girl..." He murmurs, and I reach up to hold his arm.

He says we'll discuss it when it's time for me to go, but I'm afraid no matter what he says, this isn't going to end well.

18

Stephen

"I think more marriages would be successful if people said what they wanted from the outset." I hold a green grape to Emmy's lips. They part, and she sucks it in.

Watching her makes my dick twitch. It reminds me of how expertly she pulled my tip between those pouty lips, how sexy she followed my commands.

"Explain." She reaches down and takes a cube of cheese.

She's lying with her back against my chest. I'm propped on a pillow against my embossed leather headboard. We're both completely naked, and she's flipping through Netflix.

"You married me for the money. I married you for the sex. Six years later, nobody is shocked or betrayed."

"First, we're not doing six years later." She doesn't even flinch. She's such a stone.

"For argument's sake."

"What happens if your money runs out?"

"Nope." I reach down for another grape, popping it in my mouth this time. "Despite my ridiculous salary, I have a ridiculous trust fund. Thomas Hastings ruined a lot of things in his life, but he never fucked with our money."

She selects *The Blue Planet* and hits play. "What if you get tired of having sex with me?"

Scanning her face from above, her soft blonde waves, round blue eyes, pert nose, small breasts, flat stomach. And that mouth... never forget that mouth.

"I'm pretty confident I'd be content fucking you for a long time, Mrs. Hastings."

"Always Mr. Confident."

Sitting forward, I move the bowl of snacks to the nightstand and pull her beneath me. "Stephen!" She tries to wiggle away, but I hold her down. "I want the truth now. Why do you hate me?"

She arches her back, but I'm too strong. "You're not going anywhere, cheater. I get one of my questions answered."

Finally, she stops struggling and looks at me, eyes narrowed. "I answered your questions. I told you my first kiss."

"You didn't tell me your first fuck."

Her cheeks flame red, and she starts struggling again. "Let me go."

"I told you mine. It's only fair."

"Stephen!" Her voice grows louder, but my grip only tightens around her.

"I'll let you go as soon as you give up the name. I know it wasn't Burt, because we were together before him." She struggles harder, and I lean down to kiss her neck. That makes her growl, and I chuckle. "Secrets destroy marriages."

"If you don't let me go, I swear—"

"Name." I look in her eyes, and her struggle weakens.

She turns her face to the side, and I'm not sure... Do I see a tear? Instantly, I release her, sitting back on the bed. She rolls onto her side, putting her hand over her face, and it's like a punch in the gut.

"Hey..." I dive down beside her, putting my hand on her shoulder. "I'm sorry. I was only playing."

She pushes my hand away, refusing to look at me. She's all the way on her stomach now with her arms crossed around her face. She's not full-on crying, but something's wrong.

"Did I hurt you?" My voice is gentle, soothing. My stomach is tight.

We're close, my thigh against hers, her pretty back exposed. I trace a finger up her spine. "I wish you'd look at me."

For a moment, she doesn't move. Then she turns her head, letting me see her pretty face. I trace my thumb along the top of her cheek, moving a soft wave behind her ear.

"Why won't you tell me?"

"Because it doesn't matter." She pushes off the bed and crawls up to the other side of the California king, pulling a blanket over her knees and looking at the flatscreen television.

I'm puzzled by her response. She's been so playful and open with everything else. Then it hits me like a freight train.

Crawling over to where she sits, I prop beside her, touching the top of her shoulder with my fingertip. "Did he treat you badly?"

Her head turns slowly, and she studies me. She, blinks a few times and seems to consider my question.

Could that be the reason? This beautiful girl. This smart, strong woman... My jaw tightens, and rage burns in my throat at the very possibility. How have I gone from wanting to spank her to wanting to destroy anyone who might hurt her? *How did that happen?*

"What if I said yes?" Her eyes narrow. "Would you track him down and kick his ass if I asked you?"

"Do you want me to do that?" *Would I do that?* God help me, I think I would.

"Maybe. I hate him." A grin curls her lips, and she's taunting me like it's a game.

It kind of pisses me off, and fuck it, I've got a semi. She's right. I do love fighting with her.

"Emily Barton Hastings, tell me his name."

"Stephen Hastings." She crosses her arms.

I wait.

We're both breathing faster.

Seconds tick past.

Sir David Attenborough says something about a massive sea slug, and I consider throwing the remote at the television.

Still, she watches me.

I've lost patience. "Are you going to tell me his name?"

"I just did."

"What..." My brow furrows, and everything shifts. I pause to understand the words she just spoke. "Stephen Hastings..." The bottom falls out. "Wait. I don't understand. You're saying I... It was me?"

"It was you. You were my first." Her expression is level, old anger simmering in her eyes.

I'm fumbling, doing my best to remember the details of that night so long ago. Why don't I remember it better? I would if I'd known... "You didn't act like a virgin."

"How do virgins act?"

"Shy? Scared? Like it fucking hurts, for starters." My voice rises in volume.

"Oh, it hurt." Her voice rises to meet mine. "I held on until it passed and started to feel better. Then it started to feel good."

I'm pretty sure she's enjoying torturing me this way.

"You're saying that night, in the bathroom at Ethan's..."

"You were my first. What do the boys say? You popped my cherry?"

"Don't say that." My entire body is tight, uncomfortable. "How could you let me be your first and not tell me?"

"Would you have had sex with me if you'd known?"

"No!" I throw the blankets back and stand, pacing the room with my hands in my hair.

I'm back at that night, just leaving Ximena's. She'd told me to go out, burn off some energy, and I did. Only... the minute I walked into Ethan's party, I'd wanted to walk right out again. The Dick was there being an asshole. I wanted to fight him. I should have punched his lights out.

Instead, I proceeded to drink too much whiskey until I was buzzing... Until this beautiful creature came to me. She led me to that small bathroom, and I thought it was as much an escape for her as it was for me.

Is it possible to kick one's own ass?

"That was a bad night for me. I'd just come from... I'd said goodbye to someone I cared about. I was leaving the next day for Africa."

"You definitely worked all your frustrations out on me. Then you tossed me aside like a pocket pussy."

My head snaps up. "I did not."

"You did." Her voice is louder, her eyes flashing. "You patted my arm and wished me luck."

My lips part. I want to say something, anything to defend myself. "I didn't know."

Her arms cross. She's not backing down. "What would've changed if you had?"

Stopping, I walk over to her side of the bed and get close. "I wouldn't have gone in that bathroom with you if I'd known. You can't hold me responsible for your hurt feelings when you keep a secret like that."

"I can do what I want. It was my hymen."

"And that's why you hate me? Because you didn't tell me the truth and you got hurt?"

"It doesn't matter that I was a virgin, you were still a dick." Her voice is sharp, and it cuts me down to size.

She's right.

It sucks, and my stomach twists painfully. I shove my hands into the sides of my hair, giving it a pull before releasing it.

"I was so fucking angry, Emmy." My voice is quiet. I put my fingers on my forehead and scrub. "I should've punched The Dick into next week. I hated everyone... except you. You were sweet and pretty and you wanted me. I wanted you... But I was leaving. I couldn't have another person needing me... Not that you ever did."

It's quiet a beat. I'm breathing heavily, and she seems somehow vindicated. Sir David Attenborough says sardines swim with their mouths open, filtering food from the water through their gills like little sieves.

"I was in love with you." Her voice is quiet.

I feel like I've been hit with a sledgehammer. I want to fall to my knees, but she takes it right back.

"I mean, of course I wasn't in love with you. I didn't even know you. I was just a kid. I'd built you up in my mind for a long time... I guess that part was on me."

Sharks are on the screen eating sardines like it's a seafood buffet. I glance up at her, seeing her anger has subsided a bit. I want our old banter back. I want to tease her.

"So, you agree you had some level of responsibility?" I tease.

Her eyes flash, and she grabs a little pillow off the bed and throws it at me hard. I flinch away, lifting a leg to protect my junk. "You were fully responsible. You treated me like shit."

"Seems like you came, though."

She chucks another pillow at me, but I catch it this time,

throwing it right back. She squeals and ducks. "Stop throwing pillows at me!"

"Stop throwing them at me." I'm grinning, glad she's not throwing daggers at me with her eyes anymore.

Still, she sits across the bed with her jaw clenched like a pouty little girl. I study her a moment, and shit. Something changes. I don't know what's happening to me, but this girl... This beautiful, strong woman.

I walk to the bed slowly, holding my hands out.

"I'm sorry." Shit. I might as well cut off my nuts and give them to her while I'm at it. "I was in a bad place. Can you forgive me?"

Silence is my only response. She blinks fast, and I see her eyes are shining. *Is she crying?*

Climbing onto the bed, I pull her into my arms, kissing the top of her head. "Can you?"

"Fuck you, Hastings..." Her voice is a pitiful whisper, and she pushes against my chest. "I hate you."

"I know." Scooting further in the bed, I shift her around, moving her onto my lap in a straddle. "Look at me."

She lifts her chin, and I scoop her ass, drawing her closer. "You don't have to forgive me today." Reaching up, I slide my fingers through the back of her hair. "I'll wait. Let me make it up to you."

I pull her face closer to mine and kiss her. I really enjoy kissing her this way, tasting her, consuming her. She resists at first. Then she groans and moves closer, kissing me back. Her elbows fall, and her hands cup my neck.

I have a full-on erection now, and I reach beneath her, lifting her and sliding inside her slippery heat. She whispers my name on a moan. "Stephen..."

Her hips rock slowly, and she's so beautiful riding me. Her hair is all around us, her eyes closed, her ecstasy building.

"Ride me, baby." I cup and squeeze her breast, giving her tight nipple a pinch.

She moans, rocking her hips faster, back and forth on my cock, pulling me deeper. My hands rise up her back, catching her head and guiding her lips to mine again.

I kiss her deeply, sliding my tongue against hers, curling them together. My thumbs trace her cheeks, and I cherish the sweet taste of her. Green grapes and fresh water.

She's rocking faster on my lap. Her hands grip my shoulders and she arches up. Her little noises are breathless. God, she's so beautiful. I'm so hard, so ready to go off inside her. I grit my teeth, waiting.

"Come on, baby."

"Oh, God... Oh, yes..." She says it almost like a cry.

She's right there, and I reach between us, pinching her clit, rubbing it until she breaks, falling forward. Holding my shoulders as the ripples of pleasure move through her body. I close my eyes and let her pull me along, groaning loudly as I fill her. Holding her until she's done, her breathing changing from haggard to calm.

Gently, I roll her onto the bed beside me. I'm propped on my elbow, looking down on her flushed cheeks, my cock warm and snug inside her body. I slide her hair back, and our eyes lock, blue on blue. I touch her lips with my thumb.

"I'm sorry I hurt you." My voice is something I don't recognize. It's gentle, and I fucking don't care. "I never want to do it again. Let me make it up to you."

She places her palm against my cheek. "Okay."

Leaning down, I kiss her again.

19

Emmy

"So it's a combination of resective surgery and a hemispherectomy." Stephen leans closer, studying the images on the computer screen. "They say it's more precise than the typical surgery, but it's more thorough."

I'm sitting in his lap, holding a mug of coffee. "They also say the younger the patient, the better the long-term outcome will be."

His brow is furrowed, and he's reading closely. It's a long PDF document with pictures of brain scans linked to a page on the Mayo Clinic website. It took me two days to read it, looking up the medical words and making notes for cross-reference. Stephen reads it without hesitation as if he's been practicing medicine for years.

I remember how Pike Academy made a big deal of his 170 IQ, and one of the local magazines compared him to a young Bill Gates. As a girl, I was in awe of him, thinking he would be the greatest man, imagining myself at his side.

"What do you think?" My voice is small, and my insides are tense.

He nods without taking his eyes off the screen. "I know the perfect person to talk to about this. Henry Rourke works at Weill Cornell Medical, which happens to be one of the top neurosurgery hospitals in the country. We've worked together before, and he is top of the line."

Tears fill my eyes. When he said he would help me, I still had doubt things would come together. I never dreamed it would happen this quickly. Now, reading the report with him, having him confirm it's a potential cure for Eli, seeing him put his finger on someone who can help us... it all feels so real. I believe my baby has a shot at a normal life.

I set my coffee mug on his desk. "How soon would you be able to talk to him?"

"I bet..." Stephen clicks around on his giant iMac. He actually has two giant iMacs like he's the commander of a starship. "He helped me a while back with an app I was working on for stroke victims. Henry's a good guy. You'll like him."

"Okay..." Not really answering my question...

"Let me call him. I'll have Eli here every day during the week, right?"

"Yes, but I want to go with you."

Stephen's brow furrows as he reads his calendar. "I'll call him tomorrow and see if we can get the ball rolling this week."

"Oh, Stephen!" I dive forward, throwing my arms around his neck.

He chuckles, patting my back. "Why are you acting so surprised. I told you I'd take care of it."

My eyes are closed, and I hold onto him, waiting for my heartbeat to return to normal, doing my best not to cry. "I guess I didn't believe it would happen."

He nudges my shoulder, and I lean back to meet his gaze.

"You married me so I would help your son. I always keep my word."

I think about our arrangement and our little honeymoon interlude. We've had an amazing, intimate pocket of time. And tomorrow it ends.

"I'd like to be outside in the sun. Can we walk up to Central Park?"

He smiles and touches my cheek. "Sure."

For the first time in forty-eight hours we head outside, walking four blocks west and one block east, entering the park at the Grand Army Plaza south of the zoo.

Everybody seems to be out today. The sun is shining, bikers ride past on the path, boats glide silently on the pond, children cluster around a man making long bubbles with a hoop, dancers and performers are scattered throughout.

My hand is in the crook of Stephen's arm, and we walk slowly north, in the direction of the Gapstow Bridge. I take a deep inhale of blooming flowers, cut grass, and fresh water. "It's been years since I walked these paths. We used to come every Saturday when I was a kid."

Stephen nods toward the path tracing the perimeter. "I'm here a few times a week, jogging."

"I miss all the trees. It's so far from the Village."

We pause to watch a man dressed like a mime and a woman in a black leotard and full black skirt perform a modern dance without music in front of, around, and on a fountain. A small crowd gathers, and when they finish we all clap. Stephen drops cash in their hat.

"I'll walk Eli over for lunch if you want. He and I need to get out during the day, rest our eyes."

"If you wait, I'll walk over with you in the afternoon." Lifting my chin, I meet his gaze, and we exchange a smile. It's like we're making family plans.

We continue north, past the chess and checkers house. "Strip chess?" Stephen teases.

"That would definitely draw a crowd. What could we use to hold our tips?"

He looks around. "I didn't wear a hat."

"Next time," I tease, giving his arm a squeeze.

We veer west toward the carousel. So many children are riding, laughing, and squealing.

"I've always been afraid to put Eli on the carousel," I confess softly. "All the lights and the movements. It's hard to know what could trigger a seizure, and I never want him to be embarrassed."

Stephen lifts my hand and kisses my fingers. "Hopefully all of that's going to change very soon."

My throat aches, and I look away so he can't see the tears in my eyes.

We're at the mall, so we take a seat among the statues to rest our feet. Stephen buys cotton candy from a vendor, and we take turns tearing off pieces and letting the sugar melt in our mouths.

"Are you planning to tell Burt?" He watches me, and my throat tightens.

"No." I shake my head, thinking of all the times he's said it was unnecessary. "We don't have joint custody. I don't have to get his permission for medical procedures."

Stephen's quiet a beat, and I hold my breath as I watch him consider this. "Technically you're right. It's possible he could object after the fact..."

"But it wouldn't matter then." My lungs are tight. We're so close, and I don't know if this will change his mind.

Seconds tick past, and finally he nods. "Okay. I just wanted to be prepared."

The fear in my chest breaks, and I lean forward to hug him. "Thank you."

I don't have the words to express my gratitude for his strength, for making this happen. He gives me a squeeze and another strip of cotton candy. We finish it off, and he takes my hand again, pulling me up to walk back, past the statue of Balto, the heroic dog.

"Eli would love him."

Stephen motions toward Pilgrim Hill. "He'd love the model boat sailing."

"Oh, yes! We have to bring him for that."

It doesn't even enter my mind how our time together is limited. My silly heart simply grows bigger making all these wonderful plans. I suppose we don't have to be married to keep them.

"Stephen?" A sharp female voice cuts through my daydreams. "Stephen Hastings? I thought that was you!"

Stephen's body stiffens, and we turn to see a tall woman with long, straight brown hair striding up. She's wearing skinny black pants and a long coat over a tailored blouse. She looks very rich and elegant, and I suddenly feel very casual in my ripped blue jeans and oversized white sweater falling off one shoulder.

"Alyssa." He steps forward to give her a hug.

I do not let it bother me. Why shouldn't he hug an old friend? Alyssa steps back, and her eyes zero in on my hand in Stephen's.

"And who is this?" She's trying to sound friendly, but it's coming out high and challenging.

Stephen turns to me, and he seems unsure of what to say. "Alyssa Falcone, let me introduce Emily Barton..."

I'm not really offended. It's a completely awkward situation, and we haven't discussed this at all. Should he introduce me as his wife? We're only going to be married for... I suppose it could be as long as six months, depending on the surgery. Then again, we can't hide out in his townhome for half a year.

"What's this?" Alyssa motions to my left hand holding his arm. It's too late to stuff it in my pocket. Her eyes widen, and her face goes pale. "Are you... *married*?"

Stephen clears his throat. "Yes, well, it's a recent development. I guess I should say let me introduce my wife Emily Barton Hastings."

He smiles and holds a hand out to me.

"Recent development?" Alyssa emits a strangled laugh. "How recent?"

She looks at me like I'm a bug that escaped from the zoo, and I can't decide if I feel pissed or sorry for her. I mean, of course I knew Stephen must have ex-girlfriends. He's a healthy male...

Who's taking a long time to answer her question.

"We were married last week." I jump in.

"Last week!" Her eyes flicker from me to him and back again. "You said you didn't believe in marriage."

She's so rude, I decide to lay it on thick. "Stephen and I knew each other as kids, and we reconnected at the dry cleaner where I work. Maybe you've heard of it? Miss Con-Cleaneality? It's in the Village."

"I... haven't." Alyssa smiles, but her left eye twitches, and my devilish side wants to see how far I can push her before her head explodes.

"We specialize in drag queens and pageant gowns."

"Drag queens..."

"Really, we specialize in anything beaded or with sequins or feathers. If you have any dance dresses or stripper costumes, be sure to bring them to us. Miss Con-Cleaneality. In the East Village."

I'm pretty sure she's having a mini stroke.

"Okay, then." She backs away quickly. "I guess it's good to see you, Stephen. I hope you're happy."

Biting my lip, I'm holding on tightly so I don't burst out

laughing. Whoever this bitch is, clearly she expected Stephen to be with someone super high-class. And while I grew up in that world, she doesn't have to know it.

"Good to see you, too." Stephen's voice is mild.

She spins on her heel and takes off as fast as she came. I cover my mouth with my hand and snort.

He pulls my hand in his arm again, giving me an extra tug. "That wasn't very nice."

"She was not happy to meet me. What's her story?"

We're crossing Fifth Avenue, heading south toward his townhome. "Alyssa Falcone and I dated for about nine months last year."

"Nine months!" My jaw drops, and I look up at him.

He only shakes his head. "She started pressuring me for a ring, and I finally told her I had no intention of getting married. Ever."

"Oh..." I feel a teensy bit bad for Alyssa-Bitch, and a whole lot good for me. "Maybe if she were more of a harpy you'd have proposed."

Tilting my head to the side, I cut my eyes up at him. The dimple in his cheek appears with his grin. "Don't act jealous. It's not cute."

"Stephen Hastings." I jerk my hand out of his arm. "I am not jealous. That woman was a shrew."

He picks up my hand and puts it in his arm again. "Whatever you say, dear."

"I am not jealous!" My voice goes louder. "And don't call me dear! I'm not eighty."

We're back at his place, and he takes the front steps two at a time, stopping to unlock the door. "Whatever you say, dear."

"You'd better believe me." I jog up after him, ready to tell him off, when he opens the front door and spins me inside against the wall.

He kicks the door shut and looks down into my eyes, holding my jaw in one hand. I'm captive in his arms. "Are you fighting with me again?" His voice is hot and growly.

The jog up the stairs left me breathless, but the way he's looking at me now, eyes wicked with humor and lust, has my core hot and clenching. "What if I say yes?"

He pushes off the wall and takes my hand. "Let's get cleaned up. We've got some fucking to do."

EARLY MORNING RAYS stream softly through the drapes, and Stephen is asleep in the bed beside me. I'm holding my silent phone in front of my bent knees in the bed. On the flatscreen, a pod of dolphins crosses the open ocean.

ELI
He called it the desert of the sea.

I read the text, doing my best to keep an eye on the screen.

ELI
That's cool.

My thumbs move fast, and I look up and down.

How long is 3 meters in US length?

ELI
Mom. It's feet.

Sir David Attenborough describes the striped marlin, or what I would call a swordfish, diving to depths of one hundred meters.

How am I supposed to know what that means?

Stephen emits a weird, honking sound, and I snort a laugh. I want to tell Eli Stephen snores, but my stomach twists. I'm afraid to bring Eli too close to this... whatever it is. God, I don't even know what this is.

Stephen and I had sex one million times this weekend, three more times last night. Every time I move, my insides ache from his invasion. We've made plans, we've told each other things... *Shit*, I told him he was my first, and I'm still grappling with his reaction.

He was furious. He was floored. He was defensive, but ultimately, he was gentle. He said he was sorry. I have to wonder if Stephen Hastings has ever apologized to anyone in his life. Then he said he wanted to make it up to me. He made sweet love to me. He's been so different ever since.

We've drawn each other close... yet, at the same time, I know this isn't a real marriage. I married him for his medical connections and his money.

He fell in love with my kid.

Eli is the reason he proposed to me. I can never let myself forget that. He jokes that he married me for the sex, but Stephen Hastings can have sex with whoever he wants. Take for instance Alyssa-Bitch. I'm sure she was ready to give it up at a moment's notice. I certainly was.

From ten years ago to today, nothing makes me happier than being pressed beneath the weight of his body, feeling him lose control in my arms, his breath hot, his groans ragged.

Not to mention his big dick.

Or his talented tongue.

A gray bubble floats on my screen.

ELI

A sardine tornado!

I've lost track of the episode. Looking up, I see a giant whale is on the scene, gobbling up a bunch of fish. I'm awestruck.

> I thought whales ate krill?

ELI

> Depends on the size of the whale.

My smart little man. My thumbs move quickly as I text back.

> I miss you. Ready to move in here?

As much as I've enjoyed this time with my new husband... As weird as it is to call Stephen my husband... I miss my tiny apartment and Eli in bed with me watching *The Blue Planet*.

ELI

> Sort of... Aunt Lou likes kisses at bedtime!

My eyebrows pull together.

> What does that mean?

A gray bubble floats, and I don't know what to expect.

ELI

> Chocolate has milk and antioxidants. She says they're good for us.

"Oh my God." Air bursts through my lips, and I drop my head back with a groan. "Lulabell!" Quickly I tap back.

> I hope you brushed your teeth. Chocolate will also give you cavities.

I can just hear him arguing with me. Instead, his reply heats my eyes.

ELI

I miss you, Mom.

I quickly text back.

I'll be glad to see you in a few hours.

Stephen rouses, turning toward me and sliding a muscled arm around my waist. "Is it morning already?"

His voice is thick with sleep, and I can't believe how happy I feel right now.

Scooting down in the bed, I pull his arm tighter around me. "Pretty much. I was just texting with Eli. Making sure he's okay."

"Mm... Is he?"

"Lou's been letting him eat chocolate at bedtime."

"Probably because of the antioxidants and calcium." Stephen is still waking up, but I turn to glare at him. He doesn't see me when he adds, "I hope she made him brush his teeth before he went to bed. Sleeping with sugar on your teeth erodes the enamel and causes cavities."

Pressing my lips into a smile, I shake my head. He's actually going to be a pretty great fake husband for the next... however long it takes.

"Stephen, I was thinking... How long are we planning to stay married?"

He rolls onto his back, scrubbing his fingers on his forehead. "A few months? I guess it depends on what Henry says. I'd expect at the most six months."

His voice is so casual... *Jesus take the wheel.* I refuse to let my chest sink at his response. It's why we did this. I married Stephen for his money, not for my heart. My heart is going to have to stay out of this.

Tossing the covers back, I swing my legs out of the bed and head for the shower. "Let's take off in a half hour."

"I'll make coffee."

"DUE TO RISING TEMPS, sock and bra money not allowed." Stephen reads the sign in front of Miss Con-Cleaneality. "That's not a deep thought."

"It is if someone hands you a sweaty twenty." The horrified face Stephen makes cracks me up as I pull open the glass door.

"Here come the newlyweds!" Lulabell sings loudly from behind the counter.

I cringe, wishing she wouldn't do that, but my "husband" doesn't seem to mind. He does a little bow, putting his hand on my lower back.

I imagine we're an unusual pair, Stephen in his tan Armani suit and beige silk tie, and me in my usual cutoffs and a purple tank. It gets hot in here, and Lou and I wrangle heavy bags of dirty clothes all day. It's not like we're sitting around decorating cupcakes.

I'm about to duck under the counter when large hands catch me by the waist. My "husband" stops me, turning me around and pushing my back against the wood.

"I'll miss you today." He's so much taller than me. I reach up to his shoulders, but my face is still only at the center of his chest.

"Didn't you get enough of me this weekend?"

He leans down and kisses my lips. Not his usual take no prisoners kiss. This is a regular, saying goodbye to my wife at work type of kiss. It melts my knees.

"We discussed that, Emily. Have you forgotten?"

I have not forgotten his theory on long-lasting unions. He

paid me a really nice, albeit crass compliment saying he'd probably never get tired of fucking me. Such a gentleman.

I manage to put that thought away and regain my cool. "Take care of my baby."

"I always do." He looks around. "Where is Eli?"

"Coming right up!" Lulabell's tone is dreamy.

"Hey, Mom!" Eli comes cruising to the front, barely even giving me a hug.

He slaps Stephen a high-five and calls back a goodbye. Stephen gives me a little wink and the two of them stroll out into the street. I stand at the back counter watching them go feeling completely conflicted inside.

Stephen makes my knees weak, yet watching Eli walking away with him, without even a glance my way, feels like my heart has just been removed and is dragging along behind them on the concrete.

"It's hard when they start getting independent." Lou sidles up beside me, putting her arm around my waist. "Remember, that's what you want him to do."

Rocking my head side to side, I eventually make it to a nod. "I know. He's just... he's so..." I don't want to say *vulnerable*. It makes him sound weak and Eli's the strongest kid I know.

I try again. "He's just so..." *Ugh!*

"He's got to learn to spread his wings, Mamma Bear."

"You're right." I know she's right. If only I didn't fear so much for his safety.

"And let me say, that sexy new husband of yours seems like the perfect role model for him. Good work." She leans back, inspecting my face. "You're absolutely glowing. I take it he's still got it?"

"He's got something." A magic penis? No, it's more than that.

"Any mention of your first time?"

"Actually, it did come up."

Her mouth forms an *O*, and she scoots closer. "Tell me everything."

Exhaling a sigh, I follow her to the back to help carry the clean clothes to the rack. "He was defensive at first then pissed I didn't tell him... and ultimately apologetic."

"Oh, Em!" Lou clasps her hands to her chest and looks at me like I've just told her the most wonderful bedtime story. "The stars have reunited you with the man of your dreams. I'm so happy. It makes me believe in true love again."

Anxiety squirms in my stomach. I can do this fake marriage for Eli, but misleading Lulabell makes me feel sick. Especially when she thinks I'm headed for a happily ever after.

God, *again*, I'm convinced I'm making a massive mistake. As if there's anything I can do about it now.

I only hope Stephen's right and when the time comes, we're able to explain our questionable choices and the pros and cons of making them in a way the people I love will understand.

Provided I don't lose my heart in the process.

20

Stephen

y dogs are barking!" Emmy flops on my pristine white couch as soon as she arrives home from work.

"You don't have to walk home. I'll send a car."

"I don't want to get used to being pampered."

Her response is like a splash of cold water right in my face, reminding me not to get too attached. I should be grateful for the wake-up call, but instead my jaw clenches.

Eli hops up beside her. "Stephen has two computers in his office. Two!" His high voice is loud, and he's so excited, he bounces. The grin it provokes removes my irritation. This kid. "He showed me a video of a pod of orcas swimming in a group. They really do hunt like wolves! We pulled up this other video on the screen beside it, and watched them side by side. It was awesome! Think we can go to Yellowstone and see a wolf some day? They're so cool. Did you know gray wolves are endangered?"

"I think I heard about that. Goodness, you're excited." She

looks up at me, and I cross my arms, smiling at their reunion. "Are you feeling okay? No headaches or... anything?"

"Nu-uh." Eli hops off the couch and heads over to where I'm standing. "Can I show Mom the model?"

"Sure. Run get it."

He runs to the stairs, and I take the opportunity to tell her what else happened today. "I talked to Henry. He'd like to see Eli tomorrow if that works for you."

Her eyes widen, and I really love the way she looks at me, like I just rescued her from a burning building.

"Let me check with Lulabell. I'm sure when I tell her, it'll be fine." Her pretty brow furrows, and worried blue eyes meet mine. "Why so soon? Is he concerned about something?"

"I don't think so. He's done the surgery before. I sent him all of Eli's records, and he thinks, depending on how it goes, he can work him in next week."

"Next week!" Her voice is breathless, a mixture of excitement and nerves.

I get it. She's getting what she always wanted, and it's coming in fast.

"Is that too soon?" I kind of hope she says yes.

It's strange to be both proud of what I've done and miserable at the same time. Eli spent last week with me, and Emmy was here all weekend. Now, seeing them settled and happy in my home, I have unexpected pangs of sadness at the thought of them not being here.

"I guess not..."

"He's traveling to Europe the following week, and he won't be back for a month. He said we can do it next week or wait for him to return—"

"We can do it next week." She chews her lip, looking at her hands twisting in her lap. "I don't want to miss our opportunity.

I'll talk to Eli about it, and I'm sure Lou will let me have the time off tomorrow."

"I'll let him know." My lips press into a smile, but it's not my usual cocky grin or knowing smirk. It's sad. It's a smile of knowing the right thing to do is going to hurt like hell, but knowing I'm going to do it anyway. "I've arranged for us to have dinner every day at six thirty, if that time works for you?"

"Sounds great." She stands. "I'll get cleaned up and change."

"This afternoon, Ted—my personal chef—and I planned out a keto menu for our meals. We can't use half the ingredients in the pantry, but Ted loves a challenge."

"Keto?" Emmy stops at the stairs, turning back and giving me a wry grin. "Are you saying I need to lose weight, Mr. Hastings?"

"Not at all. Your body is perfect." Her cheeks flush, but she should know how I feel. I showed her several times this weekend. "A ketogenic diet is highly recommended for controlling seizures in children. I figured we'd all eat the same thing, so Eli doesn't feel strange."

For a moment, she's silent, staring at me. Then her lip trembles and she rushes forward, throwing her arms around my neck.

My hands are on her waist, and her voice is muffled at my shoulder. "Thank you. You have no idea how much all of this means to me."

A sudden ache hits my throat. *Ridiculous.* It's only food. "Well, if it's good for him, it's probably good for us, too. I'll let Ted know the time is acceptable."

She releases me, and her eyes shimmer with unshed tears. "I'll tell Eli."

We reconvene to a dinner of pork chops with green beans sautéed in coconut oil. Eli's meat is pre-cut, and he devours it like we didn't have lunch, which we did, tuna salad with celery and fresh tomatoes.

"This is good!" He spears a green bean with his fork and bites off the end. "Mom and I usually just have pizza or subs. Or burgers from Paul's."

"You don't have to tell everything we do." Emmy slices a piece of pork chop, and I give her a disapproving look. She makes a face. "Not all of us have a personal chef."

"We can have burgers for lunch tomorrow." Eli looks up, and I give him a grin. "They'll be a little different, no bun, extra cheese."

His head tilts to the side thinking, then he nods. "Okay!"

Emmy shifts in her seat. "The way we're eating is supposed to help with your seizures." She clears her throat. "Speaking of which..." She pushes her green beans around on her plate.

I know this is hard for her, but I let her do it.

"Yeah, Mom?" Eli takes an oversized bite of pork, which pokes out his cheek and gives him duck lips.

"What if I told you we'd found a way to make it so you might not have them anymore?"

Eli jumps out of his chair. "No more seizures? How?" He's beaming, and Emmy smiles, reaching out her hand.

"Sit down, buddy. Finish your dinner." He does as she says, but his eyes are fixed on her as she continues. "It would be a surgery. On your head." His brow furrows, but he listens closely. "Stephen has a friend who's a doctor, and he can do this... thing to your brain, and hopefully it will make everything stop."

"My brain will stop?"

"No, honey..." She exhales a soft laugh. "I mean the seizures will stop. We hope. For good."

Emmy looks to me with pleading eyes, and I take it as my cue to help her. "We're telling you about it because having the surgery might change things—"

"Yeah, it would! If my seizures stopped, I could ride my bike again and go skating again and..."

"What Stephen means is since it's on your head, you might have to stay in bed for a while. Until it heals. So that's kind of a downside."

He turns to her. "How long would I have to stay in bed?"

She smiles, seeming calmer. "We have an appointment tomorrow with the doctor. He can answer all your questions and tell us if he thinks it might work for you. Is that something you'd like to do?"

"Sure!"

Ted interrupts us, entering the room with a treat I know he's been perfecting all afternoon. "Dessert is chocolate chip coconut bars!"

I lean forward and speak in a stage whisper. "It helps your son likes coconut."

The short, blond chef places a bar on each of our plates. Eli scoops his up and eats it fast.

"Coconut is cool! The other kids think it's gross, but they're just dumb." Eli speaks around a big bite of chocolate.

"Spoken like someone else I know." Emmy glances at me before placing her fork beside her plate and giving him a warm smile. "As soon as you're done, hit the shower."

A FEW HOURS LATER, I stop by the blue room on my way to the third floor. Eli is tucked in bed with Kona under his arm, and Emmy sits beside him reading a book about dolphins. It's kind of perfect, like something out of a painting or one of those Rockwell prints of family life back in the day.

She closes the book and leans forward, kissing her son's head. Eli spots me, and calls out a goodnight. I wave and tell him to have pirate dreams. Emmy cuts off his light, and a projection of stars and planets covers the ceiling—another project of ours today.

We're out in the hall, and she smiles up at me. "Well, I guess I'll get some rest. I'll go in a little early tomorrow, since I'm leaving early."

She starts for the yellow room down the hall, and I frown. "Where are you going?"

Emmy pauses at the door. "I moved my things downstairs... I figured this room was for me."

"Your room is upstairs with me." Closing the space between us, I'm ready to toss her over my shoulder and carry her to the third floor where she belongs.

She grins, crossing her arms over her chest. "We discussed this before we got married, Stephen. I'm not sleeping in your bed."

She is so fucking stubborn. "You did a damn good job of it this past weekend." My voice rises, and she steps forward holding her hand in front of my mouth.

"Shh... Eli will hear you."

"And what happens if Eli gets up in the night and sees you sleeping down here?"

She looks to the side and does a little shrug. "I'll tell him the truth. I worry about him being so far from me at night. What if he needs me?"

"I expect my *wife* sleeping in my bed with me." My jaw is tight, but her expression is firm.

"Fake wife, and I'm not sleeping in your room."

"Because you're worried about Eli?" I'm furious.

"That," she nods. "And I think it'll only complicate things down the line."

Stepping forward, I place my hand on the wall and lean in close. "You can sleep here tonight. Tomorrow, I will get a monitor for Eli's bedroom and put the receiver upstairs. I want you in bed with me at night."

"Stephen—"

"End of discussion." Leaning down, I kiss her, capturing her full, pink lips with mine.

I've wanted to kiss her all day, and as I curl my tongue along hers, she sighs a little noise—those little noises make me crazy. I roll my body over hers, pressing her against the paneling. Her hands are on my chest then on my neck, then she's holding my cheeks.

Lifting my head, I look into her blue eyes. So much emotion is reflected back at me, I hold still to take it all in. She traces her fingers down to my neck, dropping her chin and her hands at the same time.

"I should go to bed now." Her voice is subdued. I'm not sure what to make of it, but I won't push her any more than I already have.

Leaning down, I kiss the side of her cheek once more, taking a deep breath of her fresh flower scent. It'll have to get me through the night. "Sleep well."

Her fingers trace along my waist until I'm gone.

Thinking back over our weekend, I kind of love our time together. I love that she was jealous when we bumped into Alyssa. I love that Eli is so comfortable in his room and excited about what's to come. I want everything to work out for him. I want him to have a good life.

I want to make it up to her that I hurt her. I want to treat her like a queen while she's here, and when the time comes, I'll let her go with a better memory of me.

I'll give her this gift, and hopefully it will make up for the past.

21

Emmy

"And this is the part I'll take out." Dr. Henry Rourke traces a small corner with his pen on a life-sized model of the human brain.

He lets Eli touch it and turn it, looking at all the places his scans show that light up when he has a seizure. He's so easy with my son, it's hard to believe he's one of the top pediatric neurosurgeons in the country. He's more like Mr. Rogers.

Eli cuts right to his most important worry. "Will it hurt?"

"Not at all. You'll be mostly asleep the whole time, and when you wake up, you'll have a bandage around your head."

"Like a pirate?" Eli gets so excited about the possibility, Dr. Rourke laughs.

"Usually, it's just white gauze, but I'll see if there's any way we can get pirate gauze." He sets the brain model on the table. "You'll have a weird haircut for a little while. We have to shave your head around the site of the incision."

Eli's eyes fly to mine, and I do a little shrug. "At least hair grows back?"

He thinks about it a minute and seems to be okay with the prospect. "I can wear a hat."

"Lots of hats." Dr. Rourke agrees. "Knit hats, baseball caps... pretty much anything you'd like."

"And I'll never have another seizure ever again?" The hope in Eli's voice pulls my chest.

"Well..." Dr. Rourke's smile fades a notch. "Do you like math, Eli?"

"Yes, sir! I'm in pre-algebra now." He's so proud. I love him so much.

"Are you familiar with percentages? Here, if I hold the brain in my hands, you would say this is one hundred percent of your brain, right?" Eli nods, and the doctor continues. "With this surgery, the success rate of never having another seizure as long as you live is about sixty percent. So a little more than half."

My heart aches. Forty percent is such a large number.

"The good news is, the younger you have it done, the better chance you land in that sixty percent range."

"Which is why I need to do it now?" Eli squints up at him, and I'm not sure how much of this he understands. He's so smart, but this is tough.

"Right." Dr. Rourke smiles and gives his leg a pat. "Also your recovery is usually easier because your brain is so young and active right now."

Stephen lingers at the back of the room, observing our interaction. His expression is serious, listening to every word, watching over us like our private protector.

After he kissed me last night, I lay in bed a long time struggling with my emotions. It was so much easier when I hated him. Our relationship, or whatever it was, was clean and simple. I could control my lust by reminding myself what an arrogant, selfish bastard he could be.

It worked.

Now everything's mixed up. Now he's a billionaire knight in shining armor, giving us what we've always wanted. He's a dominating, passionate lover, treating me the way I've always wanted to be treated. He's the man I dreamed he was all those years ago when I wanted to give him everything, believing I could make him fall in love with me just as much as I loved him...

And I'm a fool, who's going to get my heart ripped out if I'm not careful.

Every time we talk about what we're doing, our arrangement has a deadline. Six months max, he said. Then it's back to the Village with me, and back to him being the distant, wealthy entrepreneur featured on the cover of magazines. The one who doesn't believe in marriage.

"Do you have any more questions?" Dr. Rourke snaps me out of my distraction.

"I'm sorry. Yes, I do. I just..." My eyes fall to my brilliant little son sitting on the examination table blinking at me with so much trust. "I, um..."

I don't want to ask my questions in front of Eli. I can't say what terrifies me with him here. I can barely think of the risks in my mind much less say them out loud.

If anything goes wrong, Eli could be left blind or paralyzed or unable to speak or walk or with any number of cognitive issues. He could go from being my child genius, doing middle school science projects, to mentally challenged. He could die...

Oh, God, I can't even think of that possibility.

Stephen stands and motions to Eli. "How about we run down to the cafeteria and get a chocolate ice cream?"

"Okay!" Eli shouts, hopping off the table. Then he stops and squints up at Stephen. "Is that allowed on my special diet?"

Stephen's lips press together. "I don't know. But I bet it's okay if we only get a small cup."

I smile, grateful as he takes my son's hand and leads him

from the room. The door clicks shut, and I exhale a nervous laugh.

"I'm sorry. I didn't want to say anything scary in front of Eli. He's so little."

"It's okay." Dr. Rourke puts his hand on my arm. "I think I know what's on your mind, and I can tell you, I've done hundreds of these surgeries through the years. I've seen mixed results, but the vast majority provide some level of improvement."

I think I might burst into tears. "Oh, that's such a relief!"

"Full disclosure, the bulk of my work has been focused on the traditional resective surgery."

"Okay..." My voice is quiet, nervous again. "How many of the type we're needing have you done?"

"Less than a hundred." Panic tightens my chest, and I guess it's reflected in my eyes because he quickly adds. "I can say, they've all been on young patients like your son, and they've all been very successful."

"So you think it'll work?"

His lips poke out and he nods. "I think we have a good chance at a positive outcome, yes."

"How long does it usually take? The surgery, I mean..." I watch as he looks through his notes.

"Usually about two, three hours. The longest I've had was six."

"Six." Another panicky whisper. "Is it safe for him to be sedated that long?"

"Sedation isn't recommended for patients with his condition." Dr. Rourke squints at me. "Didn't you know that?"

"I guess I did..." My forehead scrunches, and I try to remember. "I've read so many articles. I'm sorry. So you'll do awake surgery? How will you keep him still?"

"He'll take medicine to make him sleepy, and I'll use

numbing medication on his scalp. The brain has no pain receptors, so he'll be awake while I work." Now I know fear is in my eyes. "I know it sounds strange, but I feel confident about this. I wouldn't say that if I didn't believe it. I've studied his records, and I think he's a great candidate."

My shoulders slump, and I nod. "It's just so scary."

Reaching out, he covers my hand with his. "Life-changing events always are."

"It's the right thing to do, right? It's a decision between a lifetime of seizures, never being able to drive, possibly never holding a good job, public humiliation..." I'm pacing Stephen's enormous bedroom, arms crossed, second-guessing everything that's brought us to this point.

"Emmy. Look at me." He catches my arms, stopping me. It doesn't help my scattered brain that he's dressed in only maroon sleep pants. I tear my eyes off his lined torso and look in his blue eyes. "You're doing the right thing. Hell, I'm doing it with you. I brought Henry onboard, I'm funding the operation—"

"And I'm so grateful—"

"You've got to stop thanking me. I have the money. I want to do it."

I exhale a laugh, feeling embarrassed.

He shakes his head, giving me a sympathetic look. "We've covered all this. Now come to bed."

As promised, Stephen planted a baby monitor in Eli's room and threatened to throw me over his shoulder and carry me up the stairs if I didn't come of my own accord.

It didn't take much persuasion.

Still... "I'll never sleep tonight." I climb into the huge bed wishing I could shut off my brain. "Burt said Julius Caesar had epilepsy, and he conquered half the known world."

"Burt is such a fucking nitwit. He's the biggest douche... A total tool—"

"I get it. But what if he ends up being right? What if we do this and something worse than seizures happens?" Dropping my head in my hands, I groan. "Oh, my Goood!"

Strong arms are around me at once. Stephen pulls me against his chest, and I rest my head against his warm skin, listening to his strong heartbeat. It soothes me.

"Eli is an amazing kid." His voice is warm. "You're giving him a gift."

"Stephen Hawking was an amazing man. And he had major medical disabilities."

Gripping my shoulders, Stephen holds me at arm's length, looking sternly into my eyes. "And if Stephen Hawking had learned of a potential cure for amyotrophic lateral sclerosis, he would have tried it."

Swallowing the knot in my throat, I practice deep breathing. "You're right."

Stephen sits across from me on the bed, keeping his eyes on me like he's ready to grab me again if I fall apart. I kind of love him for it. Placing my head on the pillow, I pull the blankets closer around my neck.

My voice is soft when I confess, "I'm so afraid."

Seconds tick past before he answers. "I'm afraid, too."

Crawling closer, I fall asleep in his strong arms. My face is pressed to his chest, and I'm pretty sure I don't move for a long time.

"Ocean travelers come in many guises, and few are stranger than this..." Sir David Attenborough's voice rouses me from a deep sleep.

Turning, I find myself sandwiched between my fake husband and my very real seven-year-old in the middle of Stephen's California King.

"Eli!" I whisper, shifting around and doing my best not to wake Stephen. "What are you doing in here?"

Blinking hard, I try to figure out what time it is. No light is shining through the curtains, so I'm guessing it's the middle of the night.

"Mom." Eli drops the remote, and I glance to see a funny, floating crab making its way across the screen. "I miss our old place."

"You do?"

"Yeah... We're really spread out here."

Propping my head on my hand, I trace my fingers down his little face. "No question about that. But I thought you liked it here."

"I do, but if Kona ever had trouble sleeping at our old place, I could just put him in bed with you." Eli's voice is very adult, not at all like it was really him who joined Kona in bed with me.

"Is Kona having trouble sleeping?"

He nods, solemnly. "He tried really hard to sleep. He slept on his side and his stomach. He even slept on his back a few minutes, but he worried a spider might drop in his mouth." My son's blue eyes are so round and serious. I don't dare crack a smile.

Running my fingers along his hairline, over his ear, I think about yesterday. "Is something on Kona's mind?"

"I don't know." Eli tilts his head to the side as if he's thinking hard. "He said he was worried I might be different after my surgery. Like I might act like a different person."

"Like your personality might change?"

"I guess." My son looks up at me, studying my face.

I know he'll see it if I'm not completely honest with him. "I've never heard of that happening, and I've read everything I can find about this surgery. Dr. Roarke seems like a really smart man, and he's only going to touch the part of your brain that's messed up."

"He'll leave the other parts like they are?"

"That's what he said. He'll just fix the broken bits and leave all the good parts right where they are." My stomach tugs, and I fight against tears. I never want him to feel afraid.

"I think Kona still wishes he could sleep with you tonight."

Chewing my lip, I look over my shoulder. Stephen is lying on his back now, and he makes a loud noise. I gently push his shoulder until he turns his back to us. In this giant bed, we have plenty of room.

"I think it'll be okay for tonight. If you don't think Stephen will bother him."

"Kona said he's been making funny noises since before you woke up. I guess Dads are louder when they sleep than Moms."

Pressing my lips together, I think about my own dad and Ethan... "Tell Kona he might be onto something."

Eli snuggles into my side, his tattered orca cuddled between us. I punch up my pillow and look at the screen where a funny red crab continues his quest to survive the open ocean.

22

Stephen

"Stephen, how could you?" Aunt Rebecca's voice is so loud on the phone, I have to hold it away from my ear. "You're my last unmarried relative. How could you marry Emily Barton and not at least let me throw you a party. You're breaking my heart."

Propping my phone on my shoulder, I scrub my forehead with my fingertips. I've been off my game today. I woke with some massive morning wood going on, ready to bang Emmy into next week. I was getting things going, when Eli popped up beside her wanting to know what was happening.

Talk about a boner-killer! I'm surprised I didn't have a heart attack. Emmy must've been exhausted, because she only then woke to realize what was up—party at her backside, motherhood at her front.

Have I mentioned how smart she is?

She immediately asked Eli what was happening. He announced I was hogging the bed, to which she agreed, giving me the squint eye.

How was I to know we had a stowaway? The benefit of having a wife is you can fuck her whenever you want... Until the kids show up.

"I assure you, Bex, I was not trying to break your heart." I'm exhausted and not in the mood for theatrics.

"And yet you have." She sounds like an escapee from the cast of *Auntie Mame.* "There's only one way you can make it up to me."

I really don't have to ask, but I do. "What's that?"

"I'm throwing a gala for the both of you. It's going to be the biggest party our circle has seen in a long time. I'll call the boathouse and make them work us into their schedule, and we'll invite everybody, just everybody! You and Emily will be the talk of the town!"

My lips part, and I'm ready to argue, but she's off to the races. "Oh, darling, you have to bring her to dinner tonight so we can talk about it. You missed last Thursday night..."

"She has a son, Bex. I don't know if—"

"Oh yes, that's right! Well, bring him along. I'd like to meet the young man. I'm sure he's delightful. His father is one of the Dickersons, if I remember correctly..."

I don't say that doesn't make him delightful. Thankfully Eli takes after Emmy's side of the family as far as I can tell. "He's on a special diet. It's really a lot of work."

"What special diet? Fax it over. Hans will make whatever he needs. We have plenty of time. I won't hear another excuse from you. I expect to see you and your new wife... your new *family* tonight for supper."

The phone line goes dead, and I stand for a moment wondering how I'm so fully capable of handling any human being who crosses my path, but when it comes to Bex, she somehow walks all over me. Did she actually ask me to send a fax?

"Where would I even find a fax machine these days?" I'm scrubbing my fingers against my forehead again. It's turning into a habit.

Is that what having a family does? Reduces you to stress-management habits that leave you old and haggard before breakfast?

"I'm headed to work." Emmy breezes into the room in a short skirt and pink silk top. She looks scrumptious, and I regret having to jerk off in the shower this morning. "Need me to take anything for you? Any suits—"

Catching her around the waist, I pull her to me and plant a firm kiss on her lips. She smells like flowers and sunshine, and she feels so good, I kiss her longer, harder, until she starts pushing against my arms.

"Stephen!" She's breathing fast, cheeks flushed when I release her.

"What's wrong, beautiful?" I'm still holding her waist, smiling down at her like the horny husband I am.

"I've got to get to work, and Eli's right over there." She tilts her head toward the kitchen.

My arms drop. "He was right there this morning, too. We need to talk to him about sleeping in his own bed."

Her face scrunches adorably. I think she's pissed at me. "I am not telling him anything like that. He's dealing with a lot of change right now, and with that surgery coming up, it's natural for him to feel insecure and a little frightened, and if you can't understand that—"

My arms are back around her so fast, and I'm pulling her against my chest. "I understand. I'm just really disappointed I didn't get to fuck you this morning."

Her eyes go round, and she slaps a hand over my mouth, looking toward the kitchen again. I look up to see Eli's got head-phones on and is watching something on my iPad Pro. I'd bet money it's *The Blue Planet*. These two have gotten me started on it, and it's addictive as hell.

"He's wearing headphones." My nose is at her ear, and I pull her earlobe between my teeth.

She pushes against my arms. "Stephen..." It's a little less forceful, and I press my advantage.

"We could fit in a quickie. Step in the bathroom. We can revisit our first time. Only I'll be more of a gentleman after."

"I have to get to work." She starts to laugh, and I lift her off the ground, kissing her neck.

She only laughs more. "Put me down, you filthy animal." Releasing her, I hold her waist as she drags me to the door. "I'll be home usual time. Sure you don't need me to take anything? I can get your suits done for free. Perks!"

"No." I lean down to kiss her lips lightly. "Oh, my aunt Rebecca wants us to come over for dinner tonight. She found out about our marriage and wants to throw us a party or something. I swear, you can't keep a secret anymore..."

Emmy jumps back like I'm an electric fence and she just peed on it. "What!" Her eyes are wide, and I'm snapped out of my lust-induced haze. "We can't do that. You have to tell her no."

"No to dinner? I always have dinner with her on Thursdays. She's a lonely old woman—"

"Not the dinner. Of course we can have dinner with her, but we can't have a big party. Stephen! Everybody will be there. We can't do have that. Think about later..."

Her voice trails off, and I straighten. "I guess it would complicate things down the road."

How odd I've already started to forget this is only temporary.

"You think?" Emmy's eyes are wide, and she gives my chest a little shove. "Tell her to call it off."

"Tell you what. We'll all go to dinner tonight, and between

the two of us, I'm sure we can figure out a way to get her to scale it down."

"Not scale it down!" Emmy's eyes flash. "Call. It. Off."

With a sigh, I cave. "I'll tell her to call it off. But you'll see tonight. Once Bex has an idea in her head, it's impossible to get it out."

I'm pretty sure I hear my bride growling, and I can't help a grin. She's so adorable. "See you tonight, beautiful."

BEX ROLLS out the red carpet for us at her Upper East Side brownstone. I'm used to the place, but even Emmy's eyes are dazzled as we walk into the well-appointed living room festooned with candles and twinkle lights.

I'm wearing the light gray suit I've had on all day, and Eli looks sharp in khaki pants and a blue blazer. Emmy is a vision in a filmy yellow dress that flutters around her curves. Her blonde hair is long and beautiful, and my mind has gone to sneaking her away for a quickie.

I have to kill that thought because my aunt enters the room. She's wearing a cream pantsuit with a long scarlet scarf, and when she sees us, she throws out her arms.

"Emily!" She crosses the space with a flourish. "I'm so delighted to see you again! You probably don't even remember the first time we met. It was at your parent's Christmas party... I think you were only four years old, and such a darling girl."

"Is this a real rooster?" Eli is on his knees in front of a bowl filled with pinecones, Spanish moss, and a taxidermized rooster right in the middle.

Aunt Rebecca is delighted. "This must be Elijah!" She gasps. "What a gorgeous child. Stephen! Why didn't you tell me Emily had such a gorgeous child? I think he looks just like you did at that age, my dear."

Eli's brow scrunches, and I'm not sure if he's more confused by the rooster or by my aunt's effusiveness.

"Thank you so much, Miss Dixon."

"Call me Bex, dear. That's what Stephen calls me." She takes Emmy's arm and leads her toward the dining room. "Elijah! You must call me Bex as well. You hear?"

"Yes, ma'am!" The little boy has moved on from the rooster to a standing grizzly bear in the corner of the library. "Mom! She has a bear!"

"Oh, that old thing." Bex groans, shaking her head. "Our father, God rest his soul, had no consideration for conservation. He killed that poor animal and then insisted on putting it in our house. I swear, our mother almost had a conniption fit over it. He won the argument, of course. He always did."

This is family business I've never even heard. "Grandpa Babe killed that bear? I always thought you bought it from a museum or an estate sale."

"Lord, if only." Bex places her palm against her chest. "I pray for forgiveness every night."

A bell rings, and I know that means it's time to take our places at my aunt's enormous mahogany dining table in the gold room with the ornate trim.

Emmy appears overwhelmed.

I walk over and take her arm. "Dinner."

Once we're all seated around one end of the long table, the servers carry out plates of food.

"Stephen told me your son is on a restrictive diet. I made sure Hans prepared something he would love."

"Rosemary garlic chicken kabobs, cauliflower nachos, and coconut chips." The paunchy chef stands back as two servers place the food in front of us.

"Wow." Eli looks down at his plate.

"This is so kind, thank you so much for accommodating us, Miss Dixon. Er... Bex."

"Nonsense! You're family now." My aunt lifts a glass of white wine and takes a long sip. "Stephen called me today and said you didn't want a party, but I couldn't believe it. What girl doesn't want a wedding party?"

She puts a hand out in Emmy's direction, giving her a knowing smile. "I know Stephen probably made you do that hush-hush wedding. He's such a bore, but don't worry. I was able to reserve the boathouse in two weeks, which means we'll have to step up the timeline. It's going to be amazing, darling. Why the Hastings are one of New York's oldest families, and your father was absolutely *adored*..."

Emmy's eyes move to mine in a desperate plea for help. I only shake my head in a way that says I've done all I can do.

"Who do you think made the first kebab?" I say, holding up my chicken. "I bet it was a pirate."

"Yeah! Pirate food!" Eli's eyes light up, and he does a little *Arr*. I have to hand it to my aunt. She knows what little boys like. She always spoiled me as a kid.

"You're really too kind, Miss Dixon. The truth is... my son is having major surgery next week." Emmy glances at Eli, who is having a ball eating his chicken kabobs. "So you know..."

Their eyes connect for a heartbeat.

"Oh, my darling." Bex's eyes grow round and tearful. She catches Emmy's hand, giving it a squeeze. "I can't even imagine how terrified you must feel."

Emmy nods, looking down. "Then you understand why I don't think a party would be the best thing—"

"Oh, but it *is* the best thing." My aunt's tone is serious, her gaze level. "It is exactly what you'll need to take your mind off the stress. It will nourish your soul to take a break and spend time with family and friends who love you and are wishing you well."

Emmy's lips part, and I know that feeling. I've been in her shoes, trying to talk my aunt out of something she's set her mind to. "I'm not sure we'll be in a position to leave him alone so soon after surgery."

Rebecca nods solemnly. "And when is the surgery?"

"Ahh... Next Tuesday."

"That's perfect. The party is set for the following Friday, almost two weeks later!" She smiles reassuringly. "He'll be just fine by then. Still, if it will make you feel better, I will have my personal physician recommend a nurse to sit with Eli while you attend. It will be my gift to you."

"Your gift..." Emmy's voice trails off.

"And the boathouse is so close, you'll be no more than a minute from Stephen's townhome at any given time."

"We should have these coconut chips at our house!" Eli's voice is a loud interruption. He holds up a chip grinning, oblivious to his mother's discomfort. "Think Ted can make us some?"

"I'm sure he'll try." I pop a chip in my mouth. "Let's ask him tomorrow."

My aunt is satisfied the topic is resolved. We finish dinner and retire to the sitting room for cognac, whiskey, or tea for Emmy.

Bex asks about her work at Miss Con-Cleaneality—which she thinks is simply *fabulous*. She was so happy with the repairs to her dance dress, and have we ever considered taking ballroom dancing? It's fantastic exercise. Bex asks about Eli's progress in school, and no surprise, she also thinks homeschooling is the absolute *best* way to educate him.

"You are very wise, Emmy." She nods at my bride. "There's so much padding in the grades. I'm sure he's leaps and bounds ahead of where he'd be otherwise."

Eli is asleep on my shoulder when we finally say goodnight and head out the door for home.

"It's such a beautiful evening, I'd almost suggest walking." If I didn't have this funny little guy knocked out on my shoulder. Little cock-blocker. I'm starting to understand why Emmy called him her best friend. Eli's great.

Emmy walks beside me in silence. I'm sure she's exhausted. "We don't have to walk. My car is right up at the corner."

Finally, my lady speaks. "Your aunt is something else... I don't know if I love her or if I want to kill her."

"It's a common problem."

"And you were no help at all. I did everything in my power to talk her out of this ridiculous party, and you're sharing pirate kebabs and coconut chips with Eli."

"They were delicious. I'll have to get that menu for Ted."

She does a little growl, and I wait as she climbs into the car before passing her sleeping kiddo across. "You were supposed to help me change her mind."

"Emmy, look at me." She turns her head, looking over Eli's sleeping noggin. "You're one of the most stubborn people I've ever met, but you are nothing compared to my aunt."

Her eyes narrow, and she turns to the window. "You're somehow able to convince me to do things against my better judgment. You don't want to tell her no or you would have."

Sliding my hand across the seat, I cover hers with mine. "Perhaps you're right. After my mother died, Bex was the only female presence in my life." My chest aches at the memory. "She and our housekeeper Ximena."

"Ximena?" Her blue eyes meet mine, and I guess she sees the pain there.

It's not until Eli is tucked soundly in his bed, and we're sitting facing each other in mine that I tell her the story. When I finish, her eyes are downcast, sad.

"I guess I understand your dad feeling angry about the watch..." Her voice is thoughtful. "He probably felt betrayed."

"He was a pompous ass. He should have given her the money she needed."

"You're right. But... Did he even know she was sick?"

"He knew." Years-old fury burns in my throat at the memory of what happened. "After he discovered what Ramon did, he wanted to send a message. I'm actually surprised you don't know. Your father mediated the case in his office at your house."

She blinks up and shakes her head. "He never shared his work with us kids. I think he didn't want to talk about it."

"He was probably bound by nondisclosure agreements." Releasing a sigh, I rotate so my back is against the headboard. "I took care of her until I left for the Navy. I'd just told her goodbye the night of that party."

"Ethan's party?"

I reach out and slide my finger down her cheek. "Yeah. I'm sorry I took my anger out on you."

"Oh, Stephen. I had no idea." Concern lines her face. "Is this why you want to help us now? Is what happened to Ximena why it's so important to you?"

Is it? I hadn't thought of it that way. "I told you, I like Eli. I want him to have a normal life, and I have the means to make it happen."

She scoots across the mattress, climbing onto my lap in a straddle, and places her hands on the sides of my neck. "You couldn't help Ximena, so you're helping him."

Our eyes lock, and so much emotion flows between us. "I'm helping you both."

Leaning forward, she wraps her arms around my torso, pressing her cheek to the top of my chest. I wrap my arms around her just as fast. It feels so good to hold her this way. She's so soft, yet firm, and she smells like heaven. It reminds me of what I've been thinking about all day.

Rolling her to the side, I lean my head down and kiss her soft lips. Her hands thread into the sides of my hair, and she kisses me back with equal fervor. It fuels my passion. I touch her waist, gathering the thin tank she's wearing in my fists and quickly lifting it over her head.

Her small breasts bounce out, and I cup them in my hands, covering her tight nipples with little sucks, bites, and soothing kisses.

She moans and squirms, and I slip my hand down, sliding it inside her panties, my fingers threading into her, circling her clit.

Her back arches and she holds my face, eyes closed as she rocks against my hand. "Yes..." she whispers. "Right there... right there."

She's fucking my hand, and it's the sexiest thing I've ever seen. I kiss her cheek, moving my lips into her hair, biting her ear. "Come for me."

Her head turns, and her lips move to mine. "I want to come on your dick."

Fuck me, that's a shot straight to my throbbing erection. "Open your legs."

She does as I say, and I rip the string of her thong aside, lining up my tip with her core and sinking it to the hilt.

We both groan at the sensation, moving our bodies in time. Her legs wrap around me, and I clutch her ass, working her body as I chase my climax.

"Stephen..." She bucks and rides, gasping as her muscles spasm around my cock.

I don't take long in following her. "Oh, fuck, Emmy, you feel so good." I pulse and jerk, coming long and hard, holding her close, never wanting to let her go.

We come down from our amazing high, drifting to sleep in each other's arms.

On the edge of unconsciousness, my chest swells with a sense of pride. I did this. I made this beautiful woman mine.

The problem with arrogance is you never see your fall coming until your face is planted in the dirt.

23

Emmy

"Dry cleaning doesn't stop for life." The sign out in front of Miss Con-Cleaneality this week is more prophetic than Lulabell knows. I take a deep breath and head inside, where a line of customers has already formed.

It's a Monday, and regardless of Eli's surgery, we're slammed as usual. I'm actually glad, as it takes my mind off the incessant worry. On the outside, I'm all smiles and confidence. On the inside, it feels like little ants are eating me alive.

The list of complications of brain surgery is on a scroll in the back of my mind—fluid on the brain... loss of memory... meningitis... stroke... Every time a complication pops into my mind, I say a prayer against it.

I read a few days ago how meditation eases anxiety, so I downloaded an app. Sitting in silence, doing my best not to think about it... I almost had a panic attack.

"I'm praying for Eli." Lou makes me jump when she touches my shoulder.

She caught me in front of my locker, fighting my thoughts. I immediately plaster a smile on my face. "Thank you."

"Oh, honey. You don't have to be strong in front of me." She pulls me into a hug, but I fight the tears. "I'll stop by the church in the morning and light a candle. Tell me as soon as you know something."

"I will." She releases me, and we hear the bell ring out front.

Stepping to the side, she calls, "We're closed."

"Just picking up the wife." Stephen's deep voice calms me. He stops at the entryway near us.

She gives him a wink. "Hey, handsome. Why don't you drop by more often?"

"I would if my stubborn wife would stop walking home." He leans against the doorframe looking absolutely perfect in slacks and a light blue oxford.

I don't remind him I'm trying not to get used to all the pampering. Instead, I manage a tease. "No blazer today?"

"It's in the car." He studies me the same way he's been doing since we met with the doctor, watching for a break.

"Well, I'm headed out." Lulabell walks to the door. "You two lock up before you go, okay?"

"Sure thing," I call after her. "Thanks, Lou!"

Despite my anxiety, Stephen's gaze, his presence, manages to light up every nerve ending in my body. Is it possible my anxiety makes me even more sensitive to him? All I know is he swooped in and proved me wrong. He is my hero.

I've really got to stop thinking of him this way.

"How'd it go today?" he asks.

"Busy as always." I pick up my purse, sliding the strap over my shoulder. "It's good to work. Keeps my mind occupied."

His lips tighten. I know he hates that I'm worried. It's just... Eli is all I have. Eli trusts me to do what's right for him, and if anything goes wrong...

I couldn't survive it.

Stephen, by contrast, is confident, reassuring. "This time tomorrow it'll be over, and Eli will be on his way to recovery and a new life."

"A new life..." I think what a relief, then I realize what that means. "We should start looking at apartments in Midtown. It might take time to find something I can afford."

"You want an apartment in Midtown?" He waits as I take off my vest and hang it in the locker, slamming the door.

"I thought it might be nice to be close after we moved out. In case we want to stop by for a visit." He's surprised, and I feel so childish and stupid. "I'm sorry. I wasn't even thinking... That's a terrible idea. I'm sure you'll want to date, and the last thing you need is a first wife and her son hanging around. Even a fake first wife."

I'm trying to lighten the mood, but God, just saying the words is like digging my guts out with a hand rake. Still, I've got to start facing reality. I've got to stop my heart's high-speed landslide into love with him.

He puts a warm hand on my shoulder, and I peek up at him. "We have plenty of time to decide what to do."

Reaching up, I put my hand on top of his. "I think I need to start thinking about it now. These last several days... I don't know. I guess I've had to work to remember this isn't real."

"About that..." The smile playing around his lips tightens my stomach.

What is he going to say? Maybe he wishes things were different, too?

"What's going on back here?"

We both jump, turning to face Burt, who's on the other side of the counter watching us with a curious smile.

A smile. Burt never smiles at me.

"How long have you..." I look from him to the glass door. "I didn't hear the bell ring."

Burt's eyes are fixed on mine, that smile firmly in place. "It rang. I guess you two are so much in love you never heard it." Sarcasm is in his tone, and I panic. *Did he hear our conversation? If so, how much?*

"What do you want?" Stephen's voice is cold.

"I want to talk about Eli." Burt finally tears his gaze off me. "I don't like having my visitation days changed at the last minute. He was supposed to be with me this weekend."

"You'll be lucky if you ever get him again." Stephen steps forward, but I catch his arm. "I'm looking into changing your visits to supervised only, if not revoking them altogether."

Burt's face turns red. "What the fuck? Is this some kind of tit for tat, Emmy?"

Angry eyes land on me, but I don't know what to say. Stephen and I have not discussed this.

Stephen is angry and determined. "I was there for what happened after his last visit with you. Every time he has a seizure, he's at risk of permanent brain damage. You don't even give him his medication."

My ex looks from me to Stephen then back to me, stepping closer. "You think you've got leverage now that you have Hastings money?" His voice drops to sinister levels. "Don't fuck with me."

Stephen catches my wrist and steps between us, facing Burt. "Emmy might have a soft spot when it comes to letting you see him, but I happen to think you're bad for Eli. I bet I can get a judge to agree with me after that head injury."

"Emmy doesn't give a shit about my rights. It's all about your money." He flickers his eyes at me. "Isn't it?"

My heart is beating so fast, I can't speak. Stephen doesn't

have the same problem. "I'm taking care of them, now. You'd better not fuck with me."

"Oh, really?" Burt grins, taking a step back. "Because you're her husband? Then why is she still working at this dump?" Flat brown eyes land on me. "Why are you still working here, Emmy?"

My eyes slide left to right, searching for any reasonable excuse. "I-I couldn't leave Lulabell short-handed. She's my friend, and I'm helping her out until she can find a replacement."

Burt looks around the room. He holds out his hands. "Then why don't I see a help wanted sign anywhere? It looks to me like your friend doesn't think you're leaving."

"Shows your level of brain power, dickhead." Stephen puts his hand on my arm I assume to keep me quiet. "What you do see is a closed sign, which means time to go."

"Stay away from my son, Hastings." Burt wheels around on him, eyes blazing. "I'm not going anywhere."

Stephen steps closer, right in Burt's face. "Neither am I."

They stand that way, practically nose to nose for several heartbeats.

My voice is small when I finally speak. "We'd better go. The neighbors call the cops if things look suspicious. They're protective that way."

As much as I want Stephen to beat the crap out of Burt, I'm doing my best to diffuse the situation. We have to get back to Eli, and I need Stephen with me, not at a police station.

Burt cracks a smile, patting Stephen's chest. "No worries, Emmy. I won't mess up your pretty new husband's face."

Grabbing Stephen's hand, I pull him toward the door.

"Let's go now." I'm shaking, but I need to get them out of here. "Burt. I need to lock the door."

My ex storms toward us, and I put my back against Stephen's chest, praying with all my might he'll just go away without another word. "I'm just curious. What's in it for you, Hastings?"

Stephen puts both hands on my shoulders. "Eli's a great kid. Emmy's done her best with him, and you're going to back the fuck up and stop jeopardizing his health. Or I'm going to make you."

"We'll see about that." He finally leaves, and I exhale deeply.

Stephen is still growly, casting an angry glance in the direction Burt took. "If I ever get the chance to kick his ass..."

I put my hand on my chest, and I'm pretty sure I've reached the top of my stress level. Tears are in my eyes, but I actually start to laugh. Stephen looks down at me, a confused smile teasing at his lips. "You okay?"

Shaking my head, I follow him out to the car. "If you ever get the chance to kick Burt's ass, I hope I'm there to see it."

"CHECK IT OUT! They have Netflix here!" Eli grins from where he sits holding Kona on the oversized hospital bed.

It's a luxurious suite, complete with a leather recliner and a large, flatscreen television. We've filled out the paperwork, Eli's checked in, and we're waiting for Dr. Rourke to come by and greet us. He wanted Eli to spend the night so they could monitor his brain and watch for any unusual activity.

I packed a bag to sleep here. I was surprised when I saw Stephen did the same. "You don't have to spend the night in this little room." I glance around at the small futon beside the recliner.

My plan is to scoot into the bed beside Eli if it's possible with all the monitors attached to his small head and body.

Stephen shrugs. "We'll make it work." Turning to my son, he

flips through the Netflix options. "What's it going to be? *Pirates of the Caribbean* or *The Blue Planet*?"

"*Pirates of the Caribbean!*" Eli cries as if we're back at Stephen's place and nothing is happening.

On the one hand, I'm glad. On the other, I hope he's not repressing any fears.

"Good call." Several flickers of the screen later, Captain Jack Sparrow appears, riding a sinking ship right up to a waiting dock.

Dr. Rourke taps on the door, and I'm the first on my feet, ready to hear what he has to say, hoping for any kind of relief.

"You all look cozy!" He grins, stepping forward to put his hand on Eli's shoulder. "How's my patient feeling today?"

"Great! You have *Pirates of the Caribbean* on Netflix!"

Henry laughs, his chin lifting. "All is right with the world." He looks around the room. "All set for the night. I'm sorry to make you sleep up here. I just want to be sure there's no unusual activity before we start."

"Whatever you need to do." Stephen clasps Henry's hand in a shake. "We're following orders."

"This doctor orders you all to get some sleep." He reaches out to clasp Eli's foot. "I'll see you in the morning, yes?"

He's so positive, I wonder what's wrong with me. Turning to my son, he leans down. "I want you to be well rested so you can help me while I work."

Eli nods, his eyes round.

I know what Dr. Rourke means. By doing awake surgery, he'll talk to Eli and use Eli's responses to map his brain. It's freaky as shit if you think about it too much, but it's the most precise option, especially with this new technique.

Talking to Eli while he operates will guide Henry to the damaged bits and keep him from destroying the parts that could change him forever.

"Betty is your nurse. She'll check in on you throughout the night. Otherwise, I'll see you bright and early." He smiles, and gives a little nod before leaving.

My stomach has gone strangely quiet. It's as if my nerves decided they've tormented me enough. No turning back now.

24

Stephen

We've watched *Pirates of the Caribbean: The Curse of the Black Pearl* and *Pirates of the Caribbean: Dead Man's Chest*. Eli is cuddled with Kona, asleep with his head on his mother's shoulder.

At some point, Emmy showered and changed into thin pants and a long-sleeved shirt. I hung my blazer in the closet and got comfortable in the recliner in my jeans and red tee. Now I'm lying awake, mindlessly watching outtakes of Johnny Depp, Orlando Bloom, and Keira Knightley goofing off in the Bahamas.

"What I wouldn't give to be there right now." Emmy's voice is quiet from the bed, and I glance over to see her watching with me.

What I wouldn't do to take her there right now. I've seen her come close to breaking down more than once since this process began, but she hides it so well.

Sometimes getting exactly what you want can be as hard as waiting for it to happen.

"You're still awake?" I pick up the remote and reduce the volume, sitting up so I can see her better.

"I won't sleep tonight." She rotates carefully, facing me with her head on her hand. "You?"

"Not happening."

"Feels like the night before a battle."

My grin is tight as I meet her tired eyes. "Or the night before brain surgery."

Eli isn't disturbed by our voices—or by what's coming in the morning. I've told him it will be okay. Emmy's told him it will be okay. Why would he question us?

God, that's a lot of pressure.

"What should we do?" I grin, hoping to distract her mind. "I guess Truth or Dare's out."

She glances around. "I don't see a chess set."

"Damn." Leaning forward, I prop my forearms on my knees. "Any good books to read?"

We both look at the bare shelves, and she shrugs. "I guess we have to talk. Or not. We could watch another Pirates movie?"

"God, no. Let's talk. Pick a topic. World events? Will there ever be peace in the Middle East?"

A small smile, and she shakes her head. "I don't know."

We're both quiet again.

Orlando Bloom hops on a log then falls into crystal blue waters.

A few more seconds pass, then Emmy breaks the silence. "I've been thinking about something since that day at the park."

I shift, slightly uneasy. "You want to know about Alyssa?"

"Not really." She scoots a little higher in the bed. "Why did you tell her you didn't believe in marriage?"

Easy enough. "Because I didn't."

"You didn't." Her chin lowers, and her eyes level on mine. "Why not?"

"I don't know. Lousy childhood? Poor father figure? Pick one." My mind travels back to something she told me. "That night at the party, you asked if I'd be like the rest of them, a wife in Connecticut and a mistress in the city."

The corner of her mouth tilts down. "You remember that night?"

"Of course, I do." I didn't know the significance of it, but I remember it.

I actually thought about it from time to time, but in those days, I dismissed my feelings as weakness.

"So, if you don't believe in marriage, what about children?"

My eyes flicker to Eli asleep in the bed. "I never thought about having children."

"What will you leave behind when you're gone?" Her tone changes to teasing. "Who will you manipulate with all your money when you're old?"

"Yes, that sounds like me, sorting my belongings, busying my lawyer." I think about those assholes constantly changing their wills.

Her grin fades, and her voice turns serious. "So no Hastings legacy?"

"My work is my legacy. I've spent time developing programs that will help people. One could argue they're far more beneficial than another human taking up space on the planet. Who knows how a human is going to turn out? Look at me."

A laugh pushes through her lips, and she rolls her eyes. "Tell me about it."

"I'd say you got lucky with that little guy." Our eyes meet, and hers are warm, appreciative.

Her hair is tied in a low ponytail, but a tendril falls on her cheek. I want to slide it back with my finger, tuck it behind her ear. I want to kiss her. I want to pull her under me and hold her.

I'm pleased she seems more relaxed now. I hope I've helped her get there.

Comfortable silence fills the room. The screensaver is on the television. It rotates scenes of the ocean, deserts, space. It's soothing, and I think she might fall asleep after all until she speaks.

"I can't say I blame you."

My brow furrows, and I think back over our conversation. "About what?"

"Marriage, love. After Burt, I was sure I stopped believing in love."

"You believe in love. I've seen you with your son."

"That's a different love. I'm his mother." Her head tilts back, resting against the mattress. "I'm talking about a one true love, a great romance that would last the rest of my life."

I study her profile, the line of her nose, the curve of her lip. I wonder how any man could take her for granted, hurt her—of course, I've met The Dick. Still, I wonder if her dreams of romance are realistic. I wonder if what she wants is possible.

"That level of commitment takes maturity, contentment with who you are." I think about what I'm saying. "You have to give up fighting old battles with yourself."

Her face turns toward me. "It sounds like you've thought about it a lot."

"When I was younger, I thought about my father and how he treated my mother. He had affairs, but she never acknowledged it. I wonder if she even knew. Perhaps that's why I gave up on it."

"Perhaps we were both hurt by bad examples."

She doesn't speak again. We're quiet for a long time, and after a while, I hear the sound of her breathing, low and easy. She's asleep. I lean my head back, closing my eyes, thinking about her long hair, her pretty lips, and second chances.

"DR. ROURKE IS ON HIS WAY!" I'm awakened by the voice of a middle-aged nurse gliding into the room carrying a clipboard and shadowed by a younger woman. "This is Maddy. She's a nursing student making the rounds with me today. It's almost time to go, Eli. Are you ready?"

"I'm ready!" The boy sits up in the bed, holding his stuffed animal. I notice *The Blue Planet* is on the TV screen and wonder how long he's been awake.

Pushing out of the chair, I step back to make room. Emmy has changed into jeans and a long-sleeved white sweater. Her hair is over her shoulders, and it looks like she's been awake a while as well.

Maddy helps with Eli's vitals, and he watches them, a worried expression on his face. "Kona's sad he can't go with me into surgery. He says he might get scared."

An ache tightens my throat, but Betty's on it.

"I don't think I've met, Kona. Hi, Kona, my name is Betty." She shakes a stuffed fin.

Eli looks down at the black and white toy. "He says hi."

"I have a very special job for you, Kona." Betty leans down. "I need you to take care of Eli's mom while he's gone. Can you do that for me?"

Eli's mouth twists with a frown, and he looks at the orca once more. A few seconds pass, and his small fingers move back and forth over the plush fabric. My chest squeezes, and I want to take away his fear.

Finally, he looks up again. "He says he can do that."

Emmy gives the nurse an appreciate smile, and she takes Kona from her son.

Betty turns to us. "The doctor is on his way. He'll check everything out, then we'll take Eli back."

The two women go to the monitors, and Emmy stands at Eli's bedside. Her tight smile has returned, the one that tells me she's quietly fighting her own fears.

"Henry said the surgery should take three, four hours tops." I hope this gives her some comfort. I look up at the clock and it's almost eight.

As I'm speaking, he enters the room. "How is everyone today?"

"Good." Emmy's voice is tense. "He slept all night."

"Very good." Henry walks over to the nurse, scanning her notes. Then he returns to the bed. "Sleep is very good for the brain. Good work, Eli."

The little boy looks pleased, and two men in scrubs enter. Emmy's face turns pale, and her hand goes to her throat. I take it as my cue to circle around and stand beside her. I know this is going to be a hard part.

"Looks like we're ready." Henry turns to me, and I nod. His eyes go to Emmy, but her eyes haven't left her son. "Tell your mom you'll see her in a few hours."

"See you in a few hours, Mom!" Eli smiles, and she forces a smile.

"I love you, baby."

Eli doesn't even protest. He holds up a little hand, and I give him a high five.

I'm standing beside Emmy, doing my best to provide her with strength, but when they roll Eli out the door, fear hits me like a gut punch. My hand tightens on hers, and I focus on our goal.

Quantum physicists should study the passage of time in a hospital waiting room. I'd be interested to know how it transforms from normal to whatever's slower than a snail's pace. I'm doing my best not to climb the walls. The television is set to a home improvement channel, and I watch a man and a woman ripping out appliances in an outdated kitchen. I wish I could crawl in and help them.

Emmy stands by the window, looking at the flowers and landscaped paths.

"It's really nice outside." She says it as if it shouldn't be.

The day your son goes in for experimental, high-risk, awake brain surgery should be overcast and gray.

I agree.

"Would you like to go for a walk?" I don't know what else to do.

"Not really."

The clock hands move so slowly, I'll be ninety before the day ends.

"Lulabell texted to say she lit a candle for Eli and filled out a prayer card." She's looking at her dark phone screen. "Ethan said they're praying. He's sorry he couldn't be here with me."

"I hope you told him I'm here."

Round blue eyes meet mine, and she nods. "I told him."

Betty comes out every hour to give us an update on Eli's progress. She's been out two times now.

The first time, she said he responded well to the medication and was in twilight sleep. Henry had removed a piece of Eli's skull, and all his vitals were good.

Emmy's face blanched, and I took her hand, holding it firmly in mine.

The second time Betty came out, she was smiling. "He's groggy, but he's awake enough to speak and help with the brain mapping." Emmy tries to return her smile. For me, it's impossible.

"Dr. Rourke is taking it very slowly," Betty says. "It's a good thing."

We thank her. I silently pray her next report will be they're closing him up, and he's headed to recovery.

More home improvement shows, more standing in front of the window watching. I try to come up with any topic for conversation, but Emmy's too distracted.

Finally, after another hour-long eternity, I see the clock has reached noon.

Shifting in my seat, my eyes strain for Betty. Emmy stands and walks to the window, looking out at the yellow flowers, the bees bobbing from petal to petal.

It's fucking torture.

Five minutes pass, and I scratch a nail along my cuticle.

Another nurse probably stopped Betty on her way to update us. Or perhaps Maddy had a question.

Another five minutes passes, and Emmy leaves the window, joining me where I stand in front of the television. Tension ripples off her in waves.

"She's usually out at the top of the hour." Her voice is strained. The fine lines around her eyes deepen, telling me she's afraid.

Reaching up, I rub my forehead, racking my brain for any reason the nurse could have been delayed. "Hospitals are busy places. She probably got tied up talking to someone."

"She should be here by now." It's more of a panicked whisper than an argument.

Emmy's hand is on my arm when the door opens. We both turn to see Henry striding quickly into the room. He isn't smiling.

My stomach is a ball of knots as he motions to a small anteroom off the main waiting area. We follow him inside. Emmy is visibly shaking. We don't sit.

I clear my throat so I can speak. "What's going on?"

"The surgery went very well. He was a great helper. He did

everything I needed, and I could see exactly where to make the extraction..."

"Why aren't you smiling?" Emmy's voice breaks.

Henry swallows visibly, and his chin drops. "I was putting him back together, stapling the cranial structures when something changed. I-I don't know what... We did all we could do, but he's slipped into a coma."

My arms reach out just in time to catch Emmy as she falls.

25

Emmy

Two days have passed.

Wires and tubes run from Eli's head and mouth to a congregation of machines surrounding his bed. They beep and hiss as they track his heartbeat, fill his lungs with air, tell us he's still with us. He's still alive.

Betty comes into the room every hour to check his stats. Dr. Rourke comes by in the evenings. He's worried because he'll leave for Europe on Sunday, and he doesn't want to leave my son this way.

He says things to me, but all I do is watch Eli, listen to the machines, try to wake him up.

"Today on *The Blue Planet* they went to Antarctica. Everything was frozen... Kona couldn't take his eyes off the screen. He wants you to watch it with him, but you have to wake up... Wake up, Eli!"

No response.

Another hiss as the ventilator fills his lungs.

Another beep from the brain monitor.

Eli's hand is in mine, and I close my eyes as I drop my face. My back aches. Every muscle in my body aches. I'm in a constant state of strain, leaning forward, watching for any change.

I can't sleep. My eyes burn, and I gaze at his little eyelids looking for a twitch, a flicker of his lashes.

Another hiss. The ventilator expands and contracts like an accordion.

More beeping. The monitors tell us his heart and brain are active.

Stephen is here. He's been here since the nightmare began.

He sits with me. He brings me food and books from the gift shop. He paces the halls.

Last night I heard him talking to Dr. Rourke. "Tell me what you need. Drugs? I can buy them. Do you need to fly in a specialist? I'll book a private jet. Tell me what I can do." Stephen's voice cracks with desperation.

"I need you to be strong." Dr. Rourke's voice is even. "I need you to drink water and rest. Eli is in there. We have to wait and believe he's going to come out of this."

In his room in the intensive care unit, I hold his little hand and search for anything that might do it. I know the longer he's unconscious, the more his chance of brain damage grows.

My voice is strong, a little loud. "They added all the Pirates of the Caribbean movies on Netflix. We can spend the whole day watching them if you wake up. I'm waiting on you to wake up, baby. Please…"

Nonstop beeping.

Nonstop whooshing of the ventilator.

Nonstop time passing.

"We need to finish that episode of *The Blue Planet*. I want you to see Antarctica with me. You gotta wake up so we can watch it,

Eli." My voice has grown hoarse. My muscles shake. I watch for
his eyelids to flicker.

Beeping.

Whooshing.

The nurse comes in.

The nurse goes out.

Henry says we're doing all we can do.

Another day passes.

I stay at his bedside.

WARM HANDS CUP MY SHOULDERS, jumping me awake. "Did I fall
asleep?" I'm horrified at myself.

Lulabell is here, smiling sadly. "You need to take a break,
honey. Step in the bathroom and take a shower. Stephen
brought some clothes for you to change into."

"Shower?" I've lost track of how many days it's been since I
last did that.

She hands me a small kit. "I put your toiletries in here. I'll sit
by his bed and watch."

"If he moves—"

"I'll break the door down to get you." Stephen's strong voice
is behind her, reassuring me.

My chin lifts, and I see dark circles under his eyes. His
clothes are different, and I realize he must've gone back to his
place to get me clothes.

Silently, I step into the full bath and close the door, washing
my body, my hair, my face, as fast as I can. I don't bother with the
blow drier. I don't bother with makeup. I quickly apply deodor-
ant, brush my teeth, and pull on the soft knit pants, the long-
sleeved sweater.

I'm back at Eli's side in less than ten minutes, hair damp, face and body clean.

"Anything?" Even I can hear the desperation in my voice.

Lulabell's eyes are watery when she looks up at me. "I'm sorry."

My heart seizes, and I push past her.

He's the same.

"Oh, God. I thought you meant..." I cover my mouth with my hand and fight. I hold my breath and squeeze my eyes shut. If I start crying now, I'll never stop.

One lone tear escapes through the wall.

It's cut off by the loud voice of Burt ripping through the quiet. "He's my son, and I want to see him!"

Stephen steps up behind me, putting his hands on my upper arms. Burt pushes into the room and freezes, his jaw drops when he sees Eli.

Then he turns his face at me, eyes blazing. "This is your fault."

My knees give out, but Stephen's grip on my arms keeps me upright.

"Get out before I throw you out." Stephen is holding me up, but his body is tense, shaking.

Burt comes closer, his voice loud and taunting. "I said no to this surgery from the start. Now look what you've done."

"Shut your ignorant mouth." Stephen is barely restrained, and I hold his arm like my life depends on it.

"You try to make me the bad guy. Now he could die. Was it worth it?" Burt is yelling, waving his arms, and a nurse enters the room. "Was it? Tell me, Emmy. Is this what you wanted?"

My insides are crumbling. I'm not sure I can take another word from him.

"Sir, I'm sorry, but you have to go—" The woman holds up her hands. "We can't have this disruption in here."

Stephen cuts her off. "Say another word like that, and I'll kill you." His voice is ferocious, and his eyes are on fire. His arms are bands of steel around me, which is a good thing, because I'm falling apart.

"No..." My voice is a broken whisper. "It's not what I wanted."

Burt's words have gutted me.

Stephen holds onto me.

Lulabell stands and pulls me into a hug as a male nurse enters the room.

"Come with me, sir."

Burt snatches his arm out of the man's grip. "If he dies—"

"That's enough." Another male nurse joins the first, and they escort my ex from the room. His voice echoes in the hall, but I can't listen.

The ventilator whooshes in.

The monitors beep.

I collapse in my chair at Eli's bedside. My insides are like strings being twisted tighter and tighter. I've reached my breaking point, but Stephen's hands are on my shoulders. He holds onto me, doing his best to give me his strength.

"THANOS HAS ALL the stones now. His return to Earth has begun..." I push a strand of hair behind my ear. "You have to wake up to see what happens next."

My eyes go to his still mouth, his closed eyes, and I speak louder. "Spider-Man's in trouble, Eli. Better wake up quick!"

Stephen enters the room, pausing at the bedside and glancing at the comic in my hand. "Anything?"

"No."

Four days.

Books are scattered around the room, half-read.

Movies are paused at the most dramatic moments.

Kona sits in front of me waiting.

Still, nothing has changed.

"If the sheer volume of cliffhangers you've left him on carry any weight..." Stephen tries to keep my spirits up, but I'm running out of hope.

"I don't know what else to do."

"You should take a walk. Go outside and get some air. Leave this room."

Anger burns in my chest. "You want me to leave him?" My voice gets louder. "What if he wakes up for one moment, and I'm not here? What if he opens his eyes, and all he sees is this empty room? What if he cries for me, and I don't hear him?"

My chest is moving fast, my stomach clenched, but Stephen catches my hands.

"Breathe." His voice is level, calm. "None of that is going to happen. I'm here. I need you to go outside and walk. Will you do that for me?"

A shudder moves through my body, and I know he's right. I know I need to move my tired limbs. I need to let my blood circulate. I need to get out of that chair.

"I can't lose him."

Stephen's eyes are pained. "You won't."

Fear cramps my stomach. "Stay with him."

"I will."

TECHNICOLOR FLOWERS STRETCH their faces to the sun. I walk slowly along the path to a wall of water, falling over and over in a nonstop, soothing stream.

A cross is positioned behind the fountain and in front is a padded altar. Gardenia kisses the air with its rich scent, and the mood is serene and peaceful. I long to be alone here to pour out my bleeding soul to any higher power willing to listen and help me.

Instead I see a woman kneeling with her hands clasped on the railing.

The closer I get, I see she's crying. Tears coat her cheeks in slick sheets, and her shoulders shudder with her sobs.

I can't help it. I reach out to touch her arm. "Are you okay?"

My voice is hoarse, and when she looks up at me, her brown eyes cringe. "We lost him. It's over." She turns her face to her hands again and resumes her silent sobbing.

Stepping back, I stand behind her, keeping my hand on her shoulder. I don't say the words out loud. I only feel them in my soul.

Dear God, help this poor woman. Help me... "Please, help us." I say the words out loud.

The woman collapses forward, and I lift my chin, allowing the rays of sun to touch my cheeks. The dam breaks, and my tears start to fall. Over and over, as rapidly as the fountain, they coat my face in nonstop streams. All the strings are broken, and I'm hollow inside. My strength is gone.

My eyes close and another rush of tears fall as I pray with all my heart. *Please, dear God. I can't lose my son. I can't lose Eli. I'll do anything if only you'll bring him back to me.*

Crunching steps on the path cause me to open my eyes. I look up to see Stephen approaching quickly, his expression grim. My stomach tightens the closer he gets until he stops right in front of me.

"I couldn't find you." He reaches forward, taking both my hands in his. "I looked everywhere."

"Why aren't you with him?" I can barely say the words through the grief clenching my throat.

"I'm sorry I put you through this. I'm sorry I said this would be easy, and it wasn't."

Our eyes lock, and I see his raw emotions. Stepping forward, I put my arms around his waist. His are around my shoulders, holding me with so much strength.

In this moment, I'm ready. "Tell me now."

His face is in my hair.

He says the words softly in my ear. "He's awake."

26

Stephen

"Antarctica has an eerie, almost magical stillness..." I'm not sure how I ever fell asleep without Sir David Attenborough's voice in the background.

"Noah said his big brother said polar bears have fur on the bottom of their feet!" Ever since he woke up, Eli's been watching and reading everything Emmy crammed into his head while he was asleep.

We've watched every Pirates of the Caribbean movie, we read all three Infinity Wars comic books—now he wants to see the movies—and we're curled up on that pristine couch in my white living room watching the "Frozen Seas" episode of *The Blue Planet*.

"He's right." I give Eli's small shoulder a reassuring squeeze. Maybe I'm reassuring myself he's here. He's awake. He didn't leave us.

Emmy is on his other side of him holding a giant bowl of popcorn all three of us are sharing. Eli's bright eyes and excited voice almost makes me fucking cry.

Only, I'm not a pussy.

"Why do they have fur on the bottom of their paws?" Emmy looks over her shoulder at me, her pretty brow furrowed.

"To keep their feet warm when they walk on ice, Mom! Duh!"

Emmy's eyes go round, and her mouth opens in pretend shock. "Did you just *duh* me?"

Eli starts to giggle, and she spins around, putting the popcorn on the floor and pulling her son into a hug. "Don't you *duh* me! I'm your mamma!"

He laughs more, and I clear my throat, walking to the kitchen for a scotch before I do cry. Damn, I'm so relieved to have him squealing and happy and back under my roof.

Once he came out of the coma, Henry immediately ordered a battery of tests. He checked everything from brain function to reflexes to memory to cognition. Eli passed them all with flying colors—like all his tests.

Emmy asked him to name a bunch of birds, which I thought was a joke, but I'll be damned. I think he named at least fifty before she told him he could stop.

Tears were in her eyes, and I just pulled her to me, holding her and thanking God I didn't break her baby. I'm pretty sure I'd never have forgiven myself if that little boy hadn't woken up.

They kept him in the hospital until Tuesday, and he continued getting stronger and better. Henry left for Europe, but his partner continued to monitor Eli's brain activity, watching for any signs of another seizure. He said if it were going to happen, it would be in the first days post-op.

A week later, and he's still seizure-free.

We're cautiously optimistic the surgery worked. Henry anticipates a full recovery. It's incredible how fast everything has changed.

"What are you doing over there?" Emmy calls to me, and I cross my arms, leaning against the large island.

"I was..." I can't say I needed to walk around before I cried like a little girl. "Want a whiskey?"

She shakes her head, and the two of them return to the screen.

The house is overflowing with bouquets of flowers from Aunt Rebecca. She sent an assortment of caps—knit, baseball, even a bowler. Ethan sent a stuffed sea lion, which Eli keeps away from Kona for obvious reasons. Lulabell sent enough chocolate kisses to last a lifetime and a hot pink beanie with *MCC* stitched on the front.

Only Lulabell and that idiot Burt knew about the coma—primarily because Emmy and I spent four days walking through the pit of hell. All our families know is he had the surgery, and now he's home doing amazingly well.

I'm still leaning against the island watching them when my phone rings. It's Bex.

"Darling! I'm so sorry I'm just checking in. I've been busy as a one-armed paper hanger finishing up preparations for the gala. I heard the little man is doing *fabulous*! Do you still need me to send a private nurse? Say the word, and I'll call Bootsie."

Bootsie is my aunt's nickname for our family physician, Will Breyer. "I didn't know he was still alive."

"Don't be rude, darling. Of course, he's still alive. My good-ness." She acts so offended, but I swear, that man has to be one hundred.

"It's only been a week since his surgery." I'm looking into the living room where Eli sits in a gray knit cap. He hugs Kona and laughs at his mom as he puts a handful of popcorn in his mouth.

"Which is exactly why you need a private nurse. I'll demand to see their résumés. Only the best for Emmy's sweet boy."

My stomach is tight, and I glance at the floor. Bex has

planned this huge event to celebrate a marriage we never intended to keep. Standing here in my kitchen, looking at those two sitting on the couch, I have an idea for something different.

"Book the nurse. Let me see what I can do."

"Are you kidding me?" Emmy's voice rises. "He hasn't even been home a week!"

"That's what I said, but you know how she is."

Eli is tucked in his bed downstairs, sleeping soundly last time I checked. Emmy has the monitor in our room turned up to eleven. It's so loud, we're picking up our neighbor's cell phone signals.

"I'm sorry." She holds up her hands. "I can't leave him."

She's so beautiful pacing my bedroom in yoga pants and an oversized tee falling off one shoulder. Her long hair is swept back, and as stressed out as we were three days ago, I want to pull her to me and fuck her senseless.

All I can think about is my alternate plan for my aunt's gala.

Going to her, I slide my hands down her arms. "I am asking so much of you right now. I know I am."

"Then you know why my answer is no." Her eyes are level, determined, so much like they used to be when she'd tell me she hated me.

I wonder if she would still tell me that today.

"Bex has put a lot of work into this event—"

"Without asking us if we even wanted it!"

"Look at me." She pauses and does as I say. "Families aren't like that. Families want to shower you with gifts and parties. This is her way of showing us her love, and it's only a few hours. Three tops."

Her cute little face twists in frustration. Then she shakes her head. "No. I'm sorry, but no."

"Think of it this way." I skip around to catch her again. "We can celebrate a successful surgery. Eli's home and doing... so damn good. Let's celebrate."

"And if something happens while we're gone?" Her blue eyes flash.

"Nothing is going to happen. Either way, we're never more than a minute away." Glancing toward the window, I see the trees of Central Park. "It's right there."

"I won't enjoy myself." Her fight is weakening, and I'm feeling encouraged. "I'll be worrying about him the whole time. It'll be a waste of a night out."

"Hey." Cupping her face in my hands, I look deep in her pretty, pretty eyes. "You deserve this so much. You've been so worried and stressed for so long. Let me give you this night out. Bex has already hired a private nurse to stay with him while we're gone."

She looks into my eyes and blinks several times while I hold my breath, then her shoulders fall. "Three hours tops. Then we're right back here."

Pulling her closer, I'm ready for a kiss. "Deal."

HELGA IS everything I would expect of a private nurse from my aunt. She arrives wearing a strict, navy suit and never cracking a smile.

I'm pretty sure she's German.

"The boy has eaten his dinner?" Her eyes go from the kitchen to the living room where Eli is propped in a multitude of pillows. Kona is on his left, and Sam the sea lion is safely on his right.

"He's been fed, bathed, and he enjoys watching *The Blue Planet* before bed."

She nods sharply. "I was told he is at risk for seizures? I completed my residency at Northwestern Memorial in Chicago, voted one of the top ten neurosurgery hospitals in the U.S."

My eyebrows rise. "I didn't see that on your résumé."

"Dr. Bronson didn't tell me I was required to provide an updated résumé. Which version did you receive? I will fax you the updated version tonight when I get home. It will include my work with Dr. Schultz on brain trauma and stress behaviors in mice."

I'm feeling better with every word. At the same time, fax? Seriously? "Any chance you could email it? Take a picture with your phone?"

I swear, I'm one of the top software programmers in the country. I can't get over all this fax nonsense.

"Of course."

She heads toward the living room, standing behind the couch and watching *The Blue Planet* with Eli. I wait in the kitchen in my tux for Emmy to emerge. She shooed me downstairs while she finished getting ready for the event.

Picking up my phone, I quickly tap out a text.

> It's getting close to nine. The car is here. Where is Cinderella?

I hear the buzz on the stairs, and I look up as I hear her voice. "I don't know about Cinderella..."

When she steps into view, I'm pretty sure my jaw hits the floor. I know my dick perks up. She's the most beautiful... the sexiest thing I've seen in my life.

Standing on the landing, her hair is swept back in a low bun. Her gorgeous shoulders are exposed and a glittering silver necklace traces her collarbones. The strapless black dress she wears is fitted to her body all the way to the floor, but starting at her waist, a full, cream-colored skirt billows around her.

It's almost as if she's wearing the dress version of my black coat and tie.

"You look..." I put my hand on my stomach. "Incredible."

Her full lips are painted deep red, and at my words, they split into the happiest, white smile. After the gift of telling her Eli had come out of the coma, this is my second favorite memory with her.

"Thank you." She does a little nod. "I guess it's time?"

"It's time."

JAZZ MUSIC PLAYS SOFTLY, and as we walk toward the three-arched entry to the Loeb Boathouse, the sound of laughter drifts through the air to greet us. I stop her in the quiet and pull her close.

"I want to kiss you."

Her red lips part with her smile. "You'll smudge my makeup."

"You should never wear makeup. You're a natural beauty."

Shaking her head, she pulls away. "Hold that thought a few minutes. I'd like to make an entrance before you muss me."

Pulling her hand into the crook of my elbow, I cut her a glance. "I'll do more than muss you."

We enter the massive gala, and at once Bex is with us, leading us through the throng, introducing us to people she says we know, but I don't. It's like a really enormous family reunion meets high school reunion meets social event of the year.

The band starts playing "Hey, Paula," and I take Emmy's hand, leading her to the dance floor. She does a little frown, but

I pull her to my chest, tucking my nose at her ear. "It's what they want."

"I never took you for such a people pleaser." Her sassy tone is back. I've missed it.

"I can count on one hand the people in this world I care to please. Bex is one of them."

We continue swaying. I love the feel of her in my arms. Her cheek is against mine, she smells like heaven, and my mind is ahead of us a few hours to what I hope comes next.

We took a questionable route to get here, but maybe it took something unorthodox to bring us to this place. We're in our own little bubble of bliss, and I'm ready to make my move when she stiffens.

My reflexes go on alert, and I look around. "What's wrong?"

Stepping back, I see her jaw is set. Her eyes are narrowed and looking past my shoulder. I pivot to see fucking Burt smirking at us from a few couples away.

The Dick. *What is he doing here?*

He doesn't waste time crossing the floor to where we stand. Peg is on his arm. "I have to hand it to you, Em. I knew you were cold-hearted, but I never expected to see you out partying a week after your son almost died. I guess that's just the sort of mercenary you are."

Emmy's cheeks drain of color, and her hand loosens in mine, like she's letting me go.

I pull her to me, stepping in Burt's face. "Why the fuck are you here?"

"Peg has her mail forwarded to the penthouse now. When I saw the invitation and realized what it was about, I realized it was my duty to set the record straight. I needed to come here and tell our unsuspecting family and friends what you two are up to."

The last thing I need is bullshit from The Dick. "What the fuck—"

But he cuts me off. "I'll take care of it now." He picks up a wine glass and begins tapping it with a spoon. "Ladies and gentleman, I'd like to propose a toast. Can I have your attention?"

Emmy shrinks back, her hand falling from mine. I turn and follow her, confused by her behavior. The music stops, and the voices slowly die down.

Standing by her side at a back table, I look up at Burt. He's on a chair, acting proud like the pompous asshole he is. Peg is beside him, and someone hands him a microphone.

"Is this on?" The speakers whistle as he taps the mic a few times. "I know, you're probably wondering why the hell I'm giving a toast for my ex-wife." He holds up a hand, nodding like he's in charge. "Actually, this is for you, and I promise, it's *rich*."

A few people laugh nervously, looking around. My aunt looks up at him, her eyebrows pulled together in confusion. I slide a hand into my pocket, doing my best to grin and not make a scene.

Burt lifts his glass, speaking loudly. "To the two greatest actors I've ever known."

Emmy is no longer at my side. She's gone quickly to where Burt is standing and is pulling his coat.

Her voice is quiet, urgent... begging. "Please don't do this."

He glances down, menace in his smile. "I have to give you credit, you're good. You made fools of us all."

My jaw clenches, and I start forward, but Alyssa steps in front of me, glaring. "Is it true, Stephen?"

Why the fuck is Alyssa here? "Is what true?"

"Burt told me. He said I should come and ask you." I put my hands on her arms, ready to move her aside so I can get to Emmy.

"Now it's time to tell your friends and family the truth." His voice grows louder with every word. "Did you marry Stephen Hastings because you were in love with him? Or did you whore yourself out for his money?"

Emmy's hand drops along with her chin, and a low hum filters through the crowd.

Alyssa's voice is in my face. "Is it true?"

Anger blazes to life in my chest, and I move her to the side, charging forward, ready to rip Burt down by his neck.

Bex signals, and large men thread into the crowd in Burt's direction, pushing bodies between me and The Dick. *Fuck.* I've got to get to Emmy.

Burt sees the men, and he grabs Emmy's forearm. "In case you think I'm making it up, we have Emmy right here to confirm it."

He leans down to her, and she turns her face away. He pulls her arm around, and I see red. Now I'm shoving people, fighting to get to my girl.

"Tell them, Emmy. Miss Emily Ann Barton. Don't lie to all these good people. Did you marry Stephen Hastings because you loved him? Or did you marry him to pay your bills?"

He holds her steady, and her face lifts. White light illuminates her features, and her expression is pure defiance. "I would do anything for my son."

Burt smiles down at her like some comic villain. "Then answer the question. Love or money?"

The mic is in her face. Emmy blinks at him. The whole room holds its breath like this is some kind of gross reality show.

Emmy's pretty lips part, and she speaks. "I married Stephen because I needed the money."

The room erupts into voices, and Burt beams with triumph. He lowers the mic, but I hear him loud and clear telling her, "Because that's what you are. A lying whore."

I'm finally through the men when he sees me. "Didn't think you had to pay for it, Hastings."

With a loud *crack*, my fist slams into his smiling, asshole face. The mic hits the ground, amplifying the *bang* as he falls.

I'm on him fast. "You're a cunty, dickish waste of oxygen." My voice is a savage growl through clenched teeth. "I'd buy her anything..."

His shirtfront is in my fist, and I pull him up as I punch him again and again. The slippery warmth of blood coats my knuckles, and satisfaction expands in my chest with every howl, every grunt, every time he begs me to stop.

"Stephen, stop this at once!" Bex claps her hands from somewhere close by, and the bouncers she summoned finally catch me by the arms, pulling me off the piece of shit I'm beating into the hardwoods.

I notice they gave me a few minutes before they stopped me.

"You're going to pay for this!" Burt's ragged screams are the least of my concern.

"If I see you again..." I sound like a savage, and my eyes lock on his. "You'd better run."

My throat is tight, and I look all around, searching for Emmy.

She's gone.

27

Emmy

Eli is asleep on the white couch when I arrive at Stephen's townhome.

Helga looks up from where she's reading a Jack Reacher novel and gives me a tight smile. "You're back early." She says it like it's an order.

"The party ended early." I go to my son and lightly trace my fingers over his head. *No regrets.*

"He's an angel of a boy." Her compliment surprises me, coming from such an imposing figure.

"Thank you." I smile, allowing my love for him to ease the pain of public humiliation.

"I'll be going then." She stands, and I see her to the door.

Returning to the couch, I lean down and lift my son onto my shoulder. His knit cap pressing against my neck reminds me how close we came to losing him as I slowly climb the stairs.

Tomorrow, I'll pack his things, and we'll head back to our place in the Village. We haven't been here long enough for it to be much of a job.

Once he's settled in bed, I climb the last flight of stairs, allowing the tears to flow down my cheeks. My insides are numb. I'm completely humiliated, and I just want to go somewhere far away from here, from Burt's cruelty.

As sick as it was, his stunt was the wake-up call I needed. I had allowed myself to get attached to Stephen, and I forgot everything we agreed to before I said *I do*.

Looking down, a piece of hair falls on my damp cheek as I fumble with the zipper on my dress. Sliding it down, the enormous gown drops to the floor. I step out of it and into thin sweat pants. I pull on a long-sleeved tee, and slip my arms into a cropped hoodie then I walk to the bathroom.

Sadness aches between my shoulder blades, but it's time to clean up this mess.

Show's over.

I wash my face, cleaning the black streaks off my cheeks and stop crying. I hang my beautiful dress in the closet, and I slip the platinum wedding band off my finger. I'd been using it to hold the still too-big diamond engagement ring in place.

Carefully, I place them in a small tray on the mahogany desk by the window. I'm standing there looking down when I see his car squeal up to the curb. Stephen dashes out, and my stomach tightens. I'm not sure what he'll say, but I know what I have to say.

Loud footsteps on the stairs, I brace myself for his appearance. I'm just not prepared for him to take my breath away when he bursts through the door. I should be used to him by now, but I've never been fully prepared for Stephen Hastings.

"Why did you leave without me?" He strides across the room, pulling me to his chest.

I'm surrounded by his arms, my face against the fine fabric of his custom-made formalwear. Everything about him is perfectly tailored, custom made, organized, and planned. Stephen Hastings is always in control.

Until now.

"I had to leave." My voice is strangely calm, considering my insides are bleeding. "I'll pack our things tomorrow—"

"Emmy, no." He holds me out, frustrated blue eyes meeting mine. He's so handsome. "You are not moving out. I won't let The Dick win."

"Stephen, it's time. I have my apartment for another week. It's closer to work—"

"You are not going back to that rat trap in the Village."

I give him a sad smile. "I won't tell Lou you said that."

"You know what I mean." He starts to say more, but I hold up a hand, cutting him off.

"It's time to stop pretending. I need to go back to where I belong."

"Where you belong..." His jaw tightens, and I feel his frustration. "You and Eli belong here with me."

"Not after tonight, not with everyone saying I'm a whore."

His voice rises. "If one of those assholes ever dares say that—"

"Most of them are your family and friends."

"I don't know half of them."

"They know you. And the way they looked at me..." Shuddering, I remember the old women pulling their wraps tighter over their shoulders and turning away in horror. I remember the young women glaring at me with disgust. I remember the older men looking at me with either lust or curiosity.

Shivering, I push their faces out of my mind. "Ethan asked us to move to Seattle."

When I look up again, Stephen's old scowl is back. "Move to Seattle? When?"

"He suggested it last week when I told him about the surgery, when he couldn't get here for it. It would be a fresh start for us." Turning away, I place a palm against my stomach. "My lease is up in a week, and I've decided we're going to do it."

Silence is at my back, and I'm not sure I can turn around and face him.

In these last few weeks, in particular these last few days, he's become so important to me. He's like the air I breathe, and his arms surround me with strength.

I let myself fall in love with him.

Again.

This one's on me.

"I need to sleep in Eli's room tonight." Turning my head to the side is the best I can do. "Thank you for everything you've done for us."

"Emmy, stop." Large hands are on me, and he pulls my back against his chest.

"Please, Stephen." My voice breaks as the tears burn in my throat. "I can't fight you."

Turning me around, he holds me in front of him. "Then don't. This is not how you really feel."

He's so gorgeous looking at me with those eyes all pissed and bossy. He's so strong. I'm so weak, but I have to think about Eli now.

"I don't know how I really feel. That's the problem. We've been through hell. Our emotions are so high, we're forgetting who we really are. But when it all comes down to it, you don't believe in marriage. I don't believe in love. What do we do with that?"

Tears are in my eyes, and my voice is strained. He stands back studying me, considering every word. He's so smart. He'll see what I'm saying is right.

He doesn't respond to my statement, instead he looks down

at his hand, which I notice is a bit swollen. "I think Burt pulled that stunt tonight to strengthen his hold on Eli."

"Oh, God." My chin drops, and I shake my head. I'm so defeated, I never even thought about why Burt did it. I only wondered how it was possible he could hate me so much. "He was already threatening to take him from me before we married."

"Emmy, look at me." I raise my eyes to his. "It won't happen. My lawyers have drawn up a motion using letters from Henry and the ER docs when Eli had his last seizure. I think we have plenty of evidence to keep Burt from ever taking your son."

Gratitude floods my chest, and my eyes heat again. "I didn't ask you to do that."

"Are you angry I did?" His voice is gentle.

"Of course not. It's something I could never afford. All of this is."

He steps closer, towering over me in my bare feet. "I told you I would help you."

Placing my palm on his cheek, I nod slowly. "I can never repay you for it."

"Good thing you don't have to." He smiles, taking my hand and kissing my palm. His brow furrows when he sees my ring finger is bare.

Our eyes meet, and my chest aches so bad. "The rings are in the tray on your desk."

He's still holding my hand. "I don't want you to go."

"But you're set in your ways. It's too late. Remember?"

His thumb traces over the place where my wedding band once sat on my finger. "I've gotten used to you being here. I like you here. I like Eli here..."

Taking my hand out of his, I have to stop this. "It's not enough. I can't stay here because of sex or money."

"It was never just that. Not even when we said it was."

I have no words left. I can't argue with him when I'm struggling with my feelings this way. Am I holding onto him because it's right or because I'm afraid I can't stand on my own?

I have to know. I have to rebuild my strength.

"Will you take care of the annulment papers?" I can't bear to meet his eyes as I ask it.

His voice is husky when he answers. "Of course."

"IF I'M WEARING a fabulous outfit and no one's around to see it, is it still fabulous?" Lulabell stands in front of a mirror in the back of Miss Con-Cleaneality.

We're ready to head over for the final night of the Lady Liberty pageant. She's dressed in orange hot pants and a silky yellow blouse. On top of it all is a shaggy, multicolor faux fur coat made of black, orange, red, and yellow pelts.

"Yes." I nod, feeling underdressed in my dark skinny jeans and black, scoop-neck tank. "You look amazing. I look like I just rolled out of bed."

"Here." She hustles to her office and returns with a bright yellow blazer. "Put this on."

I do as she says, and she rolls up the sleeves. "The heels help," I note, checking out the improvement in the mirror.

"You just needed a pop of color."

Her shoulders drop, and she hits me with those puppy-dog eyes. "I'm just getting you plugged into the fashion scene here. What will you do in Seattle? You'll be surrounded by flannel and Uggs. *Grunge.*" She shivers. "It sounds cringey."

"I don't know. There's a lot to be said for comfort clothing."

"I swear to God, if you come back smelling like patchouli, I will never speak to you again."

The way she says it actually makes me laugh, which is a first for this hell of a week. "I promise. No patchouli."

"And the doctor said it's okay for Eli to travel?"

Nodding, I recall our meeting with Henry's partner earlier this week. "He's on his second week of no seizures. They did an MRI, and all the results came back very positive. He'll meet with the neurologist in Seattle Dr. Rourke recommended in a few months, but as long as he's resting, he can take a road trip."

"Well, that's disappointing." She sees the expression on my face and quickly adds. "That the doctor said you could leave, I mean, not that Eli's doing great. I'm glad Eli's doing great! Come, we're going to be late for the big show."

We've been working the preliminaries all week. We've seen girls come and go, and through it all, I've made friends and learned so many hair and makeup shortcuts, tricks, and tips. I've picked up business cards from industry professionals, and an Elite scout even told me to call their Seattle office about a job. It's been an amazing experience. I'm being paid very well, and it's gone a long way toward bringing me out of my "whore" humiliation. I can take care of my son and me without Stephen's money. I'm not a whore.

"Eli's staying with Stephen again?" We're walking into the backstage area. My heart is a lead weight in my chest, and I'm sure Lou can see it. "How's that going?"

"Fine. Stephen loves him." Which I believe is true.

"And?"

I know what she means. "I talked to Eli about moving and how he'll get to see his uncle Ethan, his aunt Patrice, and all his cousins. He's sad to leave New York, but it's a better situation for him, a better environment. He's only known Stephen a short time." Lou's watching me, the doubt growing in her eyes. It frustrates me. "It was never real, Lou."

"It sure looked real to me."

"Maybe things aren't always how they look." I grab my smock, pulling it over my head.

"Then again, maybe they are."

The music rises, and I don't have time for arguing. Or second-guessing.

28

Stephen

"If they tap here," The young guy on my oversized iMac monitor taps his phone's face. "It takes them to the search function, and from there, they can see all the doctors in their network who are available in any given location."

The kid walking us through the beta version of my health-care app looks like he might be sixteen. I wonder if he's ever faced a medical emergency in his life.

"It also works for pharmacies?" Remington interrupts my thoughts.

We're on a three-way video chat with Remi in Oakville, me in Manhattan, and Skippy the computer programmer in Seattle.

"Yes, sir. Just tap right here..." The man-child shows how he set up the app to work exactly as I specified.

I lean back in my office chair scowling as I watch him. I should be pleased he follows orders so well. Instead, I'm annoyed.

It's been a month since Emmy moved to Seattle...

The week before she left, Eli stayed with me during the days. It was at my request, as I'm pretty sure Emmy was swamped packing boxes. Even though he'd been released by the doctors, Eli didn't need to be doing any heavy lifting.

He sat at the coffee table in the middle of my office reading about ocean mammals while I studied code and diagrammed my newest application.

At one point, I looked over to find him studying me, that little gray beanie covering his scars.

"What's on your mind, Bart?" I teased, calling him by his pirate name.

His nose squinted. "Mom says Seattle is surrounded by water. She said we might see whales there."

"It's true." I thought about the Pacific Northwest. "It's pretty rugged country."

"I don't really remember Uncle Ethan, but Mom says he's cool." He looked at his pencil a minute. "I'll get to know my cousins."

"Cousins can be fun." I leaned back in my chair, waiting to see what this smart little guy would say next.

"Thanks for what you did for us. Taking me in and helping me get my surgery." He pressed his lips together and nodded as if he got it right. "You made my mom really happy."

An ache moved through my chest, and I told him one truth I'd learned. "Nothing is ever permanent. But you never lose true friends. I'll always be your friend."

The night before they drove away, I walked through my big, empty townhome, standing in the doorway of the blue bedroom, staring at Eli's empty bed. I think he was happy here. I was happy having him here.

I think she was happy here...

I walked up to my bedroom, then I stopped as I stared at my empty bed. Why the fuck do I need such a huge-assed bed? I'm a tall man, but I'm not obese. I'm a healthy weight, physically fit. Why do I need a California King? It's bullshit.

The next morning, I got over myself and took the car down to the Village. I pulled up in front of Miss Con-Cleaneality, surprised to see Lulabell standing on the sidewalk out front looking in the direction I'd just come. A handkerchief was in her hand, and she was dabbing her eyes.

The sign above her read, "Happy Whatever-doesn't-offend-you Day." I stepped out of my car, and Lou gave me a sad smile. "You just missed her."

My chest tightened, and I turned quickly, staring up the street in the direction she faced.

They were gone.

Almost three thousand miles.

"Go get them." Lou's quiet voice pleaded.

It felt like a stab straight to my heart.

"She'll be happier there." I looked down, hating everything in the world. "She only has sad memories here."

"Are you sure?" I glanced at her, and she gave me a watery smile.

I couldn't answer her question.

"STEPHEN? DO YOU HAVE ANY QUESTIONS?" Remi is looking at me on the video screen. "Everything look good?"

Hell, I have no idea. "How about you leave it with me, Skip. I'll take it for a test drive tonight."

"Uh, it's Phillip, sir."

"Sorry?" I cut my eyes at him, and he pulls away from the screen.

"My name..." His voice is timid. "It's Phillip."

"Sorry, we got it." Remi's cheerful tone seems to relax the kid. "Thanks, Phillip."

I'm annoyed at my partner's interference. I kind of liked seeing the beads of sweat pop out on Skip's forehead.

"I'll be in touch." My tone is flat, my gaze piercing.

Phillip signs off, and Remi swivels in his chair. "Trying to scare off all the help?"

I'm angry and growly. "He has no creativity. He repeated back word for word exactly what I told him to do. Where's the innovation there?"

"If I recall correctly, the last time he tried to innovate, you bit his head off for not following the script." Remi's voice rises, and I toss a pen on my desk.

"It was a stupid change. Linking to social media adds no value to the app. It makes it ridiculous."

"It could have good marketing implications."

"Marketing." The word is a bad taste in my mouth. "You don't market healthcare. You provide it."

Remi makes that annoying face like he's psychoanalyzing me. "How long has it been now? A month?"

"What are you talking about?" My stomach clenches, and I know exactly what he's talking about.

"I can spell it out for you if you need me to spell it out for you." He sits forward, and I don't often see Remington lose his temper. "Emmy moved to Seattle a month ago? Took that little boy with her?"

"Don't fuck with me Key. I'm not in the mood." I don't want to fight with Remi.

"Well, I'm sick as shit of your tyrannical behavior. Word gets around. You'll be coding all your own apps if you piss off too many people. Nobody will want to work with us."

His expression is serious, and I hate to admit he's right.

Clearing my throat, I sit forward in my chair. "You're right." I press my lips together a moment. "I'll follow up with Skip, tell him he did a good job, offer him a bonus for... I don't know. I'll make up something."

"His name is Phillip, and that bonus is coming out of your end, not mine." He's grinning now, and it's annoying as fuck.

"Fine."

He leans back, tossing a baseball. "You know, you told me something a few years ago. What was it? Stop making things so hard?"

Standing, I straighten my blazer and reach for the mouse. "That sounds like something I'd say." I've had enough of apologizing. I need a drink.

"Stephen!" I hesitate, catching the glint in his eye. "Take your own advice. Go get her."

My hand hesitates before I end our call. I think about what she said, needing time. Is four weeks enough time?

I think about what I should have done when she was standing right here in front of me.

Nodding, I blink up at him briefly. "That's just what I intend to do."

"I'M STILL MORTIFIED by the entire thing." Bex slices a perfectly cooked piece of medium-rare salmon and puts it in her mouth. "Some of these newer families are not the good sort, I'm afraid."

My last order of business before I catch my plane in the morning is Thursday night dinner. I don't bother telling her the Dickersons have been around for generations. I tend to agree Burt is a bad apple.

"And I'm *so* disappointed in the boathouse," she continues, sipping her wine. "Their security has gotten so lax. That young man should never have been allowed to enter the party without

an invitation. I would never have invited Emily's ex-husband."
My aunt closes her eyes and shudders.

"I think the invitation was sent to his girlfriend."

"His girlfriend!" Her face is pure horror. "Who in the world
would date such an animal?"

"Peg Yardley." My tone is flat.

"Peg Yardley..." I glance up to see her frowning. "Do you
mean Margaret Yardley?"

"She goes by Peg, Bex." I take a sip of my whiskey, not really
wanting to discuss it. I'm distracted thinking about what I want
to happen tomorrow, wondering if it will go my way.

"I had no idea." She shifts in her chair. "Margaret Yardley
has an unfortunate forehead. I'm sure that's why. I've always
tried to be kind to the Yardleys... Anyway, they should never
have allowed an unauthorized person to speak on a
microphone."

"Probably not."

"People get married for money all the time. What's the big
deal?" She waves her hand as if she can shoo away what
happened.

"Nobody says it out loud." Anger burns in my throat at the
memory. "He made her look like a whore."

"Nonsense. Emily is too lovely for anyone to think something so horrible." She studies my scowl, and her eyes turn
pleading. "Darling, what can I do?"

"You can wish me luck."

The next day I'm on a plane. Mount Rainier breaks through
the clouds as my private jet approaches Sea-Tac. It's silent,
majestic, and strong. A good omen, I think. Just before I left, the
envelope I'd been waiting for arrived. I have it in my breast
pocket, and no matter how this plays out, I know I'll leave her
with one last gift.

The brunette flight attendant stops at my chair. "The pilot

has asked that you remain seated with your seatbelt securely fastened until we land."

"Thank you." I motion to the belt across my lap.

She nods and heads to the front where she'll strap in. In twenty minutes, I'll be off this plane, headed for Ethan's home and what I hope is my future.

29

Emmy

nybody up for a walk?" Ethan's voice echoes from the bottom of the wooden staircase. "I'm headed out to Lincoln park."

"Me! Me! Me!" Eli is in the hall, running and waving at my brother.

Since we arrived, my son has been in heaven. I had no idea my brother's neighborhood was so pristine. It's surrounded by hidden coves and small pockets of gray-pebbled beaches. Almost every day, Ethan or one of the boys, Kurt or David—my older brother decided to break the Barton tradition of first names starting with the letter *E*—heads down to the water to fish or skim stones or watch the boats go by.

A ferry makes daily trips out to Vashon Island and Southworth, and we have the most amazing view of the Olympic mountains. It's all so gorgeous and homey...

And I miss Stephen.

I wake in the morning, and I think about him. I go to bed at night, and I think about him. I miss the funny noises he makes when he sleeps. I miss the way he would hold my face and kiss me. I miss the possessive way he makes love. I even miss his arrogant scowl and his bossy perfectionism.

I think about how he defended me against Burt... and how he asked me to stay.

A month ago, when everything was so intense, I couldn't trust my heart when it came to him. Now, I'm afraid we've missed our chance.

I watch Eli playing with his cousins, and I know he's happy here. I see him growing stronger every day, and I know as much as it hurt, as high as the price was to pay, his surgery was so worth it.

He hasn't had a single seizure. We had a follow-up appointment with a neurologist here, and Dr. Rourke has been consulting with him by phone. Eli's surgery is so new and ground-breaking, doctors are eager to work with us.

None of it would've been possible without Stephen.

Pulling on jeans and a gray and black striped Henley, I think about the other thing that wouldn't have been possible without Stephen. Last night, I pulled out my calendar and counted off the days. I'll have to make a trip into town and get a pregnancy test after breakfast.

I don't even know where to begin to know what to do if it comes back positive.

My sister-in-law Patrice stands looking out the window at the boys walking in a line to the water. "Sleeping better?" She smiles, handing me a blue speckled mug of coffee as I enter the open kitchen area. Her red hair shines like embers in the sunlight.

"Getting there." I hold the warm beverage to my nose. "I've never had such a time adjusting. My room is lovely."

It could be a new little person is growing inside me.

"Time zones are weird." She holds her own mug, looking out

at the mountains in the distance. "The boys want to catch the ferry after while. You up for that?"

Pressing my lips together, I think about what I need to do. "If it's not too much trouble, I think I'll stay here today. I've got to follow up on some phone calls. I might have found a place for us to live."

"We'll be glad to take Eli off your hands for a few hours." She teases, and I lean my hip against the counter, watching the boys skimming the large, gray pebbles that line the water's edge. "He's such a great kid."

I couldn't agree more.

With Ethan, Patrice, and all the boys gone for the island, I make a quick trip to the drugstore, quickly passing through the aisles until I find what I'm looking for. An equally quick transaction, and I'm back at the house, upstairs in my bathroom.

"Place in urine stream for ten seconds..." The last time I did this, I was in a cramped bathroom in a college dorm.

I never expected to be doing it again.

Stephen hustled us through the marriage ceremony and all the details so fast, I almost didn't have time to swing by the drugstore and refill my birth control prescription.

Sex shouldn't have been on the table in our arrangement... But I knew myself better than that.

"So I did refill it," I say, hunched over on the toilet, doing my best to pee on the gauze tip.

Of course, I wasn't even a week into taking it when we had our weekend-long honeymoon sexcapade.

"Is it possible we got pregnant that fast?" I could just be crazy.

Every time you have unprotected sex, you risk getting pregnant. My high school guidance counselor's voice is in my head.

"Great time to be right, Mrs. Zimmerman."

Standing, I clean up quickly then put the pink plastic cap

over the used end of the pregnancy test and set it on the counter. I'm just checking my watch when someone knocks on the door downstairs.

It's probably just the UPS man. I pace the bathroom, arms crossed, waiting for three minutes to pass. A knot is in my throat. What am I going to do if it's positive? I'll have to tell Stephen, which means I'll have to see him again, which means I'll break down crying because pregnancy hormones allow no room for stoicism...

The knocking on the door downstairs turns to banging, and I drop my arms. Leaving the pee stick on the counter, I jog downstairs thinking how some people are so rude.

My head goes light when I jerk the door open and find Stephen standing in front of me scowling. "Oh, my! Jesus!" For the second time, I'm pretty sure the world stopped spinning.

"Emmy." He reaches out, catching me before I fall. "I wasn't sure anyone was here."

I'm struggling to catch my breath. "Ethan and Patrice took the boys out to the island."

"You're alone?" He's still holding me, surrounding me in that scent I know so well. Fresh soap and spicy leather remind me of every way he's ever touched me.

Pushing out of his arms, I straighten my shirt, trying to get my shit together. "What are you doing here?"

His brow lowers, forming that perfect scowl I fell in love with so many years ago. He clears his throat and looks over his shoulder, at nothing up the road. I know, because I look, too.

Suddenly, he turns back to me, and the expression in his blue eyes tells me it's all or nothing. "Emmy, I'm an idiot."

"No..." Shaking my head. "You're the smartest guy I know."

"I'm the biggest idiot." He turns toward the street, putting his hands on his hips, spreading that expensive tailored blazer away from his tight ass.

With my heart flying in my chest, I reach for him. "Would you like to come inside?"

He turns to me again with that expression I've never seen. It's helpless. "Emmy..." It's like a prayer. "I'm sorry for what I said to you."

"What you said?" I'm racking my brains. I try to remember all the things he said the last time we were together. None of them stand out as offensive.

"That night at Ethan's party. I should have run after you into that crowd."

My lips press together, and I think I might cry. "It was so long ago."

"I should have found you when I got back from Africa."

"After you left the Navy? I had already married Burt."

Scrubbing his fingers on his forehead, he walks up the short hall to the kitchen, then he turns and walks back to me again. Stopping in front of me, he's so tall. He looks down, and the heat burning between us sets my heart on fire.

"For the last month, all I've done is think about this. I was so selfish, so broken by mother's death, by what happened to Ximena. I was angry with my father... I said I didn't believe in marriage because I never wanted to put myself in the position to be hurt like that again." His hand moves from his forehead to his mouth. "You hated me. I was safe being with you because you hated me."

I blink and a tear hits my cheek. Stepping forward, he catches it with his thumb. "Now I know the truth. I need you, Emmy. I'm in love with you."

My eyes close, and fifty tears hit my cheeks. I can't stop them. "Stephen..."

He cups my face in both hands. "Do you still hate me?"

My head moves slowly side to side. "You make it impossible for me to hate you. You always have."

His full lips part, curling into a sexy grin, and the helplessness is gone. In its place is that confidence, that bossy shine in his eyes. "Impossible?"

Even in tears, I can't resist. "Maybe I spoke too soon..."

Strong arms circle me, pinning me against his chest. "You love me. Say it."

Our noses touch, and his lips are so close, I could stretch up and kiss him. "Why should I?"

"Because you do."

"So cocky, Mr. Hastings."

Leaning down, he kisses me gently, touching my lips with his tongue, lighting my insides with his touch. "I came here to get you. I want you in my life. I need you. Let me take care of you and Eli always. Come home with me today."

"I just accepted a position at Elite..."

"Give them your resignation."

"Eli really likes being with his cousins."

"We'll fly him out as much as he wants."

Scrunching my nose, I slide my hands around his waist. "Are you proposing to me again?"

"No."

Confused, I try to pull my hands away, but his arms lock down on them, pinning me in place. "I never filed the annulment papers, Mrs. Hastings."

"Stephen!" My shoulders drop, but I stop trying to get away.

"I also did this." Reaching into his pocket, he pulls out a long envelope and hands it to me.

Stepping back, I carefully take out the thick stack of folded papers. They're covered in a blue sheet, and at the top it's stamped as official government documents. Scanning quickly, I'm not quite sure what it means.

"Are these...?"

"Revised custody papers. My lawyers convinced Burt it was

in his best interest to sign. He can't threaten you or use your son against you any more."

Pressing them against my chest, I look up at him through watery eyes. "You did this for me?"

"I want to do everything for you." He reaches into his coat pocket and holds out the two rings. "Say you'll let me."

My lips poke out, and I frown. "I don't want you to do everything for me..."

"Most things, then." Catching my hand, he slides the rings back on the third finger of my left hand. "Just stay. Stay with me always. Say you'll stay."

Reaching up, I place my palm on his cheek. He lowers his chin to kiss it. "I do love you, Stephen Hastings. I'll stay." His eyes close, and he laughs, resting his forehead against mine.

I'm grinning as well, when I add, "We need to check on something."

"WHO DO you think was the first person to say 'in the family way'?" I'm lying on my back, basking in post-orgasmic bliss.

Stephen is between my thighs, both arms wrapped around my waist, kissing my bare stomach. "Some old prude who would never eat your sweet pussy."

I squeeze him with my knees, laughing as I thread my fingers in his wavy hair. "Good thing you don't say it."

Warm lips touch my skin. "How's my little girl behaving in there?"

"It's too soon to know." Leaning my head down, warmth floods my chest seeing him so happy.

When I brought him upstairs, I wasn't sure what the pregnancy test would say. My throat was tight but I took his hand, carefully leading him to the counter where the white stick lay with the pink cap firmly in place. It was an answer we'd get together.

"Is that..."

His voice trailed off, and I nodded, looking up to see so much hope in his blue eyes. Contagious hope pushed so strongly against my chest, I was almost afraid to look, afraid it might say *no*, we weren't pregnant.

I guess we could always try again...

I had barely lifted the stick, barely read the little blue *yes* when his lips were on mine. We were laughing and struggling to get our arms around each other, a tangle of limbs until he caught my cheeks and kissed me so many times. Our lips chased each other's as we laughed, tears streaming down my cheeks.

He lifted me off my feet and carried me to the bed, but he didn't make it above my waist, not that I'm complaining.

Now I can't resist teasing him. "For someone so set in his ways, I'm surprised you want another girl in the house."

He runs his nose along my navel, kissing my skin again. "She'd better have big blue eyes and long blonde hair just like her pretty mamma."

"Her pretty mamma wishes you'd make your way a little higher and kiss me."

Sexy blue eyes cut up to mine, and that naughty grin appears. The sight of it curls my toes, and heat zips through my core. I'm ready to welcome all of him when noises downstairs freeze us.

"I don't recognize the car." Ethan's voice is in the hall, and I pull my shirt down fast.

Stephen hops up on his knees. "Is Eli here?"

He's so excited to see my son, I pretty much fall head over heels in love with him all over again. "He should be."

Stephen's off the bed, leaving me naked from the waist down, headed for the door, when I stop him. "Wash your face!"

"Right." He pivots, running to the bathroom to do a quick wash, and I push myself up, shaking my head. "What did you do with my underwear?"

He re-enters the room, and scoops a scrap of pink lace off the floor, tossing it at me. "Hurry up!"

"Go on down." I grab his shoulder, pulling him back for a quick kiss, and he's out the door before I even have my jeans over my hips.

Loud noises of excitement and disbelief almost make me cry. I can hear in Eli's voice how happy he is to see Stephen. Ethan is asking when he arrived and how long he plans to stay. I finally descend the stairs, stopping halfway to smile at my boys.

Eli sits on Stephen's hip, hugging him around the neck. Stephen's talking to my brother like holding my son is the most normal thing in the world. As I watch them, I realize it is.

"Hey, sis! You didn't say Hastings was coming for a visit." Ethan looks up at me, and I smile.

"I didn't know."

Eli's head pops up, and he points to my left hand. "You're wearing your rings again! Does this mean we're going home?"

"I..." My jaw drops, and I look from my son to my brother to my husband.

My real husband.

"That's exactly what it means," Stephen says.

"Yeah," I nod, smiling. "That's what it means."

Patrice walks in and puts her arms around my brother's waist, smiling at us as we huddle together, reunited in a hug.

Stephen entered our lives thinking he'd never have a family. He was like that cold, distant mountain, majestic, aloof... and alone. He had no idea how much we needed him to complete ours. I didn't know how much we needed him.

I hated him.

Now, as unorthodox and questionable as our choices have

been, here we are, bonded in a way I know would not have happened any other way. All the challenges, the scary parts, the heartbreaking parts, the humiliating parts—they all got us here.

Looking down at my hand, I slide my finger over the heavy band and sparkling diamond ring. Stephen Hastings *is* my hero. Now he's asking me to be his.

Wherever he goes, whatever we do.

I will.

Stay.

EPILOGUE

Stephen

"Look what Stella's doing to your stomach!" Eli is on his knees beside the couch, watching Emmy's pregnant belly stretch into pointy shapes like an alien life form is trying to break out.

It really is freaky when our unborn daughter moves that way, especially when I'm trying to love on her sexy mamma, which sadly has dropped off in the last week.

We're at the nine-month mark, or the thirty-sixth week as Emmy has taught me to say. Snow is on the ground, and we're huddled in the pristine living room, the gas log burning as we watch *The Blue Planet.*

Emmy's feet are in my lap for a massage, and she finally took maternity leave from her job as a stylist with Elite Media. They were able to transfer her Seattle offer to their Manhattan office, and she's making enough money now for her own two-bedroom apartment in Turtle Bay—not that she's going anywhere.

My wife is staying right here.

Looking at the two and a half of them in my big old place cozy and warm, I'm the happiest man alive.

And the luckiest.

To think I almost lost this.

"Stella?" Emmy frowns at me from where she's propped against the opposite end of the couch. "Do you really want teenage boys standing out in the street yelling her name in the middle of the night?"

What the fuck? Fury replaces my paternal bliss. "If I catch some teenage punk yelling for my daughter in the middle of the night—"

"Whoooa!" Eli falls back on his little butt laughing and pointing. "Your stomach looks like a torpedo!"

Emmy smiles, putting her hand over the pointy little elbow pushing against her skin. Or maybe it's a foot?

"She's so active tonight. She must know her big brother's around."

His eyes go wide and he gets on his knees again, talking to her stomach. "Hey, little Stella! It's me, Eli!"

Shit, that kid. I still can't get over how sweet he is. I wonder if all little boys are that way or if he'll grow out of it. Either way, he's going to be a great big brother. He's totally my side-kick, and I do my damndest to be a good example for him.

"You realize *Stella* is short for *Estella*, so you're not really breaking with the *E* tradition if you pick that name." Emmy rakes her fingernails through Eli's buzz cut.

His hair is slowly growing back, but he still wears a beanie to cover the Frankenstein scars. I tell him it looks like he's been in a battle, like the real Black Bart. I'm not sure if it helps. Black Bart is starting to notice girls, something his mother is not happy about. I tell her to keep her shirt on. It's all part of the process.

Actually, she can take her shirt off if she wants...

I digress.

We're at the nine-month mark for his surgery as well, and no medicine, no seizures. All of us are feeling really good about Eli's prognosis. Henry is tickled pink and writing a thesis to share at his next medical conference. Emmy and I are talking about re-enrolling him at Pike Academy in January. He misses his friends. Emmy worries so much about him, but I'm trying to help her let him go. He's got to get back in the game with the other kids.

"What about Serena? I always liked that name." She grins from the other side of the couch, but Eli and I frown.

"Hard no, Mom."

"Hard no?" She looks at me with wide eyes. "Did you teach him that?"

"Serena was the mean girl who made fun of me after I peed my pants at school."

Emmy's face goes white, and I jump in for a quick save. "I knew a Serena once, and she picked her nose."

"Oh!" Eli falls back, holding his forehead.

"She ate her boogers, too."

"No! No!" Eli puts his face on his knees, and I laugh. Even Emmy starts to laugh, and I breathe a sigh of relief.

"Okay, okay," she relents, turning to me. "What *S* name do you like?"

We decided since her mother started the *E* names after Emmy's dad, we'd start with *S* names for me. Clearly, we have not had much luck with a consensus.

"While I do like Stella..." Eli and I do a fist bump. "I've always liked the name Selena. It's like Serena, but it reminds of Ximena. Yes?"

When I look at my beautiful wife, her eyes are flooded with tears. She puts a hand over her mouth and squeaks, "Oh, Stephen! It's perfect." She sniffs as a crystal drop hits her cheek. "It'll be like she's here with us. I love it."

Climbing out of my seat, I prop my hands over her and lower myself push-up style to give her a kiss. "Sounds like we found a name for the princess."

"Yes." Emmy sniffs again, nodding.

Eli and I exchange a "Jeez with the pregnancy hormones already" look, and I hop over the back of the couch to retrieve a tissue. She bursts into tears at the drop of a hat these days. I think we'll all be happier once Selena's on the outside of her sexy mom.

Aunt Rebecca is beside herself with baby prep. She calls every day with the latest details on the christening and the enormous party she's throwing for her, the latest cashmere baby clothes she's found... Emmy tells her babies don't wear cashmere. I tell Emmy just to roll with it.

"We'll put that disgusting boathouse fiasco behind us and introduce my gorgeous nephew's beautiful new family to the world without any haters trying to bring us down." Bex declares it like an actor at the end of *A Christmas Carol*, and I wonder who taught my aged aunt the word *hater*.

"Sounds amazing, Bex." I grin, and Emmy shakes her head. Still, she's smiling.

As unpleasant as my aunt's last party for us turned out, her heart was in the right place... and I'd wager a fair sum we won't have a repeat of that occurrence.

We rejected my aunt's suggestion to renew our wedding vows and have a big reception after. Emmy and I both agreed our little ceremony at City Hall, as simple as it was, was a deeply significant event for both of us. We don't want to mess with that memory.

As the day ends, I'm so thankful the most important people in my life are all here, in this big house, in my life, that was so empty without them.

I SAID I'd take care of Eli's registration this morning. Otherwise I'd have stayed in bed and pulled some strings later. It's snowing again and cold as fuck, but I know if I blow this off, it'll only fuel Emmy's worries about sending him back.

On my way out the door, I lift my phone to see it's only twenty-percent charged? How the hell did that happen? Glancing around, I see someone unplugged the charging plate. With a frustrated sigh, I check the clock. I need to go now so I can get back. This shouldn't take thirty minutes... The entire house is quietly sleeping...

I make the decision to leave it charging and head out into the cold.

It'll be fine.

I haven't gotten five blocks from the house, when I look up and see the man who sets my teeth on edge and my blood boiling.

"Well, if it isn't Stephen Hastings." The Dick stands in front of me on the sidewalk.

I'm pleased to see his nose is still slightly crooked from the night he tried to destroy my family. I divert my attention, ready to continue walking, but he steps in my path.

"What? Not even a thank you for not fighting that custody deal?" He's grinning like he has some news for me.

I wonder if some people are simply born stupid or if they're made. Nature or nurture? I'm also starting to wonder if Eli might have been immaculately conceived.

"I'm sorry, I didn't know you wanted to fight." Lifting my chin, I give him my signature scowl. "I'm always glad to beat you, Dick."

His eyes narrow a fraction before he puffs up his chest again.

I'm sure this is when I get to hear whatever shit he's dying to tell me.

"I didn't fight you because I'm sick of the bullshit. I did my best to raise Eli right. Teach him how to be a real man. Emmy fought me every step of the way."

"A real man." I look around like I'm thinking. "Oh, did you mean like you?"

"Fuck off, Hastings. I always suspected you were a closet queer."

I guess that's supposed to offend me? "Looks like you're as stupid as you are ugly. I'd say *ignorant*, but it seems like you put a lot of effort into being an imbecile."

His face reddens, and he steps closer. "Peg's pregnant. I'll be too busy with my new family to worry about some old, broken one."

My throat tightens with protective rage. My love for Eli almost drives me to finish what I started when I beat the shit out of this douchebag at the boathouse. Instead, I take a beat, look around. Emmy doesn't need me in jail for manslaughter while she's giving birth. I wouldn't be much of a role model for Eli if that happened.

"I always knew you were a dick." My voice is even and controlled. "Now I see you're a real asshole, too. Eli's a thousand times the man you'll ever be, and he's only eight."

Burt's fucking face screws up like he's about to make some obnoxious comeback. I turn on my heel and walk away, taking an alternate route to the school. Everything inside me is demanding I punch his lights out, but I'm a dad now. I have to do what's best for my family.

Damn, just thinking those words eases the fire in my veins. It cools my blood. I'm a dad to a great little boy, a baby girl on the way, and I'm a husband to the best woman I never knew I could be lucky enough to have.

I'm talking to my attorney. We're starting the paperwork so I can legally adopt Eli.

It's going to happen.

SCHOOL REGISTRATION COMPLETE, I'm walking in the door of my townhome ready to talk adoption, when I realize something has changed.

"Dad! Dad!" Eli comes running out.

I should note Emmy suggested Eli call me Dad. It caught on much faster than I expected, and I really like it. Another reason to make it official, *stat*.

My insides freeze when I see his worried face. I'm on the stairs, taking them two at a time as I shout, "What's wrong?"

"Wrong way, Dad! Mom went into labor, and Aunt Bex sent a car. Did you have your phone turned off?"

Shit. Shit shit shit. I didn't expect to run into the Dick. I figured I'd be back before anybody woke.

"Rookie mistake!" I yell, spinning in place and running back down. My chef walks out with two plates of omelets. "Let's go, bud! Ted, take the day off! We're having a baby!"

I vaguely hear his best wishes from the kitchen as I scoop Eli up, snatch my phone off the island, and we're out on the sidewalk, waiting for the car service. I'm bouncing as I hold Eli.

"What happened, buddy?"

He pushes on my shoulder, and I lower him gently. It's still such a habit to carry him, but he really doesn't like it now. Another thing Emmy's struggling with... Poor mama. He's a little man.

"She said her water broke. Then she just started yelling a lot of stuff. Some of it wasn't so nice about you." His eyes are round, and his lips press together in a disappointed face.

I pat him on the shoulder. "It's okay. She's not herself right now. You'll see. It'll all be better once Selena's here."

Inside I'm silently praying, *Jesus, please don't let me miss this delivery,* when the car pulls up at the curb. Eli and I hop in, heading north in a blink, and I'm thankful it snowed. Our pace is slow, but the traffic is light.

Finally, we're at the hospital, and I scoop Eli up so we can run. "Sorry, bud."

His head is a lot better, but he's still supposed to take it easy. We don't have time for that.

I get directions to the maternity ward. I'm running like a maniac when I finally spot Bex. Her eyes are wide, and she clasps her chest when I appear. "Oh, thank the lord! I've been praying like there's no tomorrow! Go in! Go in…"

She takes Eli's hand, and I strip off my coat, slowing down and trying not to be frantic as I enter what I imagine will be a serene, wondrous experience.

I couldn't be more wrong.

Dr. Turner is shouting from the end of the bed where she's crouched between my wife's legs. "Come on, Emmy! You're almost there… One more push!"

Emmy screams at her doctor. "I'm not having this baby until he gets here!"

My beautiful wife sits up in the bed, her blonde waves plastered to her red, sweaty face. Two nurses are on each side of her, holding her arms, and the hospital gown is falling off one shoulder.

From what I can see in the large mirror near the doctor, something dark is crowning between her legs.

"Emmy?" I'm not sure how this will go.

"Stephen!" She wails, dropping back and reaching for me. I'm across the room in two steps, replacing the nurses and scooping her into my arms. "Oh, thank God," she cries. "I thought you wouldn't make it. She's coming so fast."

I think she's crying happy tears. I turn to the doctor and give her a nod.

"One more push, Emmy, and she's here. You can do it."

Sure enough, less than thirty seconds later, the room is filled with the shrillest, sweetest, most amazing little cries I've ever heard in my life. Emmy leans her head against my chest, gasping and crying, and dammit, my eyes are wet as well.

I can't believe it when Dr. Turner holds up the tiny red bean all covered in white goo. I love her already.

"She's perfect!" The doctor sings as if I didn't already know that.

Little Selena is quickly weighed, cleaned and returned to her mother, and with the help of a nurse, she latches onto my wife's breast. Watching her eating steadily, I feel my heart grow another size bigger.

"She's so beautiful," I whisper, touching her pale hair. "Just like you."

Emmy smiles and kisses my cheek, chuckling. "She's going to have you so wrapped around her finger. I can't wait to see it."

I know it's true. Just like this woman in my arms does. "Thanks for waiting for me."

"If you ever leave the house without your phone again when I'm thirty-six weeks pregnant..." She's smiling, speaking in a calm voice. "I thought you were a genius."

Squeezing her tighter, I laugh, kissing her head. "I told you I was an idiot. Next time I'll know."

"Next time..." Emmy says it like it might be a discussion.

Speaking of discussions. "When we have time, I've been thinking about something."

Her blue eyes meet mine. "Okay?"

"We can talk about it later."

"Stephen." Emmy isn't one to sit on things.

"I'd like to adopt Eli. Legally. I'm going to talk to Don—"

Tears are in her eyes, and Emmy pulls my face down to kiss her. I kiss her good, touching her tongue with mine, pulling her closer to my chest, sealing the deal.

"You really are my hero." She blinks and a tear falls.

My throat tightens. "You think he'll like that?"

She nods, smiling as more tears join the first one. "I think he'll love it."

She's in my arms when Eli and Bex enter the room to meet Selena. Eli's on his knees, touching his sister's little head. "She's so small."

He looks up at Emmy, and she kisses his forehead. "She'll grow. And you can teach her all the cool stuff you know."

At that, he bounces around, finding the remote, ready to start her first lesson—sea creatures.

Stepping back, I watch as Bex takes her turn, cooing and doting on my daughter.

This is what a family is. It's something I didn't know I'd love so much, and it's all here because a beautiful girl said she'd stay. I knew Emily Barton Hastings was something special. I didn't know she'd change everything about me.

Life changes. Situations change.

People come and people go.

The best people are the ones who stay.

～

Thank you so much for reading STAY!

Wait for Me is a **small-town**, **brother's best friend**, romance full of angst and heat and all the **FEELS**.

Keep turning for a short sneak peek...

Never Miss a New Release!

Sign up for my newsletter and get Three Free Bonus Stories!

*Or get a **text alert** by texting TIALOUISE to 855-902-6387* now.*

(*Text service is U.S. only.)

For a complete list of all my books with a downloadable
Reading Guide, please visit TiaLouise.com/Books

WAIT FOR ME

BY TIA LOUISE

~~Dear Taron,~~
~~I should have told you this a long time ago...~~

~~Dear Taron,~~
~~Is there a time limit on forgiveness?~~
~~If there is, I haven't reached it...~~

~~Dear Taron,~~
~~I still love you...~~

A letter never sent.
Heck, I never even finished it.

Taron Rhodes was my brother's best friend.
He was sexy as sin.
But he was more than that...
He was ponytail-pulling, ice down your shirt teasing, throw you in the lake screaming...

Strong, tanned arms and blue-green eyes over a heart-stopping, naughty grin...

Did I mention his tight end?

I gave him my first *real* kiss, my heart, my everything.

I said I'd wait for him...

I'm still waiting, because Taron Rhodes is still the man of my dreams,

And I have a secret that has his blue-green eyes.

Noel LaGrange stole my heart when she was only eighteen—
pushing me off a flatbed and calling me a city slicker.

Her brother Sawyer would kick my ass if he knew how many times we made out that summer, how close we got.

Everything changed when Sawyer and I joined the military.

We were honorably discharged, but I didn't go to her.

Instead, I went back to the city... where no amount of money, no amount of pills can heal this wound.

Only her whiskey eyes and dark hair, her slim arms and her sweet scent, give me hope.

I broke her heart just as surely as I broke mine, but I'm going back to make it right.

If she's still waiting...

(WAIT FOR ME is a STAND-ALONE small-town, second-chance romance with a guaranteed HEA. No cheating. No cliffhangers.)

PROLOGUE

Noel

My momma was too beautiful to die.

At least, that's what everybody said.

Penelope Jean Harris was the scion of our town's founder and prettiest girl in three parishes. She was head majorette in high school and homecoming queen and prom queen and every other queen. She was Peach Princess, Teen Dixie Peach, and Miss Dixie Gem. She would've gone on to be Miss Louisiana if my daddy hadn't made her a Mrs.

I was eleven—that strange age between too big to play in the creek in only my panties and too little to sleep without the closet light on. I loved Dolly Parton and butterflies and picking peaches straight off my daddy's trees and eating them, jumping in the lake and running after jackrabbits with my little brother Leon.

In the summer the trees were rich green, and the sweet scent of peach juice filled the air. In the winter they were sparse, bony hands, reaching palms up to heaven. Branches like fingers spread, grasping for hope.

Momma's hazel eyes crinkled at the corners whenever she looked at me or my brothers or my daddy. Her sweet smile was warm sunshine when I got cold.

She would wrap me in her arms and sing an old sad song when I was sleepy or cranky or "out of sorts," which is how she'd put it. I pictured "sorts" as ivory dominoes I could line up and knock down or slap off the table, across the room. I'd pull her silky brown hair around me like a cape and close my eyes and breathe...

Then she was gone.

She went for a walk one crisp winter evening along the narrow, dirt road that runs past our orchard out to the old house on the hill. Frost was in the air; bonfires were burning. The man driving the truck said she came out of nowhere.

He never saw her.

She never saw him.

Six weeks later, in that same orchard with peach blossoms on the trees and dew tipping the grass, on the very spot she died, my daddy took his life with his own gun.

I guess sometimes love makes you forget things can get better.

I guess he didn't see a bend in the road up ahead.

I guess he only saw a straight line leading deeper and deeper into black.

My daddy was the star of his high school football team... but Life threw him a pass he couldn't catch with Momma's death.

Our world changed forever that winter.

Dolly says love is like a butterfly, soft and gentle as a sigh, but from what I've seen of love, I think it's more like a tornado, shocking and violent and so powerful it can rip your soul out of your mouth...

It's faster than you can run, and it blows one house away while leaving the next one peacefully standing.

I didn't know which way love would take me, quietly or with the roar of a freight train. I should've known. I should've realized the moment I saw him.

It was both. It was quiet as the brush of peach fuzz, but it left my insides in splinters. It twisted my lungs and lifted me up so high only to throw me down with a force that rang my ears and flooded my eyes.

It all started the summer before they left, a month before my brother was sent to fight in a war everybody said was over.

It all started in the kitchen of my momma's house...

Get WAIT FOR ME and fall in love with this brother's best friend, military romance today!

*It's also available **as an Audiobook.***

BOOKS BY TIA LOUISE

Filthy, 2022*
For Your Eyes Only, 2022
Forbidden, 2023*
(*Available on Audiobook.)

THE TAKING CHANCES SERIES
This Much is True*
Twist of Fate*
Trouble*
(*Available on Audiobook.)

FIGHT FOR LOVE SERIES
Wait for Me*
Boss of Me*
Here with Me*
Reckless Kiss*
(*Available on Audiobook.)

BELIEVE IN LOVE SERIES
Make You Mine
Make Me Yours*
Stay*
(*Available on Audiobook.)

SOUTHERN HEAT SERIES
When We Touch
When We Kiss

THE ONE TO HOLD SERIES
One to Hold (#1 - Derek & Melissa)*
One to Keep (#2 - Patrick & Elaine)*
One to Protect (#3 - Derek & Melissa)*

One to Love (#4 - Kenny & Slayde)
One to Leave (#5 - Stuart & Mariska)
One to Save (#6 - Derek & Melissa)*
One to Chase (#7 - Marcus & Amy)*
One to Take (#8 - Stuart & Mariska)
(*Available on Audiobook.)

THE DIRTY PLAYERS SERIES
PRINCE (#1)*
PLAYER (#2)*
DEALER (#3)
THIEF (#4)
(*Available on Audiobook.)

THE BRIGHT LIGHTS SERIES
Under the Lights (#1)
Under the Stars (#2)
Hit Girl (#3)

COLLABORATIONS
*The Last Guy**
The Right Stud
Tangled Up
Save Me
(*Available on Audiobook.)

PARANORMAL ROMANCES
One Immortal (vampires)
One Insatiable (shifters)

GET THREE FREE STORIES!

Sign up for my New Release newsletter and never miss a sale or new release by me!

Sign up now! (link)

ABOUT THE AUTHOR

Tia Louise is the *USA Today* and #4 Amazon bestselling author of (*mostly*) small-town, single-parent, second-chance, and military romances set at or near the beach.

From Readers' Choice awards, to *USA Today* "Happily Ever After" nods, to winning Favorite Erotica Author and the "Lady Boner Award" (*lol!*), nothing makes her happier than communicating with fellow Mermaids (*fans*) and creating romances that are smart, sassy, and *very sexy*.

A former journalist and displaced beach bum, Louise lives in the Midwest with her trophy husband, two teenage geniuses, and one clumsy "grand-cat."

Sign up for her newsletter **HERE** and never miss a new release or sale—and get a free story collection!

❧

Signed Copies of all books online at:
 https://geni.us/SignedPBs

❧

Connect with Tia:
 Website
 Instagram (@AuthorTLouise)
 TikTok (@TheTiaLouise)
 Pinterest

Bookbub Author Page
Amazon Author Page
Goodreads
Snapchat

** On Facebook? **

Be a Mermaid! Join Tia's **Reader Group** at *"Tia's Books, Babes & Mermaids" (link)!*

www.AuthorTiaLouise.com
allnightreads@gmail.com

Made in the USA
Monee, IL
01 January 2025

75785240R00171